EDGE OF FRIENDSHIP

THE MACBAINS BOOK 2

NAN DIXON

EDGE OF FRIENDSHIP

THE MACBAINS BOOK 2

NAN DIXON

It started with a Kiss Cam...

Michael MacBain, a grieving CFO, must focus on staying sober. But with his family tiptoeing around him like he's broken, he needs a friend. He hopes he found one.

Liz Carlson, a financially struggling MacBain employee, is appalled she kissed the CFO at a baseball game. It was wrong. But even though she worried about risking her job, she agrees to be Michael's friend. Liz knows the damage addiction can wreck on a family.

The sparks that ignited during the kiss explode and Michael and Liz cross the line of friendship. But he stumbles with his sobriety.

Can she entrust her heart to an addict?

THE OTHER TWIN

Nan Dixon will become a favorite author. Part of series but can read as a stand alone. Fun story that's hard to put down. "One more page...just another chapter..." until soon you've reached the end.

A complicated story that reflects the many threads of real life that so often includes knots of problems in addition to the gradual unraveling of past hurts when placed in the light of love and real caring. A story I couldn't put down.

UNDERCOVER WITH THE HEIRESS

So much more than a romance novel.

This was definitely a book I was not able to put down! I took the tablet with me everywhere! **Fabulous Brunette Reviews**

THROUGH A MAGNOLIA FILTER

...a heartwarming story that showcased the importance of family, following your dreams, and true love. I thoroughly enjoyed this tender heartwarming story. **LAS Reviewer**

A SAVANNAH CHRISTMAS WISH
FRESH PICK

...is a book that has you frolicking in gardens, battling storms and falling in love...A book of warmth and love. It will leave you smiling.

TO CATCH A THIEF

Not your everyday Contemporary genre, a little suspense, a little love and definitely entertaining... **Our Town Book Reviews**

A SAVANNAH CHRISTMAS WEDDING

Another winner. Love this series

For my Family

COPYRIGHT

Grinning Frog Press - May 2022

Editor: Victoria Curran. Copy Editor: Judy Roth. Cover Design: Covers by Dana Lamothe of Designs by Dana

ONE

MICHAEL HUNG BACK FROM THE CROWD OF PEOPLE STREAMING into the Minnesota Twins stadium. It was noon on Friday. Maybe he should have stayed at the office or headed home. He didn't want to be part of this group. He didn't want to hear everyone laughing because he knew they would be laughing at him.

But both his therapist and AA sponsor had advised Michael against withdrawing.

Today was MacBain Enterprises' family day at Target Field. Every employee and their loved ones wore Twins caps and golf shirts with the company logo. As CFO, he should know what this party was costing, but he'd been *indisposed* when Mom and Dad planned the event.

Indisposed. In treatment. Drying out. Fucked up.

Kate, his sister, slowed and waited for him on the sidewalk. "How're you doing?"

He hated that question. At least one family member asked him that each day.

"I should be asking you that question." Kate was pregnant. She hadn't told him until he'd gotten through treatment.

She stroked her belly, even though she wasn't showing. "We're good."

Alex, her fiancé, set his hand on her shoulder. "Should I see if there's some kind of cart for you?"

Kate laughed. "I can walk."

Alex sighed.

Michael looked away. It was hard to be around Kate and Alex. He couldn't believe his career-minded sister had fallen in love so hard and fast. Just watching them made him miss Sarah. If life had been fair, she would be by his side today.

Kate hooked her arm through Michael's and then Alex's. "Come on."

"I don't know why Mom and Dad insisted the whole company attend the game," Michael said.

"Because it's good for morale." Kate tugged him a little faster toward the queue of people at security having their bags checked. "It's a beautiful day, and we want our employees to know how much MacBain appreciates them."

"Yeah, yeah." Sometimes he didn't feel like part of the family company. Ever since he'd come back from Hazelton, he felt even more removed.

"Then how about this for a reason?" Kate stuck a bony elbow in his side. "Mom and Dad want to celebrate her oncologist's clean report."

"What? Why didn't I know this?" Michael held out his ticket for scanning.

"Sucks to be you," Kate whispered.

Alex raised one eyebrow. "I didn't know either."

At least he wasn't the only person out of the loop.

They followed the MacBain group to the concierge level.

Dad and Mom flanked the steps into their section, greeting all the people. Everyone was smiling.

His mother looked—healthy, not like she'd just finished her cancer battle. Thank God.

He bent and hugged her. "How come I have to hear from Kate that you got a clean bill of health from your doctor?"

He tried to keep it light, but hurt seeped into his voice. Hell, weren't there any privileges with being the firstborn?

"She was in my office when I got the call. I'd planned on giving an update either good or bad at dinner on Sunday." Her hazel eyes, so like his, glittered in the sunlight. "Cat's out of the bag."

His dad joined them and gave him a one-armed hug. "Great news, isn't it?"

"The best."

"Have fun today, Michael." Mom squeezed his arm, concern on her face. "Try and enjoy yourself."

Fun? He couldn't remember having much fun in the last four years. Not since Sarah found out she had inoperable brain cancer.

As he stood in the concourse, he swore everyone held a beer. His palms perspired, and a line of sweat slid down his back. He swallowed, almost able to taste the cold, hoppy brew.

"Michael, there you are." Becca, his assistant, came up to him. "I'd like you meet my fiancé."

Another woman who'd gotten engaged while he'd been away in treatment. "Congratulations."

The guy stuck out his hand. "Dave Benthal."

"Michael MacBain." Michael shook his hand, trying to come up with small talk. "What do you do, Dave?"

Becca shifted her feet.

"I'm a liquor distributor." He gave a crooked smile. "It's a family business, like yours. Genetic luck, I'd guess you'd say."

Becca's eyes were almost as large as saucers.

Michael set a hand on her arm. "I'm not going to roll him and steal any booze he's carrying."

Dave frowned.

3

"I don't … I wouldn't …" Becca stuttered. Apparently his assistant hadn't given away his secrets.

"I just got out of treatment, well, two months ago," Michael said.

"Alcohol?" Dave asked.

Michael nodded, hating this. "I've been sober for thirteen weeks."

"I'm sorry." Dave swallowed. "Is it tough to talk about?"

"No," he lied. "Today will be a test, being around other people drinking."

A whiskey to steady his nerves might help him get through the afternoon. But he was done with that.

"Congratulations on your sobriety," Dave said. "We're in the business, but we've had our share of alcoholics. I've seen what you're going through and I wish you luck. One day at a time."

"Thanks." More like one hour at a time. "You two have fun. Looks like the game's about to start."

"It's so great that your parents decided to do this," Becca said as she and Dave headed down the steps.

Becca was right. His parents were great. He moved down the stairs and found some empty seats, taking the one on the aisle and tugged his cap lower. He was like—oh what was that book called—*Stranger in a Strange Land*? He didn't feel part of any of this.

A server stopped next to him. "What would you like to order? Everything's on the MacBains today."

He *wanted* a Jameson on the rocks. "Ginger ale."

"You got it." She entered the order in a handheld computer. "Let me know if you need anything else." She flipped her blonde ponytail over her shoulder before moving to take another order.

"She's cute." His brother, Timothy, slid into the chair behind him.

"All yours." No one could replace Sarah. "How come you're late?"

"Stephen and I waited for the Moonlight Square inspector. The guy was two hours late."

"That's terrible."

The Twins were taking the field, the Milwaukee Brewers at bat. A fierce rivalry existed between Wisconsin and Minnesota. Even now, he could see the stands had more than the average number of opposing team fan gear.

"We got the certificate of occupancy—finally." Timothy clapped as the Twin's pitcher threw the first strike.

Michael tried to remember what had hung the CO up. "You and Stephen convinced the inspector the fire exits were up to code?"

"The guy was jerking us around. We didn't have any issues this time, and we didn't change anything."

The Brewer at the plate swung and missed. The crowd cheered.

"Is that seat taken?" Liz Carlson stood in the aisle pointing at the seat next to him.

Her company shirt was tucked into a pair of khaki shorts, and the ball cap stuck out of her purse. Michael gazed into familiar deep blue eyes, the most unusual eyes he'd ever seen. When she'd first joined MacBain, Kate had warned him and his brothers to stay away from her.

"Of course. Hi, Liz." He slid his legs sideways and she squeezed past.

Once Liz settled next to him, she turned to Timothy and said, "I hear Moonlight Square is a go."

"It is," Timothy said.

"I just found out." Michael frowned. "Why am I the last to get information?"

"Stephen called when he got the go ahead. I notified the signed tenants that they can finalize their move-in dates." She

5

nodded to him. "Now that we have an occupancy date, I'll re-run the financial models."

"Yeah, good." Michael should be thinking of those things first. But it took so much energy.

While Liz and Timothy discussed the newly built strip mall he tuned them out, watching the crowd and the action on the field. That was another thing that had changed while he'd been gone. Liz wasn't Kate's assistant any more. She was now the leasing manager.

The company had gotten along fine without him. Probably better than when he'd stumbled around trying to figure out his place in the family dynasty.

His ginger ale arrived. Wonderful. Now everyone would wonder what he was drinking. As he set the cup in the holder, even his brother stared.

Liz glanced at him and ordered an iced tea.

"You don't have to abstain because of me," he whispered.

"It's a little early for alcohol."

Michael waved his hand at the group. "You're about the only one."

"I'm good." She clapped as the pitcher threw a strike. In a low voice, she said, "If you need to talk to anyone, you can … talk to me. If you … need a friend."

"Thanks," he said. With her reluctance, it hadn't sounded like she wanted to make the offer. "I appreciate that. Not many people know how to act around me right now."

"I get that. I've … attended some co-dependency classes." She tipped her head. "I know how hard this can be."

"Thank you." Exhaustion stopped him from asking why she'd been at classes.

How could she understand what he was going through? To never have another drink? That was why they talked about one day at time. Forever was exhausting.

By giving up drinking, he'd lost contact with Sarah. He'd never told anyone why he drank. Never told them about Sarah.

He pretended to focus on the game but felt out of sync. He hadn't paid much attention to the Twins this season.

"Do you play sports?" Liz asked as the teams changed sides.

"Basketball. Football." Or he had. His therapist had told him to get physically active. He just didn't have much desire.

He did play pick-up b-ball games with the family. And he didn't do that very well. Everyone hated having him on their team. Or they had when he was drinking. Maybe that was a bright spot in being sober. He wouldn't be picked last anymore.

Liz had asked a question. He supposed he should reciprocate. "Do you play sports?"

"I wanted to dance, but farm life …" She paused. "I played basketball and ran cross country in high school and college."

Because she wanted to talk, he asked, "Do you still run?"

"Treadmill. Elliptical when I can." She smiled. "My neighborhood's not the best to run in, so I use the company gym a few times a week."

"Good. I'm glad people are using it."

He didn't ask the natural question—*Where do you live?* The noise of the game filled the silence between them. He'd depleted his daily conversation quota.

Timothy punched him in the shoulder. "You heard Mom's good news, right?"

"When did you hear?" Michael half-turned in his chair.

"Just now." When he leaned forward, Michael smelled the beer on his brother's breath. He inhaled the scent.

"Is your mother okay?" Liz asked.

She'd turned toward them, bringing their three faces way too close.

"All clear from the doc." Timothy pretended to wipe sweat from his brow.

"That's wonderful!" Liz's smile lit up her whole face.

"It's great," Michael agreed.

"I'm glad for your family and your mom." Liz broke eye contact. "Will she spend more time at the office now?"

"Don't know. Guess we'll find out on Sunday." Timothy clapped. "Double play. Go Twins!"

It went on like that. Short conversations during each inning. Timothy left, his brother, Stephen, took his seat. Michael went up and chatted with his family and some of his staff. They'd seen him at the office enough that they didn't stare at him like he was dying.

But other employees avoided him like he had a fatal disease. Death by drunkenness. He went to the bathroom, and someone turned with a full beer in his hand and spilled it on his shirt.

"Fuck."

"Sorry. Sorry." The guy was half-lit.

Michael tried to wash out the spill, but the smell stuck with him. He couldn't wear this all day. He headed for a shirt concession and bought a jersey. In the bathroom he changed and shoved his beer soaked shirt into the bag, rolling it down so he wouldn't smell the appealing aroma of hops.

"You weren't wearing a jersey when you left," Liz said with a smile, a dimple at the corner of her mouth.

"Just my luck, an idiot spilled his beer on me."

Liz faced him. "Your luck's not too good today."

Stephen poked him in the back. "You're on the kiss-cam, man."

"What?" Michael asked.

He glanced over Liz's shoulder and their faces filled the video screen. The camera looked like it was eavesdropping on an intimate moment between him and Liz.

The MacBain section clapped and chanted, "Kiss, kiss, kiss."

He raised his eyebrows.

She shrugged.

This was stupid.

They leaned in.

Their lips met.

In the background applause broke out through the stadium.

He put his arms around her and tipped her lower, playing up the drama.

She laughed and tapped his back.

He pulled her up and set her back in her seat.

Her eyes flashed open and she looked up at the screen and laughed.

On the screen another couple in their sixties were on camera.

"I'm sorry," he mumbled. His fingers were tangled in her hair. Her clip was half off. "I'm really sorry."

She faced the field. "It's fine. Just part of the … game atmosphere."

She dug in her bag and retrieved a small brush. Then she pulled out her clip and ran the brush through her hair. Her fingers flew as she whipped her hair back into the claw.

Hair in place, she looked at him. Her apricot-flavored mouth creased into a smile.

"You two looked good up there." Stephen's knee nudged his back.

Michael ignored his brother and stared at the field as the players returned to the field. That was a mistake.

THE GAME WAS FINALLY OVER and the Twins had won. Liz could escape her embarrassment.

She and Michael MacBain had kissed. The eldest son of her employers. The brother of her boss. The company CFO.

Michael touched her arm.

"I don't want things to be weird for us." He pointed at the stadium screen. "I wasn't hitting on you."

"Of course not." What else could she say? "Don't worry about it."

"I'm sorry." His eyes were light green today. He ran his hand through his wavy brown hair. "I seem to have a knack for stupidity."

Apparently they both did. "It's fine. Really."

"I … It was your face right there. And the camera. And the crowd." He reached a hand to her face and then pulled back. "It's a really nice face."

Okay. Now he was hitting on her. "Excuse me," she said, pulling away.

"Hey, Liz," one of the guys in engineering called as they waited for their row to empty after the game. "We're meeting at Shamus's Pub for dinner. Want to come? Umm, you too Michael."

"Thanks, but I can't," Michael said.

Liz touched her stomach. After having a hot dog and pretzel, she'd also had a taco. "I've eaten enough calories for three days."

"Then come have a beer," the guy called.

"I'm good." She climbed the steps.

"You don't have to say no because I can't drink," Michael said, walking behind her. His breath on her neck shot shivers down her back even though it was eighty degrees in the stands.

"This isn't about you." She didn't have room in her weekly budget for pubs.

"Sure."

"I don't go out for drinks." At the top of the stairs a crowd of kids rushed by, knocking her into Michael. He wrapped a hand around her elbow, keeping her from falling.

"Thanks." She shifted away from him.

They were the last of the MacBain crew in the hallway. Since they were alone, she said,

"I hope your family isn't upset by the kiss."

"They won't be." He touched her arm. "Part of the game, isn't that what you said?"

She took a step back. Michael had too much baggage. He was an alcoholic.

She knew too much about addictions. She'd watched her mom and dad's hearts break from her brother's gambling. When Jordan's problems had surfaced, she'd handed out enough Kleenexes to wipe away a small towns' worth of tears. Her brother's drama still complicated her life.

It would be a mistake to get involved with Michael. A mistake that might derail her plan of earning a promotion to MacBain's leasing director, and then helping get her family out from under debt. Because her actions had caused their financial woes.

They headed to ground level. The crowd had thinned enough that they walked side by side. She wished they weren't heading the same direction.

Michael pulled out his phone and checked a message. His jaw jutted out as he read it.

"Work?" she asked.

"Family with a dinner invite."

"I'm so envious," she said. "I'd like to be close enough to my parents to pop over for dinner at short notice. Unfortunately they're almost five hours away."

He paused, then finally said, "It's hard being around my family. They don't know how to act around me."

She understood. Before everything had fallen apart, she

and her twin brother had been close. After—she didn't trust him.

Being an alcoholic was different than what her brother had gone through, but there had to be some similarities. She asked, "Do you need an excuse?"

He stared at his phone. "I don't like lying to them."

"I'm on a quest to see more of Minneapolis." Places that didn't cost money. "I've never seen the sculpture gardens and thought I would swing by there after the game."

"By the old Guthrie Theater?"

"The what?" she asked.

"You are new in town."

"I've been here about a year and half." But she hadn't made an effort to see much.

"I'd love to tag along." He tapped out a message on his phone and then shoved it in the pocket of his shorts. "Let's go."

"Okay," she said. This might be a massive mistake suggesting they go there to together. She hadn't thought through what hanging out with Michael would look like to her boss, Kate, or his parents.

But there was a spring in Michael's step. Even though she wasn't an expert on addictions, maybe she'd helped him.

They walked to the parking ramp near the office and got into her car.

"If we go to my condo, I can drive," he said.

"That's crazy." She pulled out onto the street. "I need my car."

Under his breath he said, "Stubborn. No wonder you work for Kate."

She chose to ignore it. "I can drop you at your car, and we can meet at the park."

"Now that's crazy too. Do you know how to get there?"

"I have a thing that's known as GPS." She tapped her phone.

"You drive. I'll navigate," he said. "Turn left here."

"This will be fun," she said, forcing enthusiasm into her voice.

They didn't talk. Michael just gave her directions. She was relieved when they arrived and found parking on the street.

"I didn't know it was so big," she said as they headed to a rock path. She breathed in the sharp smell of mown grass.

"I haven't been here in years," Michael said. "This is the allée."

Trees lined the path and framed the big spoon and cherry sculpture. "It's huge," she said, struggling to find anything interesting to say.

"Wait 'til we get closer." He steered her through a break in the border of hedges and trees.

He'd led them to a spot where countless granite benches formed a square.

"It's beautiful," she said, looking at the people making themselves at home on the seats.

He held a hand out to an open bench, and she slowly sat.

"I think it's—" he closed his eyes and took a deep breath "—peaceful."

"You've been here before then?" she asked.

"When we were in high school, a bunch of us used to come to hang out." Those changeable eyes opened and looked into hers. His mouth quirked up on one side. "We'd sneak in beer and wander around."

There was that reminder of his demons. Her cue. "Did you have a drinking problem in high school?"

"No." His finger traced a dark vein in the stone seat. "Although I was part of the party crowd."

She thought about her high school, about always needing to

come home after school or practice and rush to get her chores done. Not much time to party. She'd always envied the town kids who didn't have her responsibilities. She released a big sigh.

"What was that for?" he asked.

"We come from very different backgrounds."

"Who doesn't?" He took her hand and pulled her up. "There's more."

As soon as she stood, he dropped her hand as if he'd remembered she had the plague.

They crossed the path and went through another wall of green.

"Come on," he said.

This visit no longer felt like it had been her idea.

They headed to a fence-like structure with hedges and shrubs surrounding it.

"It's Graham's *Two-way Mirror Punched Steel Hedge Labyrinth.* See how he uses the reflection of the sky to pull you in?" Michael hustled her around the opposite side of a screen and waved. "And here we can see through."

They moved through the small maze, and Liz admired the art, she guessed you had to call it, but she was more intrigued with the man who had never been this animated at the office.

He tugged her out of the maze and finally they headed to the *Spoonbridge and Cherry.* Other people shot pictures, and they waited.

A giant cherry sat on the edge of an enormous spoon in the middle of a pond. Liz pointed at the water spraying from the cherry stem. "It's a fountain."

He nodded. "The whole thing weighs three and half tons."

"Wow." She pointed at the strange way the young boy stood, his hand outstretched and his mouth open and tipped back. "What are they doing?"

"If you get the angle just right, you can make it look like you're eating the cherry," he said quietly.

Michael took her by the shoulders.

Her heart pounded. She jerked away from him.

"Whoa." He held up his hands. "I just wanted you to move behind him."

He indicated the man taking the picture.

She skirted around him and took a look. "It does look like he's eating it."

They walked along the paths, the sun warming the top of her head. The tension eased out of her shoulders—maybe he wasn't hitting on her after all—and she inhaled grass-scented air.

Trying to ease the strain that had grown between them, she asked, "How do you know so much about the sculptures? You know more than what's on the plaques."

"I've always liked the gardens." He checked his phone again. "Sorry. I've got to go."

"Hot date?" she asked.

He shook his head. "AA meeting."

She swallowed, not knowing what to say. "Good for you?"

The carefree man she'd just spent an hour walking with disappeared. Frown lines formed around his mouth and on his forehead.

"Yeah. Good for me."

TWO

"Hi, I'm Michael. I'm an alcoholic. I've been sober for ninety-three days."

He hated admitting his weaknesses. Hated the welcomes that came back from those gathered. But if this was what he needed to survive, he'd do it.

For almost two years, all he'd been doing was surviving. He had nothing to look forward to. No one to share his life with.

This meeting beat sitting in his condo. Sitting in the home he and Sarah had created. Sitting where he'd spent so many nights getting drunk and hoping Sarah would appear. That he would hear her voice again.

But he couldn't keep drinking like he had. Even two years after her death, his pain was as fresh as when he'd buried her. His life stretched long and empty without her.

A headache thumped in his sinuses.

He got through the meeting and walked out with Terry, his sponsor.

"Have you given anymore thought to our last conversation?" Terry asked.

Michael stopped on the sidewalk in front of the church. "I don't have any hobbies."

"You need something." Terry tugged on his jacket. "How's your exercise program coming?"

"Better," Michael said. "I'm exercising three times a week." Wasn't that fun?

Terry raised an eyebrow. "Good. Keep it up."

"Yeah." He tapped his fingers against the side of his leg. Crap, he was picking up Timothy's nervous habits. He tucked his hand in his jean pocket.

"Coffee Tuesday?" Terry asked, heading to the parking lot.

"That works for me."

They agreed on a coffee shop outside of downtown.

"Give some thought to what you're passionate about," Terry said. "You can't work 24/7."

"No. That's my sister's thing." Until she'd met Alex.

He didn't actually like work. He wasn't even sure why he'd gotten his accounting degree and then his CPA.

Not true. He did know why.

Sarah.

Even though he'd loved architecture, he'd love Sarah more. They'd both gotten their accounting degrees. They'd done everything together. Lived in each other's pockets. Shared a small apartment in college, although their parents pretended they hadn't known. And when they'd moved back to Minneapolis, they'd bought the condo.

His brothers had given them the nickname *Marah*. And he didn't care. He'd loved her for more than half his life.

"Where'd you go?" Terry asked, standing next to Michael's Audi.

"Trying to think of something that interests me … I'll see you Tuesday."

What the hell would he do until then? Saturday loomed empty and lonely. Sunday he had dinner at his parents', and

17

wouldn't that be uncomfortable. Then Monday he had work and meetings.

He headed back to the condo, wishing Sarah would be waiting.

After he'd gone into treatment, his sister and brothers had scoured the place. He was embarrassed they'd picked up his garbage. Cleaned up his life. Apparently he'd passed out in vomit and blood. Kate had walked into that mess.

As the eldest he should be the most responsible. The one everyone looked up to. Instead he was the family screw-up.

He threw his keys in the entry table bowl and stood there, unsure of what to do next.

The place was too damn quiet. Maybe he should get a pet. A cat? He winced. What would people think about a guy having a cat? If he didn't live downtown, he'd get a dog.

But a dog would just die too. Like Iron Man had died when he was a kid. He'd gotten to name him after his superhero. He loved that mutt. He was the one who picked him out at the humane society. Mom had been pregnant with Timothy, his youngest brother. But when Michael was twelve, a car had hit Iron Man. He'd cried like a baby over that dog.

He didn't have the Midas touch of his family, he had the kiss of death.

He hoped he hadn't infected poor Liz.

He flipped on the television, not caring what was on. He couldn't stand the silence.

He sank into the sofa, the leather creaking a little. God he wanted a drink, anything. Beer, whiskey, vodka. He gritted his teeth and looked at the screen. *Law and Order.* He tapped his thigh.

He could nuke something. He needed to eat regular meals, but it was almost ten o'clock. His dreams were already weird. What would eating this late do to them?

His stomach gave a little growl, so he pushed himself off the sofa.

Opening the fridge, he pulled out a milk carton, sniffing before he took a big gulp.

He opened the freezer drawer. When he'd left treatment, his parents had wanted him to come home. God. Going home? Mom was supposed to be focused on beating her cancer, not having the grim reaper get too close to her.

So Maria, his parents' housekeeper, had stocked his fridge with meals. Meals with heating instructions in containers that went from the freezer to the microwave.

He found chicken enchiladas. No one made them better than Maria. Peeling off the lid, he slid them into the microwave and punched in the time.

He pulled out a glass and poured himself some milk. Emptied the dishwasher and loaded his breakfast dishes. Wasn't he fucking domestic. He could set the coffeemaker for tomorrow, but then what would he look forward to on Saturday morning?

He found a hot pad and wiggled the container out of the microwave. Balancing it on the pad, he picked up his glass.

By the time he sat, the local news was on. He shoveled down chicken, cheese and enchilada sauce, burning his mouth.

Too bad he couldn't just sit and eat until he met Terry on Tuesday.

Tomorrow loomed like an empty white room. What was he going to do?

He'd lost touch with his high school friends. He and Sarah had been an island unto their own in college. His other friends hung around bars, and Terry had told him not to get back in touch with that lot.

He stuffed the final forkful of food in his mouth. He refused to burden his family's happiness with his shit. He hated their pitying looks, their questions. *How are you?* Meant *Are you drink-*

ing? You look rested was code for asking whether *he'd lain on the sofa all day.*

He couldn't deal with their concern or sympathy.

He tossed the container in the sink, running water into it. His hands fisted on his hips.

What would he do tomorrow? What would he do with his life? The days stretched endlessly empty, quiet, nothing.

Maybe—he turned on his phone before he could really think what he was doing.

"Hi," he said.

"Michael?" Liz asked. Her voice sounded fuzzy. "It's … eleven o'clock? Why are you calling on a Friday night? Is something wrong at work?"

"No, it's not … Is it really eleven? I'm sorry. I …"

What if she'd been in bed with some guy?

"Forget it. I shouldn't have—"

"Wait!" He heard her moving. "I fell asleep in front of the news. What's up?"

Could he ask this of her? "I was wondering if you wanted to do something with me tomorrow."

"Do something?"

"I just can't sit inside, and I don't want to burden my family." He was being an idiot. But being with her this afternoon had been easy. "I'm a colleague, and I shouldn't be calling you late on a Friday night. You probably have plans for the weekend. It's just that you seemed to enjoy the sculpture garden and …"

"I did plan something for tomorrow," she said.

He was an idiot. Of course she had. She probably had a boyfriend. "Sorry to bother you."

"Wait," she said before he could hang up.

A little bubble of hope started inside him. "Yes?"

"I was going to go to a museum. I got the idea when we

were at the sculpture gardens. Like I said, I'm trying to experience more of the area."

"Which one?"

"Minneapolis Museum of Art."

"I don't suppose I can tag along?" he asked.

He waited. The pause took on a life of its own.

Finally she said, "What time do you want to meet me there?"

~

LIZ WAITED on the sidewalk in front of the Children's Theater entrance.

Sure, she'd driven by the museum numerous times, she didn't live that far away, but she never imagined waiting for Michael MacBain.

He could mess up her plans of becoming the next director of leasing. The MacBains all stuck together, at least everyone but Michael. He'd always seemed odd man out. Maybe because he was the numbers guy and his brothers and dad were into construction. And Kate? She was a force onto her own.

She rubbed at the pain starting between her eyes. *Don't let this be a migraine.*

She could walk away. Send him a text that she had gotten a migraine. *She* had things to do, like laundry, and reviewing the changes to the base lease document the corporate attorney had sent on Friday. And balancing her checkbook.

But she'd made the decision to see her new hometown. She was sticking with it.

And weird as it was, Michael had been nice yesterday.

But it was all kinds of wrong to be hanging around with a MacBain. Working for Colfax had shown her that. She could visit the museum another day.

She turned to leave.

Michael sprinted up the steps, a smile on his face, a real smile. He looked more rested than Friday. Although his jeans hung a little like he'd lost some weight.

"Thank you," he said, looking her up and down and nodding. As if he approved of what she'd decided to wear—a skirt and top—which was really all she had clean since she was here instead of doing her laundry. "I probably sounded crazy last night."

Desperate more like. "I'm not sure what you sounded like. I remember watching the weather and that's it. Then the phone rang."

She hoped she sounded diplomatic. She wouldn't tell him what she really thought. That he should be talking with his family. Maybe she understood him a little more because of her brother. She and her brother used to talk a lot. Not anymore.

"I was hoping we could check out their Prairie School exhibit and then after lunch see the Purcell-Cutts house. It's by Lake of the Isles."

She'd never seen him so ... engaged. She let him pull her to the doors.

She slowed her steps and he almost dragged her along. "Wait."

He turned. Then looked at her face. He dropped his hand and took a step back. "Yes?" His voice was low and quiet.

She felt like she was kicking a puppy with her most pointy-toed shoes. "I'd just planned on wandering through the painting exhibits."

He winced. "If that's what you want to do."

"What's a Prairie School? A sod schoolhouse?"

His lips twitched. "A school of architecture and design. Think Frank Lloyd Wright."

"Oh. I guess we can do that."

She held the door open for him, but he pushed the glass

back with his hand above her head and she walked under his arm. Men. Although she liked the way he smelled, a limey woodsy smell. So much better than when he used to smell of old whiskey. "I didn't know Wright built anything here."

"He did. Purcell was one of Wright's teachers. Wright, Purcell and Elmslie built more buildings in the Prairie School than anyone else. The museum has a collection of furniture, stained glass windows and other objects in the style."

Michael put a twenty dollar bill in the donation box and took a museum map. "I ... apologize if I sound obsessed."

She followed him up the stairs. He dropped an impersonal hand on the small of her back, gently guiding her to the right exhibition. "I thought we'd spend an hour or two here. Then have lunch and spend the afternoon at the house."

"Okay," she said.

"You really haven't been to this museum yet, have you? I could spend days."

She hadn't done any of the things the Twin Cities had available. She'd focused on getting her career established. "No. My family wasn't that kind of family. Now if you want to know about a tractor pull, I'm your gal."

"I'll keep that in mind."

They moved through a wood-paneled hallway. "The wood-work is beautiful."

As they stood in front of a room complete with furniture and stained glass windows, she said, "I didn't know they had furniture exhibits in a museum."

"The furniture are pieces of art. This era of architecture is one of the cleanest. Other than shaker furniture, of course." Michael kept walking and talking. He was better informed than the signs.

She could identify types of cattle, but Michael had a major interest in furniture styles and architectural schools. She wasn't too gauche. Her high school had bused to the Des

Moines Art Center, but she'd focused on the paintings and photographs.

Her family had been about survival. Should they give in and start a hog operation. Should they extend the irrigation? How many acres of corn versus soybeans and could they afford to let a field go fallow. Then there were the battles between the prairie restoration group and the nearby farmers. The prairie burns sometimes got away from them.

Her stomach rumbled a little.

"It's almost twelve-thirty" Michael said. "Shall we get something to eat?"

She laughed, embarrassed. "I guess I am hungry."

"How about Greek food? There's a restaurant around the corner. It's nice enough to walk."

She'd didn't remember ever eating Greek food. "Sounds good."

The day had warmed up. She pulled off her sweater that had been handy in the museum's cool halls. She was glad she'd thrown on a simple T-shirt and skirt.

"Thanks for letting me tag along," he said. "Lunch is on me."

"You're welcome. That was fun this morning." She added, "I wouldn't have checked out those exhibits."

He smiled. He'd smiled more in the last couple of hours than she remembered in the six months she'd worked for MacBain.

They found a table immediately. She looked over the menu. There were descriptions for each dish, but she would butcher the pronunciations when the waitress asked her what she wanted to eat. Did the mud from the farm have to cling so stubbornly? She wanted to be sophisticated; wanted to be just like Kate or Mrs. MacBain. Whoops—Patty. It was hard to break the habit of calling people her parents' age, mister or missus.

"What looks good to you?" he asked, folding his menu.

"What do recommend?" she asked.

"I'm thinking of having spanakopita and adding a salad." He looked up. "If you picked out the moussaka and maybe some kabobs, we could share and taste a lot of different foods."

She repeated the pronunciation. *Moussaka*. The ingredients looked tame enough: beef, eggplant and potatoes. "Okay."

She let Michael order for them.

"What got you interested in the designs we saw?" She sipped her Diet Coke.

"I took drafting in high school, and one of our projects was on different architectural styles." He drew designs on the table-top. "I did a paper on the Prairie School."

"I don't know anything about architectural styles, other than what I learned this morning." She twirled her knife. "But I can do a mean present value statement."

"Weird, isn't it?" He let out a sad laugh. "That should be my forte. But Kate was always so excited to use the tools she'd learned and flash her fancy MBA. You're following in her footsteps."

"I've always liked that part of my job, but why doesn't your department run the projections?" At Colfax, not that she would ever want to model anything on that company, the finance group had controlled the models.

Something shadowed his eyes. "You and Kate are closer to the lease terms."

"True." But it didn't make sense to her.

"When did you move here?" he asked, changing the subject.

"A year and a half ago." She blinked at the thought so much time had passed. "I went to Iowa State, in Ames." On scholarship. It was that or take out thousands of dollars of loans. "Majored in finance with a minor in entrepreneurial studies."

25

He leaned forward. "That's a lot."

"I needed one more semester to double major." She shook her head. "I thought I'd gotten all my classes lined up, but I couldn't get into a class the first semester of my senior year. The professor was a real ass—I mean ... jerk."

"I'm pretty sure I've called some people assholes. I've probably said it to my brothers." He chuckled. "Recently."

"But ... I really shouldn't. It's not proper business language."

He laughed.

Her face heated up.

"Come on. We're in the construction business. Male- and testosterone-dominated and all that."

She sipped her Coke, hoping it would cool down her blush. "I work in leasing. I don't want to get in the habit of using that kind of language."

"You're not kidding."

She couldn't look into his eyes. Today they were more golden than green. And no longer bloodshot.

Maybe he'd really stopped drinking.

Of course her brother always swore he'd stopped gambling. Then he'd come 'round looking for money, saying he just had to get even. He would quit once he got even.

Talk about an addiction. Getting *even* had never happened in the six years Liz had known about her brother's problem.

"I'll watch my language," Michael said. "So you had a jerk of a professor."

She took a breath. "I finished in August instead of May, so a lot of the new grad jobs were gone. I found an internship in Des Moines." They hadn't paid much, but it had been enough to share an apartment with a college acquaintance and still send money home. "It was in a private company, like MacBain, but much, much smaller."

He nodded. "How come they didn't snatch you up?"

"They did offer me a job and I worked there for another year, but I wanted … more."

"And after that you worked for Colfax for a while, right?"

She studied her napkin, unfolding it and placing it on her lap. Organized her cutlery. "Yes. Not quite a year."

"With Jerry."

Luckily the server came with the lunch before Liz could reply. She set empty plates in front of them and then placed the food in the middle of the table. "Enjoy."

"Goodness, if this is a lunch portion, what would dinner be like?" She stared at the massive amount of food.

"Bigger." He laughed.

She spooned some of everything onto her plate. He did the same.

"We hardly made a dent," she said, looking at their leftovers.

"Dig in."

The time flew by. The server refilled her water glass and his coffee, twice.

"I wasn't sure about the eggplant," she finally said. "Not sure if I liked the texture."

He wiped his mouth with his napkin.

Had she ever noticed he had such full lips?

"So what else is on your list of places to see?" he asked, sipping his coffee.

"Umm." Opening her phone, she looked at her list. "I hear the arboretum is beautiful. And there's a conservatory."

"Next to Como Zoo. In Saint Paul."

"Someone suggested walking around Lake the Isles was fun."

"There's some stunning homes over there." He tipped her phone and read her list. "If you like all the outdoorsy things, you should add Minnehaha Falls."

"Thanks." She liked them because they were free.

He leaned his elbows on the table. "I could show you what you're missing … if you'd help keep me away from my triggers."

"Your triggers?" Her mouth dropped open. "I can't be responsible for that. I can't keep you from anything."

He shoved his hands through his hair. "I'm screwing this up. You wouldn't be responsible for my sobriety. I am. I know that."

She rubbed the front of her neck. Was it hot in here?

"It's not good for me to just sit in my condo, and being with my family—it's like they want to breathalyze me every time I see them." He gripped the arms of his chair. "We'd be helping each other out. I get … out of my condo and my head, and you get to learn more about where you live."

It might be nice not to do everything by herself. But with Michael?

She finally said, "I'll think about it."

THREE

Liz stuck her head into Kate's office. "Do you have time to review my ideas on rearranging the upper floors of the Daschle building for Thornton Harrington?"

"Please." Kate shifted away from her computer and moved to her conference table, waving Liz in. "That will be a lot more fun than going through the diligence materials on the building Dad's thinking of buying. Their leases are old school. If I see many more therefores and wherases I might scream."

"Anytime you want me to help, let me know." Liz set down a packet of papers and took a seat.

Kate settled into her chair. "I figure once I get through one, I can identify the important clauses and pull the key issues into a spreadsheet. Although I'll want someone to look at the loan information. I have a suspicion the bank can call the loan if the current owner sells the building. We'd need to get Michael's department involved in the cash flow projections."

Liz's fingers tightened around her pen at the mention of Michael.

"So, what have you come up with?" Kate asked.

Liz spread out the Daschle blueprints she and Stephen had

worked on. "I'm ignoring the floors that won't be touched, but I have them here if we need them."

Kate scooted sideways so she could read the renderings. "And to think this all started with you talking to your real estate friend."

"I'd take credit, but I was lucky." Liz's Realtor friend had gotten the law firm heir apparent, Mitch Thornton, interested in the Daschle building. Kate had used the leverage to lock in a ten-year lease extension with another law firm. Now they had one of the biggest regional law firms looking for space in their building.

"We have almost a hundred and fifty thousand square feet open or coming up for renewal. The problem is the floors aren't adjacent to each other. We can fit in the new firm, but tenants will have to move and we'd need to offer them concessions. Here's the list of tenants we'd move."

Between her and Stephen, they'd probably put in over fifty hours trying to find 100,000 square feet in the building.

Kate sorted out the floor layouts. "We can't get them on eighteen through twenty?"

"I know they wanted the top floors, but the cost would be prohibitive. Plus, they really want stairs between their floors, and Stephen says it won't work between nineteen and twenty."

"So, we offer them floors sixteen through eighteen." Kate looked at the list. "You have this staged over six months."

Liz pointed at one of the spaces on the sixteenth floor. "This tenant's lease is up at year end. I've been checking with their office manager, and the company is amenable to staging their move. The Harrington lease is up in January, so this made sense."

Kate leaned back and rubbed her nonexistent baby bump. "I like this plan."

Liz tried not to stare. Kate had shared her shock when

she'd discovered she was pregnant. Now she was enjoying it. And her wedding was in less than two weeks.

"Okay, enough admiring my phenomenal skills." Liz handed Kate another packet of information and then opened her laptop. "Let's review the numbers."

They spent another thirty minutes running through the estimated costs, the concessions for the displaced tenants, construction and moving costs.

"With the tweaks we've made, let's schedule a meeting with Dad and get his approval." Kate organized all the information. "This is your project. I'll want you to present our proposal."

Liz didn't even try to hide how good that made her feel. "I'll check with Bernice and set up a meeting."

Kate filed the printouts into a folder but didn't stand.

"How are the wedding plans coming?" Liz closed her laptop. "Anything I can do to help?"

Kate's auburn curls bounced as she nodded. "I was hoping you might be my personal attendant."

Liz almost choked and ended up in a coughing fit with Kate standing and patting her on the back.

"Absolutely," she managed to sputter.

"That's great. I didn't want to ask my cousin." Kate grimaced. "She's so … negative. I'll have her handle the guestbook. I want happy people around me on my wedding day."

Happy people. That made Liz smile. "What do you need help with?"

Kate retrieved her iPad from her briefcase. "You don't have to help with stuff, but if you're willing …" she opened a spreadsheet. "Tomorrow night we're putting together the programs. Then next week we're finishing the favors."

"I'm in." And it wasn't because Kate was her boss. It was because she thought the world of her as a friend.

"And don't forget the bachelorette party this Friday," Kate said.

"I got the hipster-themed invitation and already RSVP'd. I can't wait," Liz said.

"I found a great dress at Second Hand Rose on University."

"I may have to check it out," Liz said.

She returned to her new office. Now that she was a manager, she had walls and a door on her cubicle. Next she wanted the title of director.

Even if she had to help her friend Kate move up in the company. But that was Kate's dream too.

Patience wasn't her strong suit. She'd been patient all her childhood. She'd had to share her birthdays. Share her room with a cousin. Even had to share some clothes with that same cousin.

She'd had enough sharing and waiting to last a lifetime.

She called Bernice, the CEO's assistant. They meshed everyone's schedules and set up the meeting within the hour.

She and Kate walked to her parents' conference room.

"Liz. Kate." Michael put away his phone. He was the only one at the table.

Liz blinked. "Are you sitting in?"

"Dad asked." Michael looked at her without any indication they'd spent most of Saturday together.

As she took a seat, she checked his eyes. Still clear. No evidence of his falling back, but what did she know. She only knew how Jordan had ripped her family apart. "I'm sorry, I need to make another copy of the terms and present value statement."

"It's okay. We can share. If I need more, you can send me a copy." Michael inched his chair closer to hers.

"Sure." She pulled out the copies she'd made, sent one across the table to Kate and one to the head of the table where Mr. MacBain always sat.

Mac walked in. "Sorry I'm late." His graying brown hair

with a hint of red was windblown. He wore a MacBain golf shirt and tan pants. "I was at The Towers. The damn inspector's trying to rewrite the building code."

"Shouldn't Timothy be handling that?" Michael asked.

Mac ran his hands through his hair, making it stand up. "I knew we were having trouble. I thought my being there might help."

Kate made a note. "Guess we won't have the certificate of occupancy this week."

"Not unless I can make enough trouble and prove the guy's an idiot."

Mac pulled his chair to the table and swung the packet Liz had put together in front of him. "What have you got?"

Kate nodded at Liz.

"We've looked at the Daschle building's tenants and how we could adjust the floors and provide the square footage that Thornton Harrington is requesting." Liz walked everyone through the changes, which tenants would need to move and the staging.

Kate described the offer terms. Then Liz jumped back in with the present value analysis, presenting the assumptions and then the cash flow. She and Kate both answered questions.

Michael looked at the numbers, jotting notes on the pages they shared. His shoulder bumped Liz's as he flipped the pages back and forth. "We'll be eating thirteen dollars a square foot in build-out expense?"

"It's the going rate," Kate said. "Although I thought I would start with ten dollars a square foot on the first pass."

"This is an opportunity to get another big-name tenant in the building," Liz added. "We know that both Thornton and Harrington were in their previous locations for over twenty years. Once we lock them in, it will be harder for them to move."

"Why are they moving again?" Michael turned toward her,

and she could almost count the gold flecks dotting his hazel eyes.

She swallowed. "Once the merger is consummated, they want a new location. In their previous locations, they thought there would still be a we/they environment."

He nodded. "That makes sense. Do we know how many other locations they're looking at?"

"Three." That sounded a little too certain, so she added, "We think. I know the Realtor showing them property."

"But of course Daschle is the best location," Kate said.

Mac grinned as he slid back in his chair. "This is a good proposal. Nice work."

Liz couldn't help it: she felt great. When she had been at Colfax, positive feedback had been rare.

"Just so you know, Liz is taking the lead on this project." Kate patted her belly again.

"You've got my approval." Mac pushed out of his chair and touched Michael's shoulder as he headed out of the conference room. "See you tomorrow?"

Michael nodded.

"Great." Mac left the room.

Liz started to stand, but Michael caught her hand. "Got a minute?"

"I—"

"I've got to run," Kate said, checking the clock. "We'll catch up this afternoon, Liz."

Liz settled back in her seat, slipping her hand away from Michael's.

His sea green eyes took a slow trip around her face, leaving her a little breathless. "I had a nice time on Saturday."

Nice? Yes, it had been … nice.

He leaned forward. A hank of brown hair slipped down on his forehead. She watched it, clenching her fingers in her lap.

"It was a spur-of-the-moment thing, but somehow it felt,"

he pressed a hand on his chest, "right. I'd like to help you see the Cities. You know some of what I've gone through, what I'm going through. I don't have to explain why I don't drink. You know about Mom's cancer."

He didn't even mention his fiancée. Wasn't losing her a defining moment in his life?

Maybe he didn't know the staff gossiped about him, about why he drank. The receptionist, Jenny, thought he was pining for his dead fiancée. Jenny thought it was romantic.

"Well," Liz said slowly, "I guess we can give this buddy thing a try."

~

MICHAEL HANDED Terry a coffee mug and slid into the chair opposite him. His knees bumped the small table. Luckily, nothing spilled. "Thanks for changing the time."

"No problem. Good to hear you're busy." Terry took a sip of his coffee and grinned. "Almost as good as a twelve-year-old scotch."

Michael took a sip of his own and shook his head. "Not even close. How can you do it? How can you joke about drinking?"

Terry leaned back, jarring the table again. "It's my way of coping. If it's always on my mind, I'd rather joke with people, so they're not uncomfortable."

Yeah. Everyone was uncomfortable around him, Michael thought. Even his parents and siblings didn't know how to talk to him. He snorted. Had they ever? Maybe he'd never fit into the family.

"Tell me," Terry said.

"What?"

"Tell me what you were just thinking."

Michael stared at the other man.

"You've got to open up. I know it's hard. In our culture, men are strong and silent. That's what got you here. That and an addictive personality."

Michael rubbed his chin. "Yeah."

"So what just went through your head?"

What had he been thinking? "People are uncomfortable around me. They don't know what to say. But my family's been that way for a while."

"Why do you think that is?"

He was different. He didn't live and breathe MacBain. "I'm the odd man out."

"Have you talked to them about this?"

They'd had family discussions in a group during his rehab. But that had really been about his reaction to Sarah's death and Mom's cancer. "No. It's not something that comes up."

Terry raised an eyebrow. "Don't you think it should?"

Michael's fingers rattled against the tabletop. "Not really."

"Guess what, that will be something you need to work on."

"Great," Michael said under his breath.

"So, what about our chat last Friday? Have you thought about taking up a hobby, finding something you're passionate about?"

Michael pushed away his coffee. "I've thought about it."

"And …"

Michael talked about the exhibits and the house he and Liz had toured. Weird, she hadn't seemed uncomfortable being with him. About the only person in the office who wasn't. Michael scratched his chin.

"So, who's this Liz?" Terry asked.

"She works for MacBain."

"Are you dating?"

"No." Michael shook his head. "No. She wants to see more of the area, and I told her I needed a friend outside of my drinking buddies. Outside of my family."

Terry didn't speak for a moment. He crossed his arms and finally said, "That's good, 'cuz I don't think you're in a good place to start a new relationship. You need to figure out how to be sober. You need to like being sober before taking on a relationship."

"I'm not talking about a relationship." Michael leaned back in his chair. Besides, no one could replace Sarah in his heart.

~

"HOLY MOLY." Liz peered at the MacBains' house. It wasn't a house, it was a mansion. The rock pillars and fascia gave the home an impression of a mini-castle.

She parked her car on the edge of the curved drive that led up the hill from the street and set the parking brake. No way was she leaving her rusting Corolla under the big portico when there were two expensive cars already parked there. Mammoth red doors guarded the MacBains from the riffraff.

Climbing the drive, she stood before the front doors and pulled in a deep breath.

When she rang the bell, a bong sounded in the house. Trust the MacBains to have an unusual doorbell.

She stood taller as the door opened.

"Liz?" the woman asked.

"Yes." She'd seen the dark blonde before. "You're Meg, right?"

"Yup! It's great to meet you." Meg held out her hand. "I hear you grew up on a farm in Iowa. I can't wait to find out more about you."

Liz followed the woman into the house, the impression of big, the only thing coming through. "You're pulling my leg, right?"

Meg turned and shook her hand. Light brown curls bounced around her face. "No. Why would I?"

"Because, hello—Iowa—and farm."

Kate joined them. "Meg, don't grill Liz. I don't want her running away screaming until after we finish the programs."

"Ha ha." Meg rolled her big blue eyes and tucked her arm in Liz's. "Don't let the pregnant lady scare you."

They walked into a dining room that could seat twenty plus. Large windows overlooked a rolling backyard. There was the full-sized basketball court the MacBain family sometimes talked about. Two men played, one looked like Mac but she couldn't identify the second player. At least now when they were talking, she could visualize the fenced in green court at the bottom of a hill.

Stacks of printed pages lined the dark wood table, along with vellum, ribbon and blank heavy stock. She'd seen the sample program, now they would put all the pieces together.

Kate stared at the program pieces. "What was I thinking?"

"You were thinking that you're marrying this great guy and want to make the day memorable," Meg said.

"But no one cares about the programs."

"We do." Meg pointed. "Sit."

Kate slid into the chair, cradling her head in her hand.

"We care, don't we Liz?" Meg said.

Liz nodded.

"And with three brilliant women, we will knock these suckers off in no time."

Liz looked at the stack and all the components. Then looked at Meg.

Since Kate had her back to the two women, they both pulled a face. "How many are we putting together?" Liz asked.

"Three hundred."

Liz sank into the chair. Okay. One hundred each. They could do this.

"We should each put one together, and then check who has the nicest bow," Meg suggested.

They split up the papers. Liz took a piece of heavy deep violet stock paper, stacked the printed ivory programs on top of that and then the vellum. She waited as Meg punched two holes at the top of all the papers. Then she strung lavender ribbon through the two holes and tied a bow.

Kate frowned, holding up her program with a lopsided bow. "How come your bow's better than mine?"

Meg held up hers. The bow looked like it had been through a battle and lost.

"4-H. I used to tie ribbons in my friend's horse's mane." Liz wiggled her fingers. "I can do a mean braid too."

"Looks like I'll be stacking paper," Kate said, pouting.

"I'll punch holes as soon as we get the ribbon cut." Meg scrunched up her face. "I wanted to tie bows, but I accede to your experience."

She and Meg cut the lavender ribbon. When she had enough to get started, she settled into a rhythm. Tamp the stack together, align the holes, thread the ribbon and then tie a bow.

Meg ran a finger over a completed program. "These are pretty."

"Do you have something to put these in?" The completed stack slipped as Liz added a program.

Kate pointed to a large wicker basket on the floor. "It's not beautiful, but it will do."

"I can spruce that up if there's enough ribbon."

"You're elected." Kate took in a deep breath. "I don't know why I decided to do all these futzy things. I am not a crafter, but the magazines make it look so simple." She pointed first at Meg and then Liz. "Don't let me make this kind of mistake again."

Everyone laughed.

Kate pushed out of her chair. "I need to pee. Anyone want anything to drink or eat?"

"Beer," Meg piped in almost before Kate finished her sentence.

"Sounds good." Liz tied another bow, then cut more ribbon.

"So 4-H, huh?" Meg said.

Liz sat for a minute, smoothing the bow and then set the program with the others. "When you grow up on a farm, you join 4-H. Every kid's in it."

"The idea of living on a farm seems so romantic to me. I envy you."

"Romantic?" Liz laughed. "If by romantic you mean hard work, then yes, it was very romantic. My family raises corn most of the time, but sometimes soybeans. We had a few dairy cows, so you're tied to milking twice a day."

"But it was automated, wasn't it?"

"Yeah, but that doesn't mean the cows work the machines themselves."

Meg cursed as the hole punch slipped and she had to toss one of the sheets of paper. "I said it sounded romantic, not easy!"

"Mom has a kitchen garden. She makes the best strawberry jam. Award winning jam." Liz smiled at the memory. "I was either milking at five or weeding that garden or moving the cows from one field to another. Or babysitting my cousins."

"Me too. The babysitting, I mean." Meg set another program in the center of the table for Liz to tie. "I hated it."

"Oh, do you have a big family?"

"Not so big, but I grew up having to babysit a lot. I guess that's the blessing and curse of being older than most of the kids on my street."

"At least you learned the value of a dollar early." Liz reached for more ribbon.

"Sure. And negotiating with kids to stay in bed helped me prepare for a career in law."

They both laughed.

"After my aunt's divorce, she and her two kids came to live with us. I was eleven."

"Ah."

"My mom's sister." As much as she loved the farm, since she was young she'd known it barely supported her parents and aunt.

"Do you have any brothers or sisters?" Meg asked.

"I have a twin brother, Jordan." She didn't want to talk about herself anymore. "How about you? Siblings?"

"I'm the oldest, and wisest of course, of three girls."

Liz laughed. "And do your sisters acknowledge your superiority?"

"They aren't smart enough to recognize it. Even if Carly is in med school and Kim is finishing her MBA."

Liz placed another program in the basket. "And you're an attorney, right?"

"Yes." Meg picked up another stack of paper. "Sometimes I wonder if this is my true calling."

"Wait, don't you work for Thornton?"

Meg nodded, almost standing to punch holes in the next program.

"Will you be affected by the merger?"

"No, I'm an SEC attorney." Meg lined up another set of paper. "My client base is pretty stable, unless they merge. Then I might lose a client or take on the new corporation. Otherwise, it's pretty boring."

SEC. Security and Exchange Commission. Liz hadn't had much to do with their regulations. All the companies she'd worked for had been privately held. There was so much about business she would like to learn.

Maybe she should go back for her masters. Although she had no clue how she would pay for it. Would an MBA even help her move up in a family company? Maybe it had been a mistake to work for MacBain, but she was learning so much.

"You think your work is boring?" Liz asked.

"It wasn't at first. Now ..." Meg held up her hands.

Liz was about to ask why when Kate returned, followed by Michael. His dark hair was tousled, and his T-shirt had a centerline of sweat.

"I found slave labor in the kitchen," Kate said.

Michael carried in a tray with water, two beers and snacks.

She bit her lower lip. What did Michael think when he was carting around alcohol?

"Hey, Meg, Liz." He twisted the caps off the beers. "Bottle or glass?"

"The bottle's fine." Meg picked up a beer. "No need to dirty dishes for me. No sir."

Liz watched as Kate kept her eye on Michael. Did Kate worry he would fall off the wagon if people drank around him.

"I don't need a glass," Liz said. Did that sound like she drank all the time?

Michael handed her the opened bottle and gave her a little smile. She took a big swallow, hoping the beer would cool the heat on her cheeks.

Meg looked at her and then Michael and raised her eyebrows.

She wanted to tell Meg, *It's not like that. He just needs a friend.*

He picked up one of the completed programs. "Wow, what is this?"

Kate explained.

Liz watched Michael. He pulled out a chair to sit and stretched his long legs, crossing them at the ankles. He wore loose gym shorts, which revealed a lot of his long, wiry body.

She ripped her gaze back to her task, tying bows. Keeping her head down, she made her fingers fly.

"Liz?" Kate asked.

"Hmmm?"

"How many have we finished?" Kate asked.

Liz checked her piles of twenty-five programs each. "One-hundred and twenty-five."

"That's all?" Kate frowned. "No more bathroom breaks for me."

Like a pregnant woman could control that.

Michael watched for a while as they worked. "I don't think the slowdown is from putting the papers together," he said.

Liz fumbled with the ribbon she was threading through the holes. How had the holes shrunk? She finally pushed the ends through and tied the bow.

"It's Liz," Michael said.

"Hey," she complained, "I'm working as fast as I can."

He waved his hand. "That's not what I meant. It's that you have to get the ribbon into the holes and then tie." He looked at the three women. "I could help."

"You're my favorite brother." Kate blew him a kiss.

Michael snorted. "Right."

"Why don't I cut and thread the ribbon." He moved next to Liz. "You keep tying your knots."

"Bows. Umm, sure." Liz tried to shift away from him, but the chairs were too heavy.

After finishing another twenty-five, she rewarded herself with a swig of beer. Then she shot a guilty glance at Michael. She shouldn't be drinking in front of an alcoholic.

The beer bottle rocked a little as she set it down.

"It's not a problem," he said.

"I shouldn't drink in front of you," she whispered. Luckily Meg and Kate were laughing about something on the other side of the table.

"It's all right. They teach us how to say no." This time his smile didn't reach his eyes.

She chewed her lip. What else could Michael say?

43

He pushed a stack of threaded programs to her. "Come on, Liz. Don't flake out on me now. I need someone to treat me normally."

"Were you working out?" she asked, trying to act *normal*, whatever that was.

"I helped my dad move some furniture, getting ready for the influx of relatives for the wedding. Then we played a little one-on-one."

"What's with all you MacBains and basketball?" She counted the next batch of twenty-five programs. With Michael's help they were making a dent.

"Best game ever," Kate said.

Meg shook her head. "They're all crazy."

Michael actually smiled. "We're tall, so that helped in school ball. Dad always had a hoop for us. Even at the old house we could shoot hoops in the basement during the winter."

In the basement? The basement of her family's hundred-year-old farmhouse was dark and small. She remembered when they'd poured the concrete floor. "What if you didn't want to play?"

Kate pushed another set of programs to Meg to be hole-punched. "It got me out of babysitting the younger brothers. I loved the game. Still do."

"She cheats," Michael said. "Dirtiest player in the family."

Kate grinned.

"I don't know why you want to play a game where you jam your fingers." Meg checked her manicure.

Liz couldn't help but agree and nodded.

Michael turned to her. *"Et tu, Brute?"*

"Mais oui!"

"That was Latin, not French," he said.

The three of them laughed and Michael seemed to drop ten years. His gray T-shirt made his eyes glow the soft color of new corn plants after a rain. A green so sharp, it always made her cry. She hadn't seen spring at home in way too long.

She clung to the ribbons, keeping her hands to herself. Butterflies filled her chest, making it hard to breath.

"Sorry, Liz." He gave her shoulder a quick massage.

She wrenched away from his hands. Her pulse beat too fast.

Liz nodded at Kate and Meg. "I'll remember you all laughing at me. Especially when I'm pinning your hems with sharp pointy objects."

Meg clutched Kate's hands. "Are you sure you want her as your personal attendant?"

Kate laughed again. "Absolutely."

"I'd wondered how you'd got sucked into the wedding vortex," Michael said.

"And I want you to come to the rehearsal dinner. That's in two weeks," Kate said. "But don't bring any of those sharp pointy objects."

"I'm not really part of the wedding party."

"You are now," Kate insisted. "It's at Alex's parents' place on Lake Minnetonka. He's sending out the directions tomorrow. Bring a date."

Liz refused to look up from the ribbon she was tying, hyperaware of Michael's presence beside her.

Kate looked at Meg. "Have you decided?"

Meg leaned a little harder on the punch. "David."

Kate shook her head. "Three million guys want to date you, and you pick your *go-to* guy."

"Go-to guy?" Liz asked.

Meg smiled. "Whenever I need a date or he needs a date, we help each other out. We're friends. It's great. No pressure, no expectations."

"Lake Minnetonka. Nice. I'll pick you up," Michael said to Liz.

The three women turned and stared at him.

"Y-you don't have to," Liz stuttered.

"It's a long way out there. Plus, I can be your designated driver."

His gaze held hers, daring her to say no. She wanted to roll her cool bottle of beer across her forehead because the way he was looking at her raised the temperature in the room another five degrees.

"Sure," she said.

Apparently Michael was her *go-to* guy.

FOUR

Michael plugged Liz's address into his GPS. Over the last two weeks he and Liz had visited the Como Conservatory, the Stone Arch Bridge and the University's Arboretum. The roses had been gorgeous, but he liked the Japanese gardens the best. If he owned a house, he would spend more time there, in his own garden.

That would mean leaving the place where he and Sarah had lived. He couldn't do it. Damn it, Sarah should be here with him.

But hanging with Liz had been—nice. They'd visited places that didn't constantly remind him of Sarah's absence. Sarah had preferred spending time at either of their parents' cabins or taking in shows or movies. He'd just wanted to be with her.

Liz was still tentative about hanging around together. Even yesterday she'd suggested she drive out to the groom's dinner on her own. He'd convinced her it would be a waste of gas. They were on the edge of friendship, and he didn't know what else he could do to tip her into true friendship. At least helping Liz explore the area kept him from sitting alone in his condo. What had Kate called the guy Meg was bringing to this groom's dinner? *Go-to?* Yeah. He and Liz were almost friends. Buddies.

He pulled up to the old house where Liz lived. The place had nice lines. Three stories, a big wide porch that wrapped around three sides. Great shaped windows but they probably leaked and made heating and cooling a bitch.

Pity someone had converted it to rental property, but the house had probably become too inefficient and it wasn't on a street that would warrant a restoration into a single family home. The owner had painted the old Victorian all beige when it should have had a great color scheme to show off the leaded windows and porch railings.

He moved up the sidewalk, avoiding the spot where the roots from a century old oak tree had heaved up the slab. He checked the mailboxes. E. Carlson was in unit 5.

He walked into a dark central hallway. Units one and two were on the main floor. He headed up the stairs. Three and four flanked the second-floor landing.

No wonder Liz had such great legs. She climbed three flights of stairs every day.

His breath was puffing a little as he stopped at her door. He should start using the stairs at his condo to help get back into shape.

He knocked.

In the apartment, he heard the clip of her heels.

The locks clicked. That was good since there wasn't any security in the entry.

"Hey, Michael." Liz's reddish-blonde hair floated around her shoulders and down her back. He hadn't realized it was that long. Long enough to brush the top of her breasts.

He yanked his gaze up to her eyes. "Hey."

"You should have called. I would have come down."

She leaned back in the doorway and picked up a shawl and small purse. He got a quick glimpse of the room behind her. A small floral sofa was angled into an alcove formed by the pitched roof. He'd probably bump his head on the side of the room, but not Liz. She barely came up to his chest.

Wait, this afternoon she did. She was wearing spikey heels. He could see her painted toenails. They were the same color as her dress and eyes, that blue that was named after a flower.

"Cornflower," he muttered.

"What?"

He waved his hand at her dress.

She looked down, giving him a chance to look too. Her dress knotted at her side, the material crossing and highlighting her breasts.

"Oh, the color." She looked back up at him before moving to the door. "I'm ready."

"Good." He shuffled back and stood in the hallway as she locked the door.

"Are you sure we aren't going to be early?" she asked.

"It's a long way." And he liked to be on time.

He held the door and then hustled down the porch steps to his car and opened her door.

She already had her seatbelt on by the time he'd gotten in. She asked, "Does it feel strange, Kate getting married?"

There had been so many changes in their lives over the last few months.

"Between Mom's cancer and Kate's engagement ..." He glanced at Liz.

"And Kate's pregnancy?"

He nodded. "I wasn't sure you knew."

"I guessed the second time she ran to the bathroom and threw up during a meeting."

He shivered. "I don't need the details."

"I'm sure she's glad to be over that stage." She glanced out the side-view mirror as he changed lanes. "But you didn't answer my question."

"Right." He changed lanes again, taking the entrance onto the freeway. "Well, between all that ... and my ... problem, things are feeling a little surreal."

"Surreal." She nodded. "That's what my first job in the Cities was like."

"At Colfax?" He'd had a sense that things hadn't gone well there.

"I really loved the job. They had quite a few new projects coming on line and I got to work with clients, walk through their new rental properties and help with the design." She ran the chain that was her purse strap around and around. It must have been a complete circle.

"Why did you leave?" Although he could ,guess. He knew the owner's son. The guy was an asshole, married but always hitting on other women.

They used to visit the same bars.

"Everything was going great. I liked my boss, I liked my job, and then I was introduced to Jerry." Now her finger tapped against the purse, making the chain rattle.

He took one hand off the wheel to still her hand. It was soft, and he had the urge to link their fingers together. *His buddy's fingers.* He took the wheel back firmly in both hands. "I kind of guessed you had trouble with Jerry."

"Trouble?" She let out a strained laugh. "That's an understatement."

Now her leg bounced up and down.

Her nerves reminded him of his brother Timothy.

"I'm sorry," he said.

"Jerry had trouble taking no for an answer."

The hair crawled up the back of his neck. Had Jerry forced himself on Liz? Was she fired over this?

"Did you talk to anyone?" He checked the traffic and passed the car in front of him.

"I ... I couldn't. He was part of the family. I ..." Her head was going back and forth like a perpetual motion toy. "Who would they believe? A new employee or the son? I updated my résumé and left."

"You should have talked to someone. The head of HR, your boss, someone."

She rubbed her arms. "I didn't want to."

"But he shouldn't get away with that crap," Michael said. "Even if he is the owner's son."

His stomach twisted.

"You don't ... I'm not acting like Jerry, am I? Do you feel pressured to hang out with me?"

She turned to face him and tucked one foot under her other leg. She touched his arm. "You're not like that. You're not like Jerry."

"Thank God for that."

She laughed. "You've got your own set of problems, my friend, but sexual harassment isn't one of them."

"Good to know."

And thank goodness she couldn't read his mind.

"HOLY COW," Liz gasped as Michael drove through the open gate. "I thought your parents' home was impressive, but this ... my apartment would fit in the gatehouse with room to spare."

"Nice summer home," he said.

"This is a summer home?" Boy, when she grew up she wanted to live like this. She might have to set her goals a little bigger than getting another promotion and sending more money to her parents.

"I'm kidding." He grinned. "This place is huge."

"Can I drop you off, borrow your car and head home?" She smoothed a wrinkle on her dress, the dress she'd found on the sales rack.

"Come on, Liz, I've never seen you nervous before."
Michael parked the car on the long drive. "Where's your can-
do attitude?"

"It disappeared when we drove down that peninsula.
Michael, they have their own bridge."

"And how many acres does your family own?"

"Nine hundred."

"That's more land than everyone who will attend this party
owns combined." He shut off the car. "Come on. You know
my family. Alex's can't be that different or Kate wouldn't have
fallen in love with him."

But it was different. A maid answered the door. Sure, she
wasn't in the short black skirt with a frilly white apron, but she
wore tailored black pants and a white blouse that probably cost
more than Liz's dress.

The woman looked perfectly at ease in the huge marble
entry, which was bigger than the farm's kitchen, soaring three
stories above their heads. A massive chandelier sparkled with
lights. Light-colored wood stairways wrapped up both sides of
the entry to the second floor. The beautiful, curved bannister
was polished to a high gloss. The air carried a soft scent of
lemons.

"If you'll head down the hall and turn left, you'll find
French doors to the patio," the maid said.

Michael set a hand on her lower back. "Come on."

"Do you think Alex and his sisters slid down the bannister?" Liz whispered.

He laughed. "I would have."

Her heels echoed on the hallway floor, the same light wood
as the staircase. A massive abstract painting hung at the end of
the hall, the colors bold blues and reds.

Michael stopped in front of the piece. "Wow, an early
David Anderson."

She shook her head. "You're supposed to make me feel more at ease."

He bumped her shoulder. "We'll check out his work at the Art Institute the next time we go."

He aimed her toward the French doors.

This time she was the one who stopped. "Look at that view."

The double set of doors framed Lake Minnetonka. A pair of sailboats raced around the tip of the peninsula. Gentle waves lapped at the shoreline. She hugged her arms around her waist. "This is different from how I grew up."

She finally pulled her gaze away from the water. The flagstone patio was huge and swarmed with staff. Each table was set with centerpieces of deep purple irises paired with gerbera daisies and white and pink lilies. A bar anchored one side of the space.

Past the patio, green grass rolled down a hill to a smooth area. Kids could play soccer down there.

"This is incredible," she said.

"Come on." Michael held open the door for her.

An older woman hurried over to them. She had a dramatic silver streak on one side of her black hair. "Welcome! Welcome!"

Michael held out his hand. "Michael MacBain, brother of the bride."

She took his hand and used two of hers to shake his. "Natalie Adamski, mother of the groom. Sorry we didn't meet you earlier."

"Well, I was a little tied up in rehab."

Liz's mouth dropped open.

Natalie laughed. "I hope that wasn't literally tied up."

Michael shook his head.

Natalie held her hand out to Liz.

"Hi, I'm Elizabeth Carlson, Liz. Umm, personal attendant to the bride."

"Oh, make sure you wear comfortable shoes. I was a personal attendant for my cousin." Natalie winced. "I think I ruined my feet for life."

"I'll remember that."

Natalie wrapped an arm around Liz's shoulders. "They're setting up the snacks and the bar. What can I get you? You get first pick since you've even beat the bride and groom."

"We did?" Liz swallowed.

"I need to check with the caterers." Natalie walked them to the bar. "Enjoy yourself."

Liz looked at Michael. "We're that early?"

He shrugged. "I like to be early."

"How early are we?" she whispered.

"Maybe ten minutes?"

She checked her phone. "Try twenty." She looked at the array of glasses and liquor. "As long as I'm here, I'll see if I can help with anything."

"You don't have to do that."

"Maybe Natalie can use another pair of hands." She'd be more comfortable working this party than attending. She eyed the bar. "Will you be okay here?"

"I'm fine." Michael glared at her, understanding perfectly what she was asking. "I'll walk down to the dock. I wouldn't want to be seduced by the call of the alcohol."

She rolled her eyes. Turning, she headed through the door Natalie had taken. The air conditioning made her shiver.

"You're here!" Kate, in a lavender sundress, called from the hallway.

"I am."

Kate pulled Liz back out to the patio with her.

Liz tried to pull away. "I thought I'd see if your mother-in-law-to-be needed any help."

"We're here to have fun." Kate stopped and stared at the patio. "It's gorgeous ... Oh God, I'm getting married." Kate fell into the closest chair. She pressed on her stomach. "Tomorrow."

"I seem to recall that."

"Can you believe this place?" Kate waved her hand. "When Alex introduced me to his family, my mouth hung open for the first hour."

"Thank goodness, I thought it was just me." Liz chuckled.

"Are you kidding? Look at this place! I thought Alex's music office was incredible, but Natalie's takes up more square footage than my condo."

"Their entry is bigger than my whole apartment."

"Speaking of apartments, I'm putting my condo on the market. You could walk to work from there." Kate fingered one of the irises in the floral arrangement. "We could work out a good deal."

Liz had been there a couple of times. Kate's place was gorgeous. "I can't afford it."

Kate frowned. "With the current low interest rates, you should think about buying. Run the numbers."

Maybe. Liz hadn't thought about owning her own place. But if she made that kind of commitment, it might stop her from sending money to Mom and Dad. She had to help pay for the mistakes she'd made.

"Listen, I won't have a chance to do anything about it until after the honeymoon." Kate gave herself a small hug and grinned. "But you should really think about it."

"I will," Liz said. But couldn't risk not helping her parents.

"Tonight I want to introduce you to Alex's best man," Kate said. "He's pretty hot."

Before Liz could respond, Alex came out on the patio, his arms around two women who had hair as black as his. Probably his sisters. And Michael came up the walk from the shore and rejoined her.

From that moment on, it seemed every time she turned around she was meeting someone new. This wasn't an intimate groom's dinner with only the wedding party as guests. This party included both the bride and the groom's extended families.

Michael leaned closer. "I haven't seen some of the cousins for years."

"It's nice that the families can get together, not just for the wedding." Homesickness swept over her like a storm through a cornfield. She hadn't been back since Christmas.

"We need the wedding party," Alex's voice boomed over the noise of the crowd.

Michael handed his glass to her. "I guess that's me."

She couldn't help it. She sniffed his drink. It wasn't that she thought he might be drinking. His eyes looked too clear. It's just —she didn't trust addicts.

The bubbles made her nose itch. She took a sip. Ginger ale. Her cheeks heated. It wasn't her responsibility to keep her non-date, buddy sober. Although, he was her ride home.

While Liz took a seat at one of the tables, the priest had the wedding party practice their parts. Michael escorted one of Alex's sisters. Stephen the other. Timothy made a female cousin laugh as he tugged her down the pretend aisle. Meg took the arm of the best man. They skipped toward the rest of the wedding party.

The best man was good-looking, with a great haircut and easy smile. She looked between him and Michael. A little zing went through her.

She wasn't supposed to be *zinging* for Michael.

Then finally Mr. and Mrs. MacBain brought Kate down the aisle. Halfway down, Kate ran up and placed her hands in Alex's. Everyone laughed.

There were discussions with the wedding party the onlookers couldn't hear. Instructions for tomorrow, probably.

A server passed Liz's table and offered her a glass of champagne. It was nice having a designated driver, even if she felt guilty for drinking around Michael.

Finally Kate and Alex ran up the aisle. Alex picked her up and dipped her into a massive kiss. Everyone clapped. Liz set her glass down and joined in.

"He's so romantic," a woman next to her gushed. "They're so cute together."

Liz turned in her seat. Brunette, brown eyes, a cousin on Kate's side, but she couldn't remember her name. Too bad they didn't have name tags. "They look good together."

The woman shook her head. "I never thought Katie would get married. All those summers we spent at the lake she always swore she would marry the company if she could."

"I'm sorry, I've forgotten your name," Liz confessed.

"Oh, me too." She laughed, pushing away her empty champagne flute. "Wait, I mean I've forgotten your name, not my own. I'm Courtney from the MacBain side of the family."

"Hey, Courtney, I'm Liz."

Courtney's eyes widened. "You work with Katie, right?"

Liz nodded.

"I'm jealous. She's my hero." Courtney left the table she was sitting at and sat next to Liz. "I would love to work with her, but I need to graduate first."

"What's your major?"

"Finance and entrepreneurial studies. I have one more year left. Well, not that many credits, but I'll be a May grad."

"Kate had a double major too."

"I know. I admit I copied her academic path," Courtney said.

Liz twirled her champagne flute. Kate's maternity leave was only a few months away. Would Kate consider bringing on her cousin for an internship, or was that too much family? And would Liz be training her replacement if she recommended Courtney? Courtney was family after all.

They talked about the courses Courtney was taking. The wedding party returned to the patio, and Michael joined their table.

"Hey, Courtney, haven't seen you in—years," Michael said.

Courtney jumped up from her seat and gave him a hug. "I've been busy growing up."

"You've done a nice job." Michael looked at Liz. "Do you have my pop?"

Liz checked the table. "I set it down while watching the rehearsal. The serving staff must have picked it up. I'm sorry, I'll get you another."

He frowned at the two champagne flutes. "No, that's okay. We're eating soon."

"I can—"

He stopped her by catching her hand as she started for the bar, setting off a flight of goose bumps. "It's okay."

"Oh, wow, this is nice." Courtney waved a hand between them and sighed. "You work together. It must be so romantic."

Liz glanced around, hoping no one had heard Courtney. She didn't want that kind of rumor running through the MacBain family. "We're just friends."

Courtney pouted. "Really? But you're cute together."

Michael rolled his eyes.

"You said the same thing about Kate and Alex." Liz couldn't help laughing again. Being around Courtney made her feel old. "What color is the sky in your world?"

"Blue and sunny every single day."

"She's always been like this. The eternal optimist," Michael confirmed.

Wouldn't that be wonderful? People used to call Liz an optimist. That had all changed when Jordan ended up in the hospital. And it had been her fault. The memories slammed into her.

"Mom! Dad!" Liz rushed into the ER waiting room and hugged her dad and then her mom. "What happened?"

"Someone beat him up." Her mother squeezed her close. "Why would anyone hurt him?"

"No!" But she knew why, or guessed.

"Carlson family?" a nurse said from a doorway.

They hurried over to the woman.

"You can come back now."

They followed the woman to a room.

Jordan lay on a gurney. His swollen nose was taped. Dried blood coated his neck and face, and his arm was splinted.

"Jordan." She went to take his hand, but it was bandaged too.

"Hey Lizzy." His words were barely recognizable.

"Did Rudy do this?" she asked. Maybe if she had told her parents how bad Jordan's gambling had gotten, he wouldn't be here.

Jordan glared at her. "You promised me."

Mom and Dad stood at the foot of the bed staring at her and her brother.

"What's going on?" Dad asked.

She was done keeping Jordan's secrets. For his sake, she had to tell them. "Jordan's gambling is out of control."

"Shut up." Jordan's words slurred.

"Look what's happened to you. You can't keep doing this. You need help."

"Liz?" Michael waved his hand in front of her face. "Everyone's sitting down."

People were finding their tables.

"What happened?" he asked.

"I was … just thinking of … stuff." She started to move to her assigned table, but Alex's dad held up a microphone. He had a full head of silver hair and stood inches over six foot tall. He must be a real force in the courtroom.

59

Feedback rang over the patio; people covered their ears.

"Sorry about that," Mr. Adamski said. "I should have left this to the experts."

Everyone laughed. A few people toasted Mr. Adamski with their glasses raised.

"If you'll find your seats, we'll get the food out here. I know I'm starving." He patted his stomach. "Natalie and I are glad you're joining us to celebrate with Kate and Alex."

Again the glasses went up, and all eyes turned to the couple.

"I wish you joy and happiness." Alex's father lifted his champagne flute. "To Alex and Kate."

"To Alex and Kate," everyone repeated.

Liz glanced at Michael as he tucked his hands in his pocket.

"Father, could we ask you to say a few words?" Mr. Adamski asked.

As the priest moved from the back of the crowd, Michael directed her to a different table. The last time she'd looked, her name tag had been next to the best man.

"Did you rearrange the name tags?" she asked.

His eyes went wide. "I don't like what you're insinuating, Elizabeth."

She shook her head. "Right. You never touched the name tags."

The priest blessed the gathering and the food. Lowering her head, Liz laced her fingers together, letting his gentle words soothe her. She'd been brought up Lutheran, so she wasn't familiar with all the gestures, but Michael followed along.

Their salads were already set: grilled asparagus on a bed of field greens with golden and red beets. "This is beautiful," she whispered.

Michael already had a forkful in his mouth. "And it tastes good."

They were sitting with cousins from both families. The only one Liz had met was Courtney, and she sat on the opposite side of the table. The couple to her left were newlyweds from Alex's side who kept feeding each other. Michael sat to her right.

"Wine, ma'am?"

Liz looked at the young man holding out a bottle. "Please."

She forced herself not to look at Michael.

Michael covered his wineglass. "None for me."

"Of course, sir. Would you like something else?"

He asked for more ginger ale.

The waiter moved around the table, filling glasses. Liz focused on her salad.

Michael leaned close. His cologne smelled almost as delicious as the food being placed at the table behind them.

"Stop thinking I'll freak out every time there's alcohol around. You were supposed to be someone normal I could hang with. Turns out you're as bad as my family."

"Doesn't this bother you?" She pushed her salad out of the way and waved at her wineglass.

He leaned toward her. Their faces were so close she could see his pupils dilate. He had a small scar under his eyebrow.

He exhaled, feathering the hair off her face. His gaze dropped to her lips.

She jerked, turning back to her plate. The MacBain family was all here. She didn't want her friendship with Michael to hurt her career.

He finally said, "No, it doesn't."

"Excuse me?"

Silver chimed against china. People's conversations buzzed. She looked across the table, and Courtney had a grin on her face. She gave a thumbs-up.

Liz blushed.

"No, seeing other people drinking doesn't bother me,"

Michael said, his voice a low rumble. "Stop worrying about drinking in front of me."

Right. If she'd learned anything from her brother, it was that addicts told you what they thought you wanted to hear.

~

LIZ DIDN'T BELIEVE HIM. Michael nodded as the server took away his empty salad dish. Right behind him, another server set his entrée in the empty space. Liz didn't believe he could be around people who were drinking.

Yeah, he wanted to feel that first hot slide of whiskey. Have it hit his empty stomach and loosen his muscles. But he wasn't in it for the thrill. He'd always wanted the oblivion. He wanted that point right before he passed out where he could reach out to Sarah. Reach out and talk to her, touch her.

God, he missed her so fucking much. Missed belonging to her. Missed the dreams and plans they'd made.

He pushed on the ever-present ache in the middle of his chest. Two years next month. Two fucking years. They would have been married almost four years if Sarah hadn't wanted to wait after she'd been diagnosed.

They might have had a kid. Or Sarah might have talked him into two. She'd always been able to talk him into everything.

He'd wanted to make her happy. One smile from Sarah made his whole day.

He looked at Liz. Her back was turned to him as she talked to his cousin Margaret and her husband.

Hell, earlier if they hadn't had all these witnesses, he'd almost kissed Liz.

He was a mess. He didn't want to give up Sarah, but he wanted to kiss Liz.

He could be around all these people while they drank, 'cuz

that wasn't his problem. It was in the dark when he wanted Sarah.

After the entrée was cleared, dessert appeared. He talked with Alex's cousin. They didn't know he'd been through treatment, so they didn't look at him as if he would steal their drinks out of their hands like his aunt and uncle had done earlier.

Worse, like Liz had looked at him.

And all the time they talked about the weather and tomorrow's wedding, he was hyperaware of Liz sitting inches away. It was like she had a magnetic hold on him.

"This is not the way I set the tables up," Kate said, placing a hand on his shoulder.

Liz turned toward his sister standing behind him. He clenched his teeth, seeing the regret and embarrassment on her face.

"Oh, w-well," Liz stuttered.

Kate tipped her head at the table behind them. "I wanted you to eat with Gabe."

Gabe, that slick ad guy? Kate was trying to set Liz up with that asshole?

He closed his eyes. They would probably be good together.

Liz glanced at him. "I enjoyed sitting with Michael."

Kate's fingers squeezed his shoulder. "Oh, sure. That's … nice. I thought you and Gabe …"

See, even his sister knew he wasn't any good for Liz.

"It was my fault, Katie. I switched the cards." He didn't want Kate thinking any less of her employee.

"What time do you want me at the church?" Liz asked Kate.

"I'll be there at noon. That gives makeup and hair three hours to get everyone ready. We're bringing in food, so don't worry about lunch." Kate put a hand on her stomach and took in a deep breath. "I'm getting married tomorrow."

Liz grinned. "This will be fun."

His baby sister was getting married. Something twisted inside him. He and Sarah had never gotten there.

He stood and hugged her. "I'm happy for you."

She held on. "Shoot. You'll make me cry. Then my makeup will run."

"Better now than tomorrow."

"I'll be wearing waterproof makeup tomorrow. We'll see how good it is."

She stepped away. Her hazel eyes stared into his. "I'm so glad you're here. I'm glad you're … better."

"Me too." He wished to God he wasn't lying.

She hugged him one more time. "Okay, I've got to talk to our guests."

Alex walked toward Kate, and her eyes brightened. Love burned in his eyes as he took her hand.

The ache in Michael's chest turned into a sharp pain.

He wanted Sarah. He wanted his soul mate. He wanted her by his side as he tried to figure out his place in the family.

He was firstborn and didn't know what he wanted to be when he grew up. His sister was better prepared to lead the company.

A drink didn't sound too bad after all.

"Are you all right?" Liz asked softly. She stood next to him. A breeze took her blue dress, cornflower blue, and molded it to her breasts.

"Fine."

"You're not fine." She touched his arm. "You look sad."

He shook off her hand. "Yeah, I'm fucking sad."

She took a step back, and her eyes widened. "I didn't mean to intrude." She twisted away from him.

Just as she took a step away, he caught her by the elbow.

"Let go." Her eyes glittered.

"Wait." He let go, holding his hands out in front of him. "You caught me in a bad place."

She crossed her arms over her chest. He kept his eyes on her face this time.

Swallowing, he said, "I was thinking about my fiancée."

"I'm sorry," she said stiffly. "Do you want to talk about it?"

There were too many guests who could eavesdrop on their conversation. Moving to the table, he picked up her wineglass and shoved it in her hand. "Let's walk down to the dock."

She stumbled and he caught her by the elbow a second time. Once she was steady, he tucked his hands in his pockets. No need to touch that soft skin.

"Are you sure you want to talk about her?" she asked. "You seem … angry … pushing and shoving. Don't take your anger out on me."

He nodded at one of his aunts. "I'm sorry."

He would just … he wanted to talk about Sarah. So he wouldn't forget.

He headed for the dock, but she pointed to a wooden swing on the lower tier of the lawn.

Her heels must be giving her problems because she walked on her tiptoes.

"You could take them off," he suggested.

"I don't think so."

She slipped onto the seat, angled her body and faced him.

"So …" she prompted.

"I was engaged." He closed his eyes. "I proposed about four years ago."

She nodded.

"We'd known each other," he swallowed, "forever. We'd known each other forever." Even he could hear the longing in his voice.

She waited. Music started on the patio. A burst of laughter floated to where they sat.

"Like high school?"

He shook his head. "Grade school. First grade."

Sarah's family had moved to the neighborhood after Christmas. They'd been assigned the same reading group. They'd been best friends and then more.

"Wow. Grade school." The words seemed like they were dragged out of her mouth.

He nodded and stared at the lake. There were so many boats clogging the bay, the place needed traffic patrols.

And why did people say that water looked blue? He'd been looking into Liz's eyes moments ago. That was blue. The lake looked dull gray in comparison.

"Once we graduated and moved back here, she started having headaches. Thought they were migraines. She ignored them for two years."

He sensed that she nodded.

"Stage three brain cancer. Eventually, glioblastoma. We spent the next two years in and out of hospitals, surgeries, treatments."

Her hand rested on his forearm. "I'm so sorry. It must have been horrible."

He let her hand rest there. He didn't have the energy to push it away. God, did anyone ever touch him anymore? Sometimes he felt like he wore *Do Not Get Close* signs.

"So when you thought I looked sad, I was thinking that Sarah and I should be celebrating our fourth anniversary. I look at my sister and think she might have been an aunt by now. I look at my sister and Alex and see everything I've lost."

He stood, and her hand fell to the seat of the swing. He headed to the dock. "Go back to the party."

LIZ SANK BACK against the wooden swing. Michael's fiancée had died. She'd known that. But now it was … real.

Michael walked away, his hands in his pockets, his shoulders hunched.

He was alone. And he didn't want help.

She set her wineglass on the grass, and it immediately tipped over. She couldn't swallow anything right now anyway.

Sarah, his fiancée's name was Sarah. She'd died almost two years ago but had battled her cancer for two years before that. No wonder Michael never smiled. Had he been grieving this long or had watching Kate's happiness brought on his sorrow?

She rubbed at the ache in her temple.

Brain cancer.

Leaning over, she picked up the wineglass and headed back to the party. It was what Michael wanted.

She looked one more time at the lone figure silhouetted on the dock.

Pain seemed to radiate off him. He was so alone and she wasn't able to help.

Just like she could never help Jordan. She wasn't an addiction counselor. She didn't know how to stop people from digging themselves so deep a hole that they couldn't come up for air.

Back on the flagstone steps, she forced a smile on her face as another couple headed down to the beach.

"There you are," Kate called.

Her boss and friend looked so darn happy, Liz couldn't help smiling for real.

"Come and meet Gabe."

Kate pulled her into a knot of people standing near the area now opened up for dancing. Alex towered over everyone. Hard to believe that someone six-foot-six could create such wonderful music.

"I found her," Kate called out.

Alex tucked Kate into his side and brushed a kiss on the top of her head. Liz held in a sigh. What would that kind of adoration be like?

"Gabe, this is the Liz I've been telling you about." Kate held out a hand to a tall brown-haired man. "Liz, this is Gabe Mauer."

"Not related to the baseball player," voices chorused around the group.

She laughed. "What a pity. You would be the life of the party."

He held out his hands. "I'm not the life of the party? Damn."

He had an easy smile. Trouble didn't hover behind his gray eyes.

"I don't think you're supposed to be the life of a groom's dinner party," Liz said.

"That makes sense." He stepped a little closer and she could smell his cologne, warm and expensive-smelling.

"Do you have your speech ready for tomorrow?" she asked.

Gabe looked at Alex. "I'm giving a speech?"

Everyone laughed.

Gabe snatched up her arm. *What was with all this grabbing?* "Tell me about this speech while we dance."

She let Gabe tug her to the dance area. The four-piece combo played music her grandparents used to sing.

Gabe pulled her into his arms, a little closer than respectable. With Gabe, she didn't worry about whether she would say something wrong, or long to hug him, just to soothe his sadness.

"So do you have your best man's speech ready?"

"Pretty much. I'm an ad man. Full of BS."

Right. She'd heard Gabe worked for an ad agency. "Would I recognize any ads you've worked on?"

"Maybe. One of my favorites is a campaign for Larson

Lighting." He spun her in a tight circle, moving like he'd trained as a dancer.

"I've seen their commercials. That little girl is so cute."

"Alex wrote the jingle."

"I'm impressed." They moved around another couple. "How has social media changed what you do?"

"We have to accelerate the way we get product info out there. It's a kick to look at how many hits a YouTube video receives or find out it's trending on Twitter. But the pace is mind-boggling."

"I'll bet." She'd thought some of the negotiating they did on leases could be stress-filled. "I guess every field has its share of adrenalin-inducing moments."

"Kate tells me you were promoted."

Her boss really was trying to set them up. "Yes. It's great working with her."

He watched Kate and Alex as they swayed together. "I've never seen him so happy. His ex-wife did a number on him."

"Kate's happy too."

He pulled her a little closer, and she lay her head on his chest. He smelled good. She took a deep breath and laughed.

He looked down at her. "Hey, what's the joke?"

"I was thinking how good you smelled and how bad spring can smell on the farm."

He tilted his head, frowning.

"The fertilizer."

"Oh. Oh," he said, finally getting it. "You're comparing me to fertilizer."

He made her laugh. Again.

She patted his back. "You're a nice man."

"Just keep those compliments coming. Next you'll compare me to a brother or cousin."

She grinned. He did feel like family.

He tugged her back into his chest and turned them in a circle.

As they spun, she caught a glimpse of Michael standing on the periphery of the dance floor. All alone. His arms were crossed and even though he leaned against a pillar, there wasn't anything relaxed about him.

A chill moved down her spine. What did Michael need from her? And why did she want to lead him onto the dance floor and just hold him?

"DID YOU HAVE A NICE TIME?" Liz asked Michael as they drove away from the party.

The car rattled over the bridge as she waited for an answer. Any answer that took this long wasn't going to be lighthearted.

He stopped at the stop sign and waited for his turn to pull onto the main street. "It's nice to see Mom looking healthy, and Kate happy."

"Everything's clear with your mom's cancer?" she asked, even though she knew the answer. It seemed better to keep Michael talking.

His smile glowed greenish from the dashboard lights. "Yeah. Still a clean bill of health. What a relief."

"She wasn't off all that long."

"She took a couple of months off during her radiation treatments. Dad would have liked her to take more time, but she was antsy to get back to work." He shook his head. "It was terrible seeing her so … fragile."

"She looks great now."

He pulled onto the highway.

Liz closed her eyes, letting the rhythm of the tires on the pavement lull her into a near-sleep.

"You know what bugs me the most?" he said.

She forced her eyes open. "What?"

"The looks people give me. How can I expect you to act normally around me when my own brothers don't know how to deal?" He ran his fingers through his hair, making it stand on end. "Timothy actual shoved a beer behind his back. I fucking hate this."

"How did the treatment staff tell you to handle these situations?"

"Assure people that I'm good. And if I wasn't strong enough to say no, to stay out of situations where I would be tempted."

"So you told me. Have I changed the way I react?"

He glanced at her. His eyes glowed bright green from the car's dash lights. "Sometimes. But you still stare at the glass in my hand and look like you want to sniff it."

"Maybe I wanted a sip. I was thirsty tonight, and every time I set down my glass, the waitstaff scooped it up."

"Right." He dragged the word out.

She couldn't stop a little laugh from snorting out. A rude sound that kids would have freaked over.

Michael laughed too. A deep rusty laugh.

"Next time take a sip." He actually grinned.

His laugh and his smile made her happy.

"Hopefully tomorrow everyone will have gotten over seeing you and wondering if you're drinking. Although I wouldn't hang next to the bar. That would make people talk."

"Yeah, that's a plan." She watched him in profile as he drove. "I got a chance to talk to Alex's dad about the house and how they designed the place."

He described how the Adamskis had made use of the lake view as they'd laid out the house. Just like when they'd been in the museum he grew animated talking about the home design.

Why was he in finance? His eyes didn't light up when he

71

talked about budgets or forecasts. Sure the glow from the car lights had some effect, but this was something inside Michael.

But she didn't ask. She didn't want him to think in case it made him quiet and sad.

"I talked the entire drive to your house," he said as he pulled in front of her apartment.

"I enjoyed it." She gathered her purse. "I'll see you tomorrow."

His hand dropped to hers before she could open the door. "So, you have to be there around noon?"

She nodded.

"I'll pick you up at eleven-thirty."

"I can drive. You probably have a lot to do."

He rolled his eyes. "Come on. I'll be your designated driver. It will be fun."

She didn't want to see him lose this energy. "Sure."

FIVE

Liz pulled the basket she'd created over the last two weeks out of the backseat of Michael's car.

"I can get that for you." He came around to her side of the car.

"I've got it. You have your tux to worry about."

"I don't understand why the women need all that stuff," he said, opening the church door.

"You never know what kind of emergency will come up."

She had pins, thread, water, aspirin, ibuprofen and scissors. There were bandages, hairspray and deodorant, granola bars, Imodium and antacids. Baby wipes and stain remover. And she'd found a small sample bottle of Kate's favorite perfume. She'd even included a coloring books and crayons in case the ring bearer and flower girl got bored.

Timothy paced inside the church entrance. "Can I take that for you?"

"No. Just point me to the bridal room."

"Follow me. Michael, the guys are down here too."

He led the way down the steps.

She was glad she'd thrown on shorts and flip-flops for the

first part of the afternoon. Before the wedding, she would change into her dress and sandals, the most expensive dress she'd ever purchased. Hopefully she would fit in with the crowd a little better than yesterday. The salesperson had said the pale lavender made her eyes almost look violet.

Timothy knocked at a door on the left. "Male of the species coming in."

Laughter broke out on the other side of the door.

"We're decent," someone called out. Possibly Meg.

Timothy held the door. "Into the dark side you go, Liz. If you need help, just follow this hallway. We're the second room on the right."

Michael peeked in. "Good afternoon, ladies."

"Alex better not be out there," Kate called.

"Nope. Stephen and Gabe are picking him up right now," Timothy said.

"Hello." Liz entered a room full of mirrors, chairs and women.

Everyone was dressed casually; shorts, yoga pants and T-shirts. A gray salon cape covered Kate. The makeup artist sprayed on what looked to be a base coat. Meg was in another chair with the hair stylist creating an intricate up-do with her light brown hair.

Kate's two cousins ate sandwiches on a small sofa.

"What on earth did you bring in that basket?" Meg asked.

Meg left her chair and pawed through it, holding up a water bottle. "This is fantastic." She raised her voice. "Kate, you won't believe what Liz brought. If I was ever going to get married, you would be my personal attendant, Liz."

She couldn't help smiling. "Sure thing."

Courtney and another MacBain cousin came over. Courtney exclaimed, "Holy cow. Put me on your list."

"Me too," said the other cousin. Liz would have to get her name.

Liz tucked the basked on a counter. "What do you need me to do?"

"Have a sandwich," Kate said. "Then can you wait upstairs for the photographers? They'll be here in about twenty minutes. The wedding planner is delayed."

"Will do." Liz took what looked to be a turkey sandwich.

And that was the last chance she got to sit for the next two hours.

She made a run to buy support wear for the mother of the groom. Looked like a torture devise to her. She tracked down the florist and brought the bouquets to the women and then pinned boutonnieres on all the men. Her feet were already starting to hurt, and she hadn't changed out of her flip-flops.

"Okay," she checked over the list of photos Kate wanted, "mother of the bride, mother of the groom and Kate. Then we're done with your group and you can head back inside."

She would head out with one of the photographers to make sure they didn't miss any of the pictures with the men.

Denise and Faye, the two photographers, closed in as the mothers flanked Kate. Her bouquet of pinks and purples added a splash of color in front of her ivory dress. Kate's mother had chosen a bold pink dress, Alex's purple. They looked perfect.

The photographers fired away.

"That's great," Denise said. "Time to move on to the men."

She and Faye draped their camera bags on their shoulders.

Kate, her mother and her mother-in-law linked their hands together. Kate dropped her head on her mother's shoulder.

Two flashes went off. The three women blinked in surprise.

"That picture will be fantastic," Denise said.

"I guess that's what the day will be like," Kate said. "I'll be seeing spots all night."

Faye took another picture as Kate tipped back her head

and laughed. "And the pictures will all be beautiful," the photographer added with a smile.

"On to the men." Liz checked her watch and then led the way back inside and knocked on the men's door. "Everyone decent?"

"No, but come on in." The voice had to be Gabe's.

What an array of male gorgeousness. They all wore tuxes, although they didn't all have their bowties tied. Alex paced in the corner.

"Anyone need help with their ties?" she asked.

Two hands shot up. She helped Stephen first. "Turn around."

He crouched in front of her. The guy was big, even from this angle. He was the biggest of the brothers. She made short work of the tie.

"How does that look?" she asked Gabe.

"Great."

She swallowed as Michael took the position. He was slimmer than his brother, and not as tan. But boy did he smell good. Her fingers shook a little as she reached for the tie. "How's Alex holding up?"

"We gave him a beer, but that didn't calm him down."

"Yeah, Kate had a sip of champagne but is saving the rest for the reception." She gave his tie a tug. The bright blue looked great on all the men.

"Your bride is absolutely radiant, Alex," she called over.

Alex smiled. Two flashes went off. "How's she doing?"

"Fantastic." Liz patted Michael's tie in place, and he stood. "Your jaw is going to drop."

She followed the men back out to the church steps where they'd shot the bride and bridesmaids. And finally the wedding planner showed up, apologizing for her absence.

"Where are the fathers?" Faye asked.

"I'll find them." Liz headed into the church. She'd last seen the two men resting in the back pews.

Luckily they were still there. Mac tucked a silver flask in his jacket pocket. Liz raised her eyebrows, and he looked a little sheepish. Great, now she was making the owner of the company she worked for, the man who ultimately controlled her paycheck, feel guilty.

"It's my daughter's wedding," he mumbled.

"And the photographers would like you both out on the church steps."

The men headed outside. With a big exhale, she sat and set her feet up on the seat of the pew. She needed a minute.

The florist was hanging flowers on the end of each row. The gerbera daisies were a sharp contrast to the dark wood. Sprays of flowers cascaded down from stands flanking the altar. Thank goodness she didn't have to move the flowers from the church to the reception. The florists would handle that transfer.

She took a deep breath and let her feet drop to the floor. Then she pushed up from the seat. Back at it.

The men were finishing their pictures. She headed to the women's dressing room. Everyone was actually resting. "Can I get anything for anyone?" she asked.

"Sit, sit," Kate's mother called from the couch. "Have a glass of champagne. You've already run ten miles and the wedding hasn't even started."

Kate asked, "How are the men?"

"Handsome devils. Just finishing off their pictures. And the wedding planner is here." She poured a half glass of champagne and sank to the floor. "Don't scrunch your dress."

Kate stroked it smooth, spreading it over the chair she'd taken. "I wish we didn't have all this extra time."

"The church looks gorgeous. Guests are arriving." Liz

sipped the cold drink and sighed. "I caught the dads in the back of the church with a flask."

"Oh, they would." Patty frowned. Then the two moms looked at each other and laughed.

"Yeah, they would," said Natalie.

Liz dressed.

Babs, the wedding coordinator, showed up at the door. "I'm so sorry I was late, but everything seems like it's running smoothly."

"Thanks to Liz," Kate said. "She's been incredible."

Liz waved off the accolades. "I've been having fun."

"Thank you," Babs said. Turning to Kate she added, "It's time."

Liz slipped on her shoes and helped straighten everyone's dresses. She re-pinned the flower girl's halo of flowers. "Good luck," she said before she headed upstairs.

The groomsmen were doing double duty as ushers. Michael extended his arm. "Everyone ready?"

Liz nodded. "Ready and gorgeous."

He handed her a program and led her to an empty pew. "Catch you after the ceremony. Save a dance for me."

She didn't know if her feet would hold up for dancing.

The ceremony was one big, beautiful blur. Alex's face did that lighting up thing as he watched Kate walk down the aisle.

What would it feel like to be loved so strongly by someone?

The homily and music had her relaxing. Until Alex went to the grand piano below the altar.

"I wrote this for Kate," he said.

An ooh went through the crowd.

The song was about new beginnings. New loves, new lives, taking chances. Kate covered her mouth with her hand and tears streamed down her cheeks.

By the time he'd stopped, half the women there were dabbing their cheeks.

Liz should have brought the packets of Kleenex from the basket. Thank goodness Meg had some. Meg hurried over and blotted Kate's face.

Liz let the rest of the ceremony wash over her. Everyone else in church had someone sitting next to them, leaning in to whisper a word or two. Even the lady two rows ahead of her who was in her eighties and wearing a hat Liz would love to try on had a lovely older man holding her hand.

And she was alone.

Even though she'd come with Michael. Her friend.

Finally Kate and Alex were married. They kissed. Then Alex took Kate's hand, and everyone applauded as they almost ran down the aisle, their smiles lighting the sanctuary. The wedding party exited behind them, couple by couple. Michael caught her eye as he came down the aisle with Alex's sister Emily on his arm. He smiled and Liz's cheeks got warm.

She should be doing something. Helping Kate in some way.

No. She was supposed to wait and give the family time with the couple. After pictures, she and Meg would bustle the dress.

She slid to the far end of the pew, figuring she would go out the side door. Standing, she walked as quietly as she could to the door and looked through the glass. Everyone was hugging and laughing. Happy.

Look at all those beautiful people in the hall. She was just an Iowa farm girl who worked for this family. What was she doing thinking she was even part of their celebration.

Meg beckoned to her. Liz gave her a little smile and Meg waved a little harder.

Reluctantly she joined the family.

"Wasn't that song perfect?" Meg gave her a big hug. "Okay, let's get these pictures out of the way so we can parteee!"

Liz was pulled into the center of the group.

They took a picture with both families out on the church

steps. Then Babs corralled each family, making sure the moments were documented.

Finally the family pictures were done.

"Let's go." Michael hauled her into one of the two waiting limos. She was trapped next to him and Timothy on the long bench seat.

"I should make sure everything gets packed in the changing room," Liz said.

"Nah." Timothy handed her a champagne flute. "The wedding planner will check the rooms. Relax."

Michael raised an eyebrow at his brother and Timothy shifted away.

"Here we are." Stephen and Meg sat on the opposite bench. He popped the cork of one of the champagne bottles in the car. "To the bride and groom."

Liz held out her glass as Stephen poured. They toasted the bride and groom who were in the other limo. Michael held up his water bottle and tapped her glass.

"Where are we heading?" she asked, feeling a little like she was on a merry-go-round.

"The sculpture gardens," Michael said. "I was showing Kate some of the pictures, and she decided she wanted her wedding pictures shot there."

Liz pulled out Kate's photo list. This was a production. Nothing like the weddings in her hometown. At home, people got married in the church and had their reception at the American Legion hall, the biggest hall in the county. She'd never even ridden in a limo.

Michael leaned in. "You've got that look on your face."

She blinked. And blinked again. "What look?"

"The one that says you're uncomfortable. And this time it's not me causing the look."

"I just ..." She waved her hand around the limo. Meg and

Stephen were refilling glasses. Timothy was taking a picture with his phone. "This is foreign to me."

"You fit in just fine." Michael bumped her shoulder.

A shiver ran down her spine, and she took a deep inhale of his cologne. She could pick him out of a room with her eyes closed. She'd run across men who wore the same scent, but there was something different when Michael wore it. Something that drilled a hole in her chest.

She looked into his eyes. They looked green against his bright blue vest and tie. And she couldn't look away.

She finally tore her gaze away from his and sipped her champagne. She swallowed, but then guilt had her pulling the glass away from her lips.

"Don't do that," he whispered.

Her head snapped up. "What?"

His head touched hers as he leaned in. "Don't feel guilty because you're drinking in front of me. I hate that."

A flash went off.

Timothy stared at his phone. "That's a good one."

He tipped the phone toward her and Michael. She stared into Michael's eyes, her mouth open. He was smiling. There was too much of everything in that photo.

"Delete it. God." She waved her hand.

"No way." Timothy pulled the phone away.

"Send it to me," Michael said.

Why would Michael want that picture?

"Let's see it," one of Alex's sisters called from the back of the limo.

Luckily the limo slowed. They'd reached the park.

Liz climbed out of the limo behind Michael. The humidity was already doing a number on her curly hair. She would probably be one big frizz by the time pictures were finished.

The photographers were already sending them down the

paths. She helped with Kate's small train, anything to get some distance from Michael. His intensity was grating on her nerves.

The first set of pictures were taken in front of the *LOVE* sculpture. Then Alex and Kate posed by the spoon and cherry. Denise herded the bride and her attendants over to the maze while Faye took the men to the arbor.

"That's it for pictures," Denise announced. Everyone let out a big sigh.

"Wait," Kate said. "One more. I need pictures with Liz."

Liz waved her hand. "No, no. Not necessary."

"Don't argue with the bride," Kate said, grinning.

Liz stood next to her in front of a big blue rooster.

Kate took her hands. "Thank you. For everything you're doing. You are such a friend."

The word was like taking a sip of champagne, fizzy and fun.

Both photographers snapped away. Kate gave her a hug and the cameras clicked, probably getting another one of Liz's open-mouth fish looks.

She hugged Kate back. "I love helping you out."

"Good, but don't forget to have fun at the reception. I've put you at a table with my cousins. They're a little crazy and don't let Ashton hit on you. He's lying if he says that he's old enough." Kate pulled away. "Course, you could be a cougar. He's barely over twenty-one and cute." Kate fanned a hand in front of her face.

"No, thank you." Liz gathered Kate's train to keep it from bringing back half the rocks on the paths.

When they met up with the guys, she was still laughing.

"What's up?" Michael fell into step with them.

"I suggested Liz check out Ashton." Kate linked her arm in Alex's. "Hello, husband of mine."

Alex pulled her into a hug, forcing Kate and Michael to

stop as the groom planted a big one on Kate's lips. "Hello, wife of mine."

"Ashton?" Michael said as the couple broke their kiss. "The kid is sixteen."

Kate started walking again and Liz gathered her train.

"He's definitely over twenty-one." Kate elbowed her brother.

"When did that happen?" Michael shook his head. "Liz, you're too old for him."

That only made her more curious about this infamous cousin.

The limos headed to the reception.

Michael leaned over to Stephen. "Did you know Ashton is over twenty-one?"

"No way!" Stephen slapped his knee. "I remember him tagging along at the family gatherings. I suppose he would have to grow up."

"He can't be that much younger than me. A couple of years." Timothy finished off his champagne.

"I can't wait to meet him," Liz said. "Kate sat us at the same table."

All three MacBain men frowned.

"What side of the family is he from?" she asked.

"The Murphy side." Michael's voice was low, almost a growl.

"Don't you get along with them?" she asked.

"Yeah. It's ... he looks like his father."

"This is bad?"

Michael scowled. If she didn't know better, she would have thought he was jealous, but all three brothers were frowning.

Their limo arrived first, so she was waiting for Kate by the time they arrived at the reception.

"Let's get this gown bustled," Meg said, "before it's filthy."

They headed to a dressing room set aside for their use. Liz and Meg bustled, tucked and hooked the train.

"Will that hold?" Meg stepped back and looked at their work.

Liz tugged. "Assuming no one steps on the hem."

"You sure you don't need to pee?" Meg asked.

"I'm good. And I'm glad we decided against a formal receiving line. Alex and I are going to walk around and talk to everyone before dinner."

"Okay." Liz straightened the dress's full skirt. The dress was gorgeous and hid Kate's tiny baby bump perfectly. "You let me know if there is anything you want."

Kate took her hand and then Meg's. "I want you both to have a good time. You've worked hard on this wedding. Now it's time for fun."

They walked out together, arms linked, and moved down the hall, drawn like magnets to the crowd noise.

"I'd better get my table number." Liz broke away from the other two women.

Another of the cousins was handing out cards with the table numbers.

"You're Liz, right?" the pretty brunette asked.

Liz nodded, recognizing the teen from last night's party.

"I'm Alicia, a Murphy. You're at my table."

"Good to meet you, Alicia." She took her table number. "I'll see you at dinner."

A waiter came by with a tray of champagne flutes. She took one.

Another waiter, female, came by with a second tray, this one with food. "Chicken satay," she explained.

It was a long time and a couple of glasses of champagne since she'd eaten her half sandwich at the church. She took one of the sticks. "Thanks."

Just as she filled her mouth, a great looking guy with black

hair and amazing silvery gray eyes came up to her. His dark
suit clung to broad shoulders.

"You're Liz?"

She nodded, pointing with the stick at her full mouth.

He laughed. "They're good, aren't they?"

She nodded, swallowed.

"We're sitting at the same table. I didn't get introduced to
you last night, but I asked my sister to give me a heads-up
when you had your table number." He pushed his curly black
hair off his forehead. "I'm Ashton."

She almost snorted. This delicious man was the cousin the
MacBain men thought would take advantage of her? He was
gorgeous and could have any women in the room under forty.
Her included.

Wasn't that a pathetic thought …?

"Nice to meet you." She would have shaken his hand, but
she had a flute in one and an empty stick in the other.

He held up a plate. "Here, add your stick to the pile."

Now what did they talk about? She was good at meeting
clients, they always had business to talk about, but with guys,
attractive guys, not so much. "So, you're a cousin, right?"

He nodded. "My dad and Aunt Patty are siblings. On the
Murphy side."

"So, what do you do?" Liz asked.

"Assistant pro at Simon Lake Country Club."

"Golf?" Stupid question.

He nodded.

She could see it. He had a long lean build. A tan that didn't
look fake. And now that she noticed, one of his hands was pale.
"I should have guessed by your hands."

He laughed, staring into her eyes. "Yeah. I do take off my
glove, a lot, but I can't seem to match my tans."

Another server swung by with a tray of wine. He took a
glass of red. "Want one?"

She shook her head. It was still early in the evening. She planned to nurse her remaining drinks.

"Are you going to play the tour?" That was what they called it, right? Because someone who dedicated their life to golf was so out of her environment, she wasn't exactly sure of the language.

"I hope to. I'm looking for sponsors." He took a deep breath. "Maybe next year."

"Does it cost a lot to go on tour?" she asked.

A hand dropped on her shoulder. Jumping, she turned her head but knew who it was. Michael's scent was too … appealing.

"Yeah, it costs a lot," Michael said. He left his hand on her shoulder.

Ashton looked between the two of them. A smile curled his lips and a dimple popped out. The guy could be a model.

Liz took a step to the side and Michael's hand dropped away.

"Looking good, little cousin," Michael said.

Ashton quirked one eyebrow. "You too."

"I should check on Kate," Liz said, making her escape.

Liz found her by searching out the tallest man in the room, Alex.

"Anything you need?" she whispered in Kate's ear.

Kate grinned and the photographer snapped another picture. She held up her wineglass. "Any chance you could fill this with water?"

"Absolutely."

She worked her way to one of the two bars in the room. Mac, Kate's father, leaned against the counter waiting for a drink.

"How does it feel, Mr. MacBain, having a married daughter?"

His grin told the story. "Absolutely perfect. And how many times do I have to tell you to call me Mac?"

It was hard to do. "Last time, Mac."

She handed the bartender Kate's glass. "Water, please."

"You got it." The guy gave her a slow once over and winked.

This party was good for her ego, even if it was because he was looking for a tip.

~

MICHAEL KEPT TRACK OF LIZ. And Ashton.

He wanted to punch his cousin. Then he wanted to poke out the bartender's eyes. The guy had to have pictured her naked. Asshole.

Liz returned to Kate's side. At least she wasn't joining Ashton. His cousin was putting on a golf clinic on the patio.

"How's it going, bro?" Timothy asked.

"Great, just great." He took a sip of his coke. "Ashton's hitting on Liz."

Timothy's gaze snapped to where Liz, Kate and Alex stood in a group of people. Why did his brother know where she was in this crush?

"Why wouldn't he?" Timothy let a slow grin fill his face. "She's a looker."

"Yeah? Well, do you know the reason she left her last job?"

The smile dropped from Timothy's face. "I forgot. Was she really harassed by Jerry?"

"She told me about it a couple of weeks ago."

Timothy started to raise his drink to his lips, and then pulled it down fast. "So are you and she ..." He waved his hand.

"Hell no!"

His brother frowned. "So what's going on between you two?"

"I ... I thought she needed a friend." He was the one who'd needed the friend, but he wouldn't confess that to his baby brother. "It's not sexual."

Timothy's eyebrows shot together. "Are you sure?"

"Yeah."

She wasn't Sarah.

"It's just that ..." Timothy stopped.

"What?"

"She looks at you. Whenever you're not looking, she looks at you."

"She's probably trying to decide if I'm drinking again."

Timothy looked in Michael's glass and laughed. "Yeah, I can tell you're pounding back the sodas."

"Yuck it up." But his chest loosened a little. If Timothy could tease even a little about his drinking problem, maybe he and his brother could get back on track. "You know you can drink around me, bro."

Although he and his brother had spent too many hours drinking together, Michael couldn't go back there.

And if he never got to the point of passing out, he would never see or speak to Sarah again. He swallowed. As Kate would say, sucked to be him.

"It feels ... weird," Timothy mumbled.

"You have to get over that."

The silence got uncomfortable. Damn it.

Thank goodness the wedding planner announced it was time to head in to dinner. As people made their way to another room, he saw that he and the rest of the wedding party were eating on a platform. Behind their long table was a bank of west-facing windows. Maybe the sun would set and blind anyone looking at the head table. The last thing he wanted was all of the wedding guests watching him cut his steak and checking out whether he was drinking.

He'd rather be sitting with Liz. That way he could help her fend off Ashton.

He took his place next to Gabe and Stephen. The groomsmen sat in the order they'd walked down the aisle. The bridesmaids were on the other side of the big table.

Mom and Dad's table was below them. Mom looked good in her bright pink dress. She didn't look like the mother of the bride. She looked like she could be a bride.

"Mom looks fantastic, doesn't she?" Stephen said.

"That's what I was just thinking." Michael took a deep drink of water. "Hard to imagine she was going through radiation therapy four months ago."

The DJ played "Here Comes the Bride," getting the crowd's attention. "I'd like to introduce the happy couple, Kate and Alex Adamski."

At the top of a curving stairway in the two story room, Kate and Alex waited. His sister glowed. And Alex looked like he'd won a hundred-million-dollar lottery—twice.

Everyone stood. The applause drowned out whatever else the DJ said.

The couple stopped next to the DJ, and Alex took the microphone.

"Thank you all for being part of our celebration." He brought Kate's hand to his lips. "We couldn't be happier that you're sharing our joy."

He handed the microphone to Kate. "I don't know what more I can say. Thank you for sharing this day with us."

Her hand smoothed the front of her dress. Only a handful of people knew his sister was pregnant.

Kate had proposed to Alex the day she'd found Michael in his bathroom, blood pooling around his head, since apparently he'd hit it passing out.

Not a proud moment for him.

But apparently that day had brought Alex and Kate together. And wasn't it like his take-charge sister to propose and not the other way around.

He missed the end of their speeches but clapped along with the rest of the crowd.

His mother blew him a kiss.

He wanted his family to stop worrying about him. It had been their pastime for too many years. It had to stop.

Someone clinked their glass with a knife. Alex and Kate stood. He dipped her dramatically and they kissed.

He and Sarah should have had memories like this.

He felt like something was touching his neck and brushed at it with his hand. Nothing there. Maybe it was all the eyes on the front table. He looked around, finally catching sight of the cousin table and Liz staring at him.

"Red or white, sir?" A waiter stood behind him.

"None for me." He could feel his face turning red. Why didn't they hang an *Alcoholic* sign around his neck? "Just keep the water coming."

"Will do." The server moved down the row.

Then his dad made his welcome speech, his deep voice booming through the two floors. As Dad stood below Kate and Alex, love filled his face like a light pouring through a stained glass window.

Michael didn't actually listen to the words; he listened to the emotions behind the words. Dad moved from Kate and Alex back to his mother and clasped her hand. He finally said, "Let's toast Alex and Kate and wish them happiness in their new life together."

Everyone raised their wineglasses or flutes. Michael almost knocked over his water goblet before getting it into the air.

And wouldn't you know, there was his cousin Ashton sitting

next to Liz and tipping his glass to hers. And Liz grinned at his cousin's too handsome face.

Dad handed the microphone to Grandpa Murphy for the prayer.

Michael tucked his head and stared at his salad.

Grandpa blessed the couple, blessed the meal. Shit. How much longer would they have Grandpa Murphy? He'd outlived his wife by ten-plus years and never remarried. Although at the groom's dinner, he'd met Grandpa's very nice friend, Diana.

Had it taken Grandpa ten years to get over Grandma Murphy?

He didn't want to let go of Sarah. She'd been the foundation of his life, the driver. If he let go, he might crumble.

Finally the crowd echoed Grandpa's, "Amen."

The other groomsmen had shed their jackets. He slipped his over the back of his chair, then dug into his salad. At least everyone else had their salads so they were no longer staring at the front table.

"You're the financial head of MacBain," Gabe said.

Michael had just put a forkful of greens in his mouth, so he nodded.

"What's the economy looking like from your perspective?"

Michael swallowed. Since he'd been sprung from treatment, he'd spent time looking over the revenue streams. And Jessica, the controller, had done a great job of recapping the activity. "We're seeing an uptick in retail construction. The remaining gross sales leases we have are seeing an upswing in their sales."

"I didn't know anyone still had those kind of leases." Gabe took a sip of his wine.

"When they renew, we'll convert them to a straight lease. The competition has all gone that way."

They talked through the salad and the delivery of their

entrees. He must have requested the steak. He didn't remember.

"Switch with me," Stephen said.

His brother had fish that actually looked good. "No way."

"Come on."

"Why did you order fish?" Michael asked.

Stephen shook his head. "Kate said it was the best thing they tasted."

"Then eat it." Michael cut into his steak. Done perfectly—medium-rare.

"Let's go halvsies. A little surf 'n turf action."

He could do that. He drew the steak knife down the center of the meat and slid half onto Stephen's plate while his brother did the same. "Are you happy now? Do you want to change places?"

Because Stephen always sat in the same chair. It was a wonder they ever got him out of his condo and the fat ass lounge chair he'd bought for himself.

"I'm good."

Michael glanced at Liz's table. What the hell? She was handing half her fish … to Ashton.

The lights dimmed. Every few minutes someone would hit their silverware against a glass and kissing would commence. Votive candles flickered at each table. He hadn't even noticed they were there. And didn't Liz's skin look luminescent in the candlelight?

He sure would like to hear what Ashton had said that made Liz laugh so hard.

"Stop the frowning. This is a wedding." Stephen eased back in his chair and stretched out his legs. "Can I have your potatoes?"

Michael pushed his plate to his brother. "Knock yourself out."

Stephen tracked Michael's gaze. "Ashton sure has a way with older women."

Yeah, that wouldn't last. He planned to pull Liz away from that kid as soon as he had a chance.

Liz left her seat and walked toward the head table. He started to rise, but she stopped in front of Kate.

Of course. He fumbled with his napkin. Stephen shot him a look. Kate, Liz and Meg headed out of the room.

They were traveling in a pack, although with a dress that looked like a bell, Kate probably needed help with everything.

Finally the torture of dinner ended. Michael pushed away from the table and sat on the window ledge behind him, watching everyone. Dad and Kate headed to the dance floor. They looked good together. People surrounded the floor and the photographers recorded everything.

Alex and Kate then took the next dance.

Liz walked over to him, a smile on her face. The weight in his chest eased.

"Kate wants all the wedding party dancing next."

"Sure."

She held out her hand. "She wants you by the dance floor."

"On my way." He wanted to take that small hand and hold it. But she was only indicating the path to the dance floor. As he straightened his bright blue vest, he asked, "How was dinner?"

"Great. Ashton is really funny. That sea bass was fabulous. What did you have?"

"Stephen and I shared. He had the sea bass. I had the steak. It was good."

They stopped next to the dance floor. Liz said, "I'll find your bridesmaid."

"Hey, I hear we're dancing." Emily, Alex's sister, was almost as tall as he was.

"It's been a while for me."

"So, no tango? Damn." Emily smiled.

"Yeah, sorry, I forgot my dancing shoes today."

"Well, I found mine." She held up her foot. She had on flip-flops. "I'd had enough of those heels."

He looked at the other women's feet. They'd all changed into flats or flip-flops. Even Liz was wearing the pair she'd had on when he'd picked her up.

As the next song started, the DJ called off their names and the wedding party joined Alex and Kate. It was a slow song, so he took Emily in the waltz hold he'd learned in middle school. Then he stumbled around for small talk. "You play in the orchestra, right?"

"I did until we went on strike. This is not the time to play for an orchestra around the country. Everyone's asking for concessions."

"What instrument?"

"Viola."

"That's a violin, only bigger, right?"

"Basically. I've been working with recording artists lately. Although The Saint Paul Chamber Orchestra has contracted my sister, my mother and me to play a sonata Alex wrote. Not sure I'll like being directed by my brother."

"I'd like to see that."

"Good. We want to fill the concert hall."

Sarah would love an event like that. Sarah would have loved Kate's wedding. Sarah …

Was gone.

Tightening his hold, he swung Emily in a circle. They ended up next to Kate and Alex.

"Looking good," Alex called to them.

Kate just grinned.

He'd never paid attention to anyone's emotions but his own. At least not over the last four years. "You look happy, sis."

"I am." She snuggled into her husband's arms. "Oh, I am."

The song ended and the DJ called for everyone to join them and reminded guests that instead of the cake cutting, there were cupcakes set out for dessert.

"Thanks," Emily said. "I'm heading back to my so-called date, but if you want to dance again, let me know."

"Won't your date mind?"

"Naw. He's my go-to date. And he's hitting on Meg."

Even he knew Meg didn't date. He just didn't know why. But she would dance with every male who asked her.

He looked around in time to see Ashton pull Liz onto the floor. She was laughing and trying, but not too hard, to pull away from him.

Everything in his body tightened.

Michael wished he had a glass of whiskey. A tall, undoctored glass of Jameson He wanted the burn, the hit, the unconsciousness. Wanted his body to slide into that wonderful stupor.

He stalked to the bar. He couldn't watch Ashton and Liz cozied up on the dance floor.

The line was two deep for both bartenders. He waited his turn, inhaling as the man in front of him requested a glass of wine and a Jack on ice.

What the hell difference did it make? He wasn't happy. All he did was document his family's success.

He wasn't special. Not without Sarah.

SIX

L<small>IZ LET</small> A<small>SHTON PULL HER BACK INTO HIS ARMS.</small>

"You're a good dancer," she said.

"I'm going to have to thank my mom for forcing me to take dance classes," Ashton said.

The music changed to something slow and Liz pulled away.

"No, you don't," he growled low in his throat. "Come on, this is a nice song."

"I need water." She pointed at her throat.

"After this song." He tried to pull her tight to his body.

She didn't wrap her arms around his neck. She stuck with a hold that held him at arm's length.

"Ashton," she warned.

"Elizabeth," he repeated in the same tone.

"You're tenacious." But charming.

"Us dumb golf pros don't know what that means."

"Right. Dumb like a fox."

He tugged her closer and she rested her head on his chest. "Only one hen in this henhouse that I'm interested in."

She couldn't help laughing.

"I'm glad we sat together tonight," he said.

The music ended and she pulled out of his arms. "I need something to drink."

As they walked off the dance floor, he took her hand.

"Ashton." She yanked her hand away.

"Elizabeth." With his hand on the small of her back, he guided her to the bar tucked behind the staircase. "I'm just being a gentleman."

"Right. You're incorrigible." She didn't believe him.

"There's another one of those big words we don't use on the golf course." As they neared the counter, he asked, "What do you want? More champagne?"

"Water."

"Okay, both."

She elbowed him. "I've had enough to drink, thank you. You conned that waitress into leaving the champagne bottle at the table. I don't know how many glasses I've had now."

"Not enough," he whispered.

They shuffled to the counter. "Water, champagne and a Jameson."

"No champagne. Just water," she corrected.

She leaned against the bar, trying to take her weight off her aching feet. She should check on Kate. See if she needed anything.

The bartender handed her a bottle of water. Good. She could probably use two more of them. And he'd cracked the seal. She tipped it back and took deep swallows.

She wiped a drip off her mouth and looked around to see if anyone had noticed.

Michael stood at the other end of the bar, staring into a tumbler filled with an amber liquid.

A chill ran down her spine. Don't let him be drinking.

She moved to where he stood at the end of the bar. "How's it going?"

His gaze met hers. She read the pain in his eyes.

He swallowed, his Adam's apple working up and down. Then he pushed the glass back across the counter. "Dance with me. Please."

She took his hand. It was shaking. Setting her bottle on a small table, they moved to the dance floor.

"Hey," Ashton called. "I thought we were dancing?"

With her free hand she waved him off.

Even though it wasn't a really slow song, she let Michael pull her into his body. She set her head on his chest and inhaled. Did he smell of booze?

"I didn't drink it." The words rumbled in his chest. "I smelled it, but I didn't drink."

She tightened her hold on him.

Addicts were the best liars.

If he had been drinking and dancing stopped him this time, then that was okay. Although she couldn't keep him from drinking. She knew that. Michael was the only one who controlled his impulses.

"How are you really?" she asked.

He was silent, rocking in place with her because gyrating bodies packed the dance floor. "I'm okay. Just a moment of madness, but it passed."

"Madness or sadness?" she asked.

"Both. I don't want to talk about it." He pulled her arms down and took her by the hands. Then he tugged her in and guided her away from him in a four-count combination. She tripped the first time, but he kept repeating the movement. Catching on, she let her body follow his.

"I'm not much of a dancer," she admitted.

"I used to love to dance."

With Sarah.

"We're adding more now." As he said the words, he turned her under his arm. Then spun her out and spun her back in so his body cradled hers and his arm nestled on her stomach. "Not so hard, is it?"

He spun her back out and then repeated the original steps.

As she stepped into him, she asked, "What is it with the MacBain/Murphys? You all take dance lessons together?"

"Don't tangle with Ashton. Even I know his reputation with women. He's still planting his oats." Michael made quote marks with one hand.

It might have been the fizz from the champagne she'd drunk. Or the dancing. But Michael's jealousy and concern made her feel good.

Stupid. But it felt great to be popular for something other than just being Jordan's twin sister. Although being Jordan's sister had made her infamous.

That was one of the reasons she liked the anonymity of a metropolitan area. Nobody knew what her twin had put their family through. Nobody knew she'd hidden her brother's addiction until he'd almost bankrupted the family.

"Why are you frowning?" Michael asked.

She shook her head. "Nothing. Long day."

He pulled her into a turn one more time. "How about we sit on the patio. It's a nice night. If we stay inside, it's too loud to talk."

While he went to get her water, she found a small table with empty chairs outside. A couple leaned against the railing on the other side of the patio.

Across the street, the grass led down a gradual bank to Lake Bde Maka Ska. People still moved along the path around the lake even though the sun had set.

Liz set her feet on a chair and didn't hold back her groan. Thank goodness she'd taken off her heels after pictures. Her feet would be barking even harder right now.

"Here you go."

Her water appeared over her shoulder. She took a deep

drink. Michael pulled out a chair and sat. He set a glass on the metal table.

Her eyes darted to the contents of his glass. *He wouldn't, would he?*

"Ginger ale." He held up the glass. "Take a sip."

Liz wanted to believe him, but she didn't trust him. She took a sip. The sweet taste filled her mouth.

Didn't mean he hadn't slammed back a shot at the bar, but the drink he had now was ginger ale.

His smile was a little sad. "I'm okay now. For the night."

"Is it hard?" The metal chair scraped against the stone with a large squawk as she slid closer to the table.

"Most of the time I don't think about drinking. It's remembering what could have been and nighttime. Nighttime is the worst."

"I'm sorry."

"Nothing for you to be sorry about." He shook his head. "It is what it is. So, are you done with your duties?"

"Meg and I will help pack the presents into your parents' car. But that's pretty much the last of the official duties unless Kate needs anything."

"You're a good friend." He flipped his hand over and linked their fingers together. "To both Kate and me."

This didn't feel like friendship anymore. Not with Michael.

The night closed in on them. Her breath got stuck in the back of her throat. She couldn't breathe, couldn't swallow. And she couldn't look away from his hazel eyes.

A number of people came through the French doors, and she eased her fingers out of his.

Kate and Alex swept over to the table.

"Kate, can I do anything for you? Get you anything?" Liz stood, pulling out of the vortex that tugged her closer to Michael.

"A new pair of feet. Mine are aching."

Liz pulled out a chair. "Put your feet up. Do you need water?"

Kate took the chair, and Alex pulled another one up.

"Sit," Kate said. "I'm good. Just resting before we do the bouquet toss."

Alex pressed a kiss to Kate's hand. "Limo's coming in forty-five minutes."

"I am so ready." Kate kissed him.

Michael's face went blank. Probably thinking about his lost fiancée.

When he looked at her, the air pressure changed. It was like she couldn't pull her gaze away from his. What did he want from her? Somehow tonight was more than friendship. This was the edge of something else.

She needed to get up—get out. "Do you want me to get your tossing bouquet?"

"You don't have to wait on me." Kate pressed her hand, just like her brother had. "You're supposed to have fun."

"I'm your personal attendant and I'm enjoying it. I'll get that bouquet while you rest." And she'd bring Kate back a bottle of water. "Anyone need anything?"

No one requested anything, so she went to the bathroom. A mother and her daughter tidied up their makeup in front of the mirror. Their banter made Liz smile.

How long had it been since she and her mother had enjoyed themselves together? Years. Now all they focused on was money and how to meet the next mortgage payment.

Regret burrowed into her stomach. She should have told her parents about Jordan's gambling earlier. If she had, it might have saved everyone so much heartache and money. But she hadn't. Ever since she'd gotten her first real job, she'd been sending money home to make up for her mistake.

There wasn't any use thinking of that right now. She

retrieved the key to the bride's room and got the tossing bouquet.

When Liz returned to the reception, Kate and Alex were back on the dance floor and Alex was removing her garter—with his teeth. The crowd laughed and cheered.

"They're good together." Meg put her arm around Liz's shoulder. "I hate losing my best friend, but they're so damn happy."

"That's silly," Liz replied. "You're not losing your best friend."

"Have you ever been to O'Dair's?" Meg asked, ignoring her comment.

The name sounded familiar. "I don't think so."

"It's a great pub. With my BFF heading on her honeymoon, you and I will stop in for a beer."

Liz bit her lip. Maybe she could eke the cost of a beer or two from her budget. But she'd better buy a paper tomorrow so she could find coupons before grocery shopping. "Sure, I'd like that."

Alex had gotten the garter off and was tossing it over his shoulder to the group of guys standing on the dance floor.

Ashton leaped up and snatched it out of another man's hand. "All right!" He pointed at Liz and moved toward her.

Liz turned to see who Ashton was pointing to, but no one was behind her.

Meg elbowed her. "Looks like you've got an admirer."

The blush that must be covering her face actually burned. "Probably because most of the people here are related to him."

"Oh, I don't think so. You're hot, girl." Meg laughed.

Michael intercepted Ashton, grabbing him by the arm. They were too far away for Liz to hear what they were saying, but Michael was in his cousin's face.

The DJ announced, "All you single ladies, head to the floor."

"Our turn," Meg said, doom filling her voice. "I'm staying in the back of the crowd. No way am I getting my hands on that bouquet."

"Once I give Kate this, I'm with you," Liz said, holding up the bouquet.

She took it over to Kate.

"Thank you," Kate said. She climbed the stairs as Liz headed down to the dance floor.

"Okay, ladies," Kate said from the balcony. "Here it comes."

Kate threw the bouquet over her shoulder. Darn thing seemed to have wings, arrowing its way to where she and Meg stood.

They both stepped aside and one of the many cousins caught the flying flowers. She and Meg both laughed.

The DJ called out, "Time for the dollar dance. Line up and don't be stingy. It's all going to charity, Habitat for Humanity."

"Oh shoot, I need to take the money." Meg hurried over to stand in front of Alex.

Gabe was already taking money for Kate.

Liz dug in her pocket and pulled out a twenty. She'd brought money to pay for drinks but with the free bar, hadn't needed it. It would go to a good cause. The music was nice and slow, but Meg was hurrying people through the line.

When she was next, Meg leaned over. "Wow, they're making a haul. And Kate didn't want the dollar dance."

Meg tapped the young girl's shoulder who was currently dancing with Alex. The girl, who wasn't more than twelve, pouted.

Alex held out his arms to Liz. It was like walking into the arms of a bear. "Thank you for everything you've done for us."

"I've loved being part of your celebration." And she had. She liked feeling useful, doing things that other people might not think of.

As Alex turned her, she noticed Michael dancing with his sister. Kate had her head tucked into his shoulder.

"He looks better than he did when I first met him," Alex said.

"He does."

"You're good for him."

"Oh." Had both Alex and Kate gotten the wrong idea when Michael held her hand? "We're friends."

"Really?" Alex frowned.

Meg tapped her shoulder. "Times up, girlfriend."

Liz moved to the edge of the dance floor and Michael joined her. "You and Kate looked good," she said.

"I've never seen her smile so much."

They stood together, not talking. Not needing to talk. Comfortable.

The final people danced with the bride and groom, and then Kate and Alex took to the dance floor one more time.

"I'm sure you know that the groom is a Grammy-award winning composer," the DJ said into the mic. "For their last dance of the evening, I'm playing a song he wrote for Kate. 'Kate's Song.'"

The couple swayed, lost in their own world.

Liz brushed tears away. And she wasn't alone. Michael also wiped his eyes.

"Pretty nice," he whispered.

When the song ended and the applause died, the DJ announced, "Time to say goodnight to the bride and groom."

Kate and Alex climbed the stairs, stopping at the top. They waved and called out goodnight. The room erupted in applause.

As the clapping slowed, the DJ said, "We'll be playing for another half hour. Get your requests in now."

A few couples headed to the dance floor, but now that the bride and groom were gone, people were leaving.

"Buy you one more drink?" Meg asked.

"It's an open bar," Liz reminded her.

Meg grinned. "I know."

Liz shrugged. "One more glass of champagne. Although I'm not sure I've finished one all night. Maybe at dinner." But even then she'd gotten up to help Kate in the bathroom.

They both went with champagne and clinked their glasses. "To the happy couple."

The liquid cooled her throat. Smooth. Nothing like the champagne her family shared on New Year's Eve.

"Guess we should load the MacBains' car," Meg said as they walked away from the bar. She looked around the room. "Let me find out where the car is and get some muscle."

"I'll sit." Liz stretched her legs out in front of her and wiggled her toes. It had been a lovely wedding.

She didn't wait long. Meg waved from across the room.

As they reached the bridal room, Liz took in the sight of Michael and Ashton on either side of the doorway. They stood in the same poise, legs spread and arms crossed. Frowns knit their eyebrows together.

She almost turned around and walked away. Instead she straightened her shoulders and walked between them through the door.

The waitstaff had moved the presents and cards into the room on a big trolley. Liz tucked the bags Kate wanted sent home in with the presents. One trip to the car with all the gear and she could go home.

Meg said, "This is a full load."

"I'll push if you steer and pull."

"Sounds like a plan." Meg set a gift bag on the pile of boxes.

Liz did the same. When she pushed, a couple of boxes slid to one side. She lunged and caught them before they fell.

"Glad I corralled muscle. We'll have to walk on both sides." Meg went to the door. "Need you guys."

The men came into the room and suddenly the space that had seemed so large shrank to the size of a dollhouse.

Meg pointed. "Could one of you push and one of you pull? Liz and I will keep everything on the cart."

Michael shouldered Ashton out of the way and moved back to where Liz stood.

Ashton tipped his head. "Sorry to get in your way, cousin."

Meg ignored the obvious clash between the men. "Let's go. We're heading left out of the door."

The cart started moving and the packages shifted. Liz and Meg walked next to the trolley, slipping things back in place and holding a hand on packages as the cart moved.

Meg was at the front when something slipped at the back. She caught it just before it hit the ground. "I feel like I'm trying to plug the holes in tax code."

Everyone laughed, breaking the tension.

They headed down a ramp to a section of the building Liz hadn't seen before. One box hit the floor with a thump.

"Maybe we should have carried everything down," Liz muttered.

"Only one more corner," Meg said, holding a door open.

Liz wedged a bag they were about to lose next to two boxes. "I hope we haven't broken anything."

They took a short ramp into the parking area.

Meg hit the lock on the keys in her hand. "The car is nearby."

"There." Ashton pointed.

At the SUV, the men hauled the packages off the trolley, and Meg and Liz packed the car.

"Done." Liz pushed the button for the hatch and rested against the door.

"Are you ready to head home?" Michael pushed the cart out of their way.

"I am." Her feet were aching.

Ashton stood next to her. "I can take you home."

Michael did that glare thing again. "She came with me. I'll bring her home, kid."

"Kid?" Ashton took a step toward Michael.

Meg set her hands on Ashton's shoulders. "Boys. We just celebrated a beautiful wedding. Let's not ruin the evening."

Liz started pushing the cart. This was too weird. "I'll bring this back and get my stuff."

Ashton moved to help her, guiding the wobbly trolley from the front. "I'd like to take you home."

She shook her head. "Ashton."

"Elizabeth," he said.

Michael wrenched the cart out of their hands. "Give it up."

Liz dropped back to walk with Meg, who asked, "So who's taking you home?"

"This is crazy," Liz whispered.

"My go-to went home already, so Stephen's dropping me off. Once I give the MacBains their keys, I can see if he has enough room in his car for you?"

"No." Liz didn't want to be the excuse that led Michael back to the bottle tonight. But being his savior was too much responsibility.

She unlocked the bridal room. Picking up her purse, the basket and her bag, she made one more turn around the room.

Meg did the same. "All clear."

Liz turned, and Ashton was right behind her with Michael a few steps behind him. "God!" She jumped back.

"Ready to go?" Ashton asked.

"I'm going with Michael."

Michael stared Ashton down.

"Then give me your number. I'd like to call you." Ashton captured her shoulders in his hands.

She shook her head. "Have a nice night."

She tried to move away, but Ashton stepped in and kissed her.

Stunned, she let him press another kiss on her mouth before she slammed her hands into his chest.

"Good night." She stalked away. Then backtracked and set the room key on the counter.

Michael looked like he wanted to tear his cousin's face off.

"Let's go," she said. Turning to Meg, she added, "I'll talk to you next week about O'Dair's."

"Sounds like a plan." Meg gave her a hug. "Go easy on Michael. He's always seemed fragile to me."

Fragile? Liz didn't think he was fragile. She worried he might be weak. Her brother had proved too weak to overcome his gambling addiction. And she hadn't understood just how much strength and endurance it would have taken to beat it. Now she knew.

Michael had an uphill battle ahead of him.

She walked next to him, but he kept stopping and saying goodnight to family and friends.

She should Uber home. But she didn't have a clue how much it would cost or if she even had enough money to pay for it.

"I'm sorry," he said. "I'll try not to make eye contact anymore."

"This is your family, you need to talk to them." She swallowed her impatience. "In fact, I'm glad you're making this effort for them."

He stopped short and studied her. "You know, it does feel … good to be with family tonight."

"Quite a departure for you," she added, smiling.

He smiled back.

"We can take the stairs if your feet are doing okay." He tugged on his bowtie and unbuttoned his shirt. "Then we wouldn't have to wait for the elevator."

Liz nodded, exhaustion weakening all her muscles.

When she stumbled, Michael steadied her with his hand. "Maybe we should take the elevator."

"I'm okay. I think all the adrenaline just evaporated." Or maybe all the champagne she'd drunk had just hit, although she didn't feel impaired.

They started down the stairs. Michael kept his hand on her elbow, and this time she didn't mind. In her flip-flops, she worried about tripping.

On the first level, they waited in the valet line. She asked, "How did your car get here?"

"Courtney brought it over for me."

"She really is nice."

"I wish I'd known she could park in the ramp," Michael said. "Sit. Get off your feet."

"If I sit, I might not get up."

"At least you've got tomorrow to rest."

Yeah, she planned to sleep in.

Finally the valet brought Michael's car. He opened the passenger door, and she curled into the leather with a sigh.

Money exchanged hands and Michael settled into the driver's seat.

Music played faintly in the background. She was too tired to talk.

Her head sank against the headrest, and she tucked her legs up on the seat. The rocking of the car lulled her into a half-sleep.

The car accelerated. They must be on the freeway. Then she drifted. What an odd evening.

"Why did you do it?" Michael asked quietly.

She rolled her shoulders and sat up. Looking at him, he stared out the windshield. "Do what?"

"Why did you kiss Ashton?"

"Whoa. I didn't kiss him." She shook her head. She barely remembered Ashton's kiss. She hadn't kissed anyone, at least not willingly in … she didn't even know. A year? Except the kiss-cam kiss with Michael, but that was him joking around.

"Sure looked like you were kissing him from where I stood." His words were as tight as her bra strap cutting into her back.

"Well, I was the one he kissed, and I didn't kiss him back."

Michael turned onto her street. She wanted out of his car. Out of this new drama.

"But did you want to?" The words snapped at her.

"I'm not talking about this with you. You have no perspective when it comes to your cousin."

"Because he wants to sleep with you."

The words echoed in the car. It wasn't any of his business if she and Ashton got together. But she couldn't hold her tongue. "It's not your problem."

"Of course it is." He shook his head. "The kid is too young for you."

"He's a couple of years younger than me." She threw her hands up. "That's nothing."

"But … but he's only twenty-one."

"Twenty-two." Ashton had said he would be twenty-two next month. What difference did it make? She wasn't interested in Ashton. She wasn't interested in anyone.

Lies. A memory of Michael linking their fingers together and the way her body had gone on high alert flashed through her.

Michael's jawbone stuck out, like he was grinding his teeth. He jerked the steering wheel so the car settled in next to the curb outside her apartment.

"Thanks for the ride." She didn't sound very gracious, but she was tired of the drama. She got out of the car and opened the backseat door to get her things. Michael's door opened. *Now what?*

He was right behind her, trying to take the basket from her hands.

"I've got it."

He let go but caged her in between the car at her back and his body blocking the way up the sidewalk.

Too close. Even in the light from the streetlight overhead, she could see the gold sparkles surrounding his eyes.

He took a step closer, and his woodsy scent had her insides melting. Damn it.

"Michael," she whispered.

He cupped her face with his hand.

She couldn't breathe.

His thumb gently stroked her cheek. "I couldn't stand seeing him kiss you."

She opened her mouth to deny that she'd wanted Ashton's kiss, but his other hand came up along the side of her head and the words evaporated.

There was no more space between them, only heat. He leaned down and kissed her.

A little mew left her lips. Then his mouth was back, pressing harder. His hands angled her head and his tongue entered her mouth.

She moved closer. Slid her tongue along his as fireworks played through their connection.

The basket dropped to the ground and her bag slid down her arm. She snuck her hand under his jacket and ran it along the play of muscles on his back.

He pressed her against the car. Breaking the kiss, he ran his tongue down her throat, stopping at her collarbone.

All she could do was cling to his arms. Her legs were too wobbly to hold her up.

He kissed her again. This time her head rested against the top of the car, and her legs were definitely shaking. His mouth was so agile, so perfect.

He pulled away, his head resting on her forehead. "God, Sarah."

Sarah?

She tried to back away, but since she was flush against the car, there was nowhere to go. She shook, claustrophobia setting in. "Michael, let me up."

She pushed.

He stumbled back.

She bent for her things. Could she be more of an idiot? "I'm not Sarah."

"What?"

"You called me Sarah."

"I ... I ..."

"I can't believe this." She started up the sidewalk.

He caught up to her.

"Michael, we're done for the night."

"I'll walk you to your door."

"No!" She turned, her finger pointed at his chest like a gun. "This wasn't a date. You're not over Sarah. We shouldn't have kissed, and you are not walking me to the door."

She jerked her keys out of her purse.

"Come on, Liz. It's almost one in the morning. That was a mistake."

"That was honesty. You've been sad most of the night. I understand." She shooed him away. "Go home."

He opened his mouth and she walked away. Walked through the door and pulled it closed so there was metal and glass between them. No more heat from his body, no more tortured eyes, no more wishing the world was different and she could invite him to her apartment, to her bed. He was still in love with his dead fiancée.

She stumbled up the stairs. It was sad, but she couldn't handle being attracted to Michael and having him long for Sarah.

If Michael called again, looking for a friend, she would say no. She couldn't be around him.

Reality was a bitch.

MICHAEL THREW his jacket toward his bedroom armchair. It slipped to the floor and he left it.

He'd kissed Liz. Then called her Sarah. He was an asshole.

He wanted a friendship with her. No, he *needed* a friendship with her. Now he'd gone and screwed it up.

Ashton had known Michael was ready to tear his face off, and he kissed her in front of him.

He ran his hand through his hair. Could he ever fix this with Liz?

Maybe if it had only been a friendly brush of their lips together. But he'd soul-sucked her mouth. He hadn't kissed a woman like that since … Sarah.

He dropped onto the bed. His hands worked the bowtie from under his collar.

Sarah. He couldn't remember what she tasted like. He swallowed. Liz tasted like apricots and champagne.

Sarah had always worried she was too flat-chested for him. He hadn't cared if she was a B or double D.

Liz's breasts, cushioned against his chest, had been heaven.

His head sank to his chest. He was forgetting Sarah. Forgetting her scent, her taste. He was losing his soul mate.

He pulled off his shoe and winged it toward the closet. It smacked into the wall, leaving a scuff on the cream paint.

NAN DIXON

They'd wanted kids. They should have been married and pregnant by now. Or even had a child. A baby. With Sarah.

He wanted to hold her again. Smell her hair, taste her. Goddamn it. He wanted to hear her laugh. Her voice.

He brushed at a tickle on his cheek, and his hand came away wet.

Unless he got drunk again, he would never hear Sarah's sweet voice calling his name.

He kicked off his other shoe and added another mark to the wall.

He shuffled into the kitchen, his socks whooshing a little on the wood floors. All he needed was one bottle. One bottle could bring Sarah back to him. One sweet word from her to keep him going.

He opened cupboard after cupboard, searching for liquor. Nothing.

His siblings had gone through his place after he'd committed to treatment. They'd thrown out every bottle.

He slammed the last door and it bounced back, hitting him in the face. He touched his cheek and his fingers came away bloody.

Stumbling back to his bedroom, he collapsed on the bed. Now what?

SEVEN

"Liz Carlson," she said, answering her desk phone.

"I'm so glad I caught you at the office."

"Meg?" Liz wasn't sure if she recognized her voice.

"It's me. Kate has been gone for two weeks. What are you doing?"

"Getting ready to head home."

"It's Friday night," Meg said. "Meet me at O'Dair's."

"That pub you talked about?" Liz flipped through her wallet. She had about forty dollars. The good news was she'd had enough business lunches this week, she had some extra cash.

But she could also send her parents a little more money when her next check came.

"You promised."

"I'm not sure I did," Liz said. Michael had sent a text, wondering if she wanted to do something this weekend.

She never replied.

"What the heck, why not," Liz said. Then she wouldn't feel so guilty about not responding to Michael "What time and where is this place?"

Meg gave her the details.

Liz decided to walk. It wasn't that far away.

She'd easily survived Kate's two weeks away. And successfully avoided Michael by staying chained to her desk or visiting leasees. There was plenty to do. When she wasn't fielding calls, she was updating models.

Her only encounters with Michael were stilted conversations in the break room. And she hated it. Each time she saw him, she remembered their kiss.

Best kiss ever.

She found the pub right where Meg said it was. She hoped Meg was already here. She didn't want to sit in a bar by herself on a Friday night.

A bell jingled when she opened the door. The scent of beer and … lemon greeted her.

It was inviting. There was a large central bar with a brass railing and hooks under the counter for coats or purses.

Meg waved to her from a high top table.

Relieved, she hurried over.

Meg threw her arms around her. "I'm so glad you're here."

"Are you going through Kate withdrawal?" Liz tugged off her sweater and hung it on one of the extra chair backs.

"I'm just looking for intelligent conversation."

"I'm still exhausted from the wedding," and not sleeping because of Michael's kiss. "I'm not sure if I'll be a stellar conversationalist."

A server stopped at their table and handed out menus. "Happy hour drafts are three dollars for another twenty minutes. I'd recommend the summer ale."

Happy hour prices would help her budget. Yay.

They both took the server's suggestion.

"I'm glad you were free," Meg said. She turned on her barstool. "I think this place is so much fun."

There was a nice energy to the pub. On the far side of the

room was a small stage. Through large glass windows she could see big copper stills. "Do they brew their own beer?"

"Yes." Meg pointed at the cute guy behind the bar. "Sean O'Dair. Brew master."

"And have you grilled him on how to make beer?" Liz asked.

Meg laughed. "Don't believe everything that Kate says about me, but yes. I thought it was fascinating. I even watched the bottling process. Sean and Mitch Thornton from my firm are close friends."

"I miss being able to see my friends from home," Liz admitted. Not when they whispered about Jordan but her true friends. "If I ever run into anyone from home in the Cities, we're always shocked."

"Now that we're connected, you can run into me."

"Thanks."

When their ales arrived, Meg held up a mug and said, "To our new friendship."

"To us."

Their conversation was easy and fun. Even though it was summer, Liz ordered the Irish stew and one more beer during happy hour pricing. That should last her the night.

"I figured I'd find you here." Stephen walked up behind Meg, stealing one of her fries that had come with her mushroom burger.

"Hey." Meg covered up her plate. "Get your own."

"I plan on it." He slid Meg's chair to the side and pulled one of the empty chairs to where she had been sitting. Then took her second beer and a large drank.

"You're paying for the next round," Meg growled.

"Why do you do that?" Liz had to ask.

"What? Steal her food and drink?" He rubbed his knuckles on the top of Meg's head. "'Cuz it drives her nuts."

Meg pushed his hand away and straightened her hair. "It's like you're still ten."

"I didn't care about driving girls nuts when I was ten." Stephen looked at her over the edge of his beer mug and held her gaze for a long minute.

The server came over. "Hey Stephen. What can I get you?"

He rattled off an order. "Thanks, Amy."

Stephen kept glancing around the pub, like he was looking for someone.

"What brought you here on a Friday night?" Meg asked.

"I heard you were going to be here." But his gaze kept panning the room.

There was an awful twisting in Liz's stomach. She used to get warning calls about her brother. "Is it Michael?"

Stephen locked eyes with her. "Why?"

"He … was so sad at the wedding. He kept talking about everything he'd lost." Then he'd kissed her and called her Sarah.

"I don't know how to help him. I don't know how …" Stephen, the biggest of the MacBain brothers, seemed to crumple in front of them. "Ever since the wedding, he doesn't say much."

Liz had found that checking up on Jordan had never helped. It had torn their relationship apart. They used to have so much fun together, now it was all accusations and anger. "Is he here?"

"I got a text, but I haven't seen him. From here I can watch the door."

Meg made a point to lighten up the conversation as Stephen's food arrived, but Liz couldn't help noticing that Stephen kept glancing around the pub.

Maybe this was what was bugging Michael, his family monitoring him.

Maybe he was drinking again. There had been such a look

of longing on his face at the wedding as he'd stared into that glass of whiskey. He'd said he'd only sniffed it, but she wouldn't know if that was the truth.

"I need to find the ladies' room."

Meg pointed. "The lass's room, you mean. Don't go in the door with the leprechaun."

"Thanks for the warning." She headed down the hall and passed a back room where people played darts and pool.

And there was Michael. Slouched in the corner, a glass on the table in front of him.

Instead of confronting him, she headed to the bathroom, not a leprechaun but a beautiful fairy in stained glass. Then she checked again as she scurried by the archway. Michael was throwing darts.

She was going to let Stephen deal with his brother. Michael wasn't her friend anymore.

Meg was saying something and Stephen stared at her. It made her think they were together, but she knew Meg didn't date.

Liz stopped next to the tall table. "He's playing darts."

Stephen set his mug down. "Did you talk to him? Is he sober?"

"I didn't."

"But …" Stephen stood and pulled out his wallet. "Meg. Can you get the bill? Tonight is on me."

"Thank you," both she and Meg said.

"Can you come with me?" Stephen asked.

"Oh. That's not a good idea," Liz said. "We aren't really talking lately."

Not since he'd called her Sarah.

"Please." Stephen held up both hands. "You two seem to have a connection."

Leaving was so tempting, but Stephen looked … lost.

"Fine," she said.

"Thank you. Really, thank you." Stephen set his hand on the small of her back, hurrying her through the crowded pub. "If you need anything, if there's anything I can do for you, let me know."

She couldn't think of anything. "No need."

Michael was still playing darts, his back to them as they came closer.

"Hey bro'," Stephen said.

Michael turned. He was holding a dart in one hand and a tumbler in another. "Stephen. Liz."

He turned back and tossed the dart. Triple 20.

"Nice game, MacBain." A man slapped a five dollar bill in his hand. "Didn't think you could do it."

"I can hold your drink while you put away your money," Stephen said, pulling the glass from Michael's hand.

"Hey!" Michael said.

The four people playing pool looked up and another group of four looked over at them.

Stephen took a sip, closed his eyes and shook his head. "Fuck. Why Michael?"

"Oh Michael," Liz couldn't help saying. "You've been doing so well."

"Did you two come here to check on me?" Michael tried to rescue his glass, but Stephen held it away from him. "Stop embarrassing me!"

"Stop embarrassing the family." Stephen dragged him out in the hallway. At least there, no one eavesdropped on them.

Liz felt like she was watching an accident happen.

"Did you call your sponsor?" Stephen said.

"He didn't pick up."

"Then you should have called me, or Timothy."

Michael snorted. "You guys don't know what to say to me."

"Then someone." Stephen paced a few steps down the hall,

but a server came out of a swinging door with a full tray. They all backed against the wall.

"I tried a friend." Michael glanced over at Liz. "I didn't get an answer."

"Me? You can't blame this on me." She pointed her finger at his chest. "You made the decision to come to a bar. A bar!"

"It was one drink."

One drink. One bet. One anything. She wrapped her arms around her stomach, suddenly cold. "There is no *only one.* You know that."

Michael hung his head. "I know."

"Let me take you home," Stephen said.

"Why not. Little brother to the rescue." Michael avoided her gaze as he and Stephen walked to the main section of the pub.

She watched as Stephen stopped by the table and stuffed his credit card in his wallet. Michael just stood with his head down.

Once they left, she rejoined Meg.

"Are you okay?" Meg asked.

"He blamed drinking on me." Liz still couldn't believe it. "Because I didn't answer his text."

"That's not right," Meg said. "He looks so lost. I'd thought he'd looked better over the last few weeks."

"It must be a battle." Liz gathered her purse and sweater. "But I can't be responsible for his sobriety. He can't hang that on me."

"IT HAPPENS," Terry said again, twirling his coffee mug. It was Saturday morning, and they were meeting in another coffee shop. "But instead of heading to a bar, you should have gone to a meeting."

"I know." Michael shoved at his hair. "I screwed up."

"Yeah, you did." Terry handed him a card. "There's my work phone number. Try either number next time."

Michael didn't want a next time. Hell, he'd been so embarrassed that Stephen and Liz had found him with a drink in his hand, he never wanted that to happen again.

"Why did you go there? To O'Dair's?" Terry asked. "Did you want to get caught?"

"I ... Maybe." He knew Meg went there a lot. And Stephen.

But he'd never seen Liz there before.

"My sister's wedding was hard. Sarah should have been there with me." He ripped the napkin under his Danish. "We should have been married and had kids by now. I miss her."

"I get that." Terry tapped his finger on the table. "But taking a drink is never the answer."

"I fucking know that."

"What are your plans for today?" Terry asked.

"Not to drink. Go to a meeting." The new pattern of his life.

"Do you want to get together tomorrow?" Terry asked.

"I'll call if I need to."

"Make sure you do," Terry said.

LIZ PILED the last of her laundry from the dryer into her basket. She'd left the task for Sunday night. She'd fold everything in her apartment. The basement was creepy.

She hadn't heard anything from Stephen or Michael over the weekend. She hoped Michael was getting the help he needed. Hoped he wouldn't fall off the wagon again.

She climbed the stairs. At least on laundry day she got her steps in.

On the third floor, she turned the corner and gasped.

A man sat in front of her doorway, his head down as if he was in deep thought. Or sleeping.

Turning, her basket hit the railing. She dropped it and her clothes spilled out.

The man's head popped up.

She ran down the stairs, hoping her neighbors on the first floor would let her in.

"Lizzie," the deep voice filled the hallway. "Lizzie, wait! It's me!"

Her foot slipped on the stair tread and she caught herself on the railing. "Jordan?"

"Yup."

"What are you doing here?" Liz slowly returned and righted her laundry basket, picking up her clothes.

Her brother's eyes had deep circles under them. He hadn't shaved in a while by the length of his stubble. And his clothes looked like he'd slept in them—for a week.

"I had to get out of town." He picked up the duffle he'd been sitting on. "Thought you might have a spare room for me."

"Spare room?" She frowned. "I live in a one-bedroom apartment."

The locks squeaked as she opened them one at a time. She wiggled the door handle until it popped open. "Do you think I live in the lap of luxury?"

"Sure." He looked around before stepping into the apartment behind her. "You got that big new promotion."

"Well, I don't." She dropped the basket in her bedroom. "Do Mom and Dad know you're here?"

"Kind of." He set his bag at the door.

She threw the Diebold and door locks. How far they'd come from leaving the farmhouse unlocked all the time. Well, this wasn't the fields of Iowa, was it?

"How are they?" she asked.

"Good. Waiting on rain." He prowled her small space. "I tried to pick up more hours at Jake's shop, but there just aren't enough vehicles coming."

He updated her on their aunt and cousins. Then he asked, "Do you have a place for me to sleep?"

"There's a couch in the alcove you can sleep on." It would give him a little privacy. "Why are you here?"

"I … I can't keep living on the farm. I'm dying there." He caught her by the arm. "I need to make money, and I'm hoping you can help."

"Me? What can I do?"

"You work for a big corporation. They've got to have something."

It was always like this. Jordan got into a jam and expected her to help him out. "I don't know of any positions. I guess I can ask at the office tomorrow."

"Thanks." He sat at the table and propped his head up with his hand.

"You look exhausted." She went to the closet and pulled out a set of sheets. She didn't have another blanket, so he would have to make do with the throws on the sofa. She grabbed the second pillow off her bed and pulled on a clean pillowcase.

She wasn't set up for guests. Grimacing, she brought the sheets and pillow out to him. "There's an extra towel in the bathroom closet."

She looked around her small apartment. This was the first place she'd ever lived alone. Now her small sanctuary was gone. "Please don't leave clothes lying around. Keep the apartment clean."

"Thanks, sis." He took the linens and set them on the sofa. Then he pulled her into his arms for an awkward hug. "I owe you."

Just like Michael, he felt as if he'd lost weight.

She patted his back. He was her twin. They'd once been so close. Now it was like they were strangers. Maybe living together again would bring them closer.

She finished folding her clothes. "I'm heading to bed."

"So early?" he asked. "It's not like we've got cows to milk."

"No, but my boss has been gone on her honeymoon, and I want to make sure everything is up to date when she gets back." It would be nice to see Kate again. "I'll see you in the morning. Coffee's in the fridge if you wake before I do."

There was the one high point of living with Jordan. He made better coffee than she did.

She took that thought with her as she brushed her teeth and crawled into bed.

And with her brother here, she couldn't obsess over Michael.

"STEPHEN, DO YOU HAVE A MINUTE?" Liz asked, spotting her prey as he walked down the hallway.

"Sure." He walked into her office and filled one of her guest chairs. "I'm actually early for this morning's staff meeting."

She was beginning to understand how the brothers worked. Stephen was usually late. Michael, early, and Timothy? Timothy was all over the map.

She'd gotten lucky this morning. Maybe Stephen didn't have a lot on his plate this Monday morning.

"What's up?" he asked. "Is one of our leases looking for a remodel?"

That had been her and Stephen's usual encounters since he ran the MacBain construction arm. "No. It's personal."

"Really?" He leaned forward and set his arms on her desk.

The man was so big, she almost slid her desk chair back a couple of inches so she had room to move. Instead she laced her fingers together. "My brother's looking for a job. I don't know how you're situated for crew, but I was wondering if you had anything open?"

She glanced down. Her knuckles were white. She tried to relax her fingers, but she hated this. Hated using her position to get her brother a job. If he screwed up it might affect her career.

"I might. Plus, I owe you for helping with Michael on Friday night."

"No, you don't."

"I do," Stephen said. "Is he a carpenter?"

She tucked her hands under her thighs. "We're farm kids. He can do about anything. Build a barn, repair a tractor, drive a harvester, and of course, milk a cow."

Stephen smiled. "Well, I don't have cows on any of my jobs, but sure, I'll talk to him. We're always looking for good people. I know Katie thinks the world of you."

She bit her lip, wanting to confess that her brother had a problem. But she couldn't. Maybe if he got this job, he'd clean up his act. Maybe this would be a turning point in his life.

She swallowed back the lump in her throat. "Thanks."

"Have him call my cell." He checked the time. "Better yet, have your brother meet me at Swallow's Ridge around one?"

She nodded. Hoping she wasn't promising something her brother couldn't handle. "Thank you. I'll let him know."

"What's his name?" Stephen asked as he stood.

"Jordan."

"Great." Stephen started out, but someone stopped him right outside her door.

She picked up her phone and texted her brother the time, the address and Stephen's name.

"Liz?" Michael asked.

She glanced up and both brothers were looking at her.

"Did you hear the question?" Stephen asked.

She shook her head, trying not to stare at Michael.

"Mom and Dad want you to join the staff meeting," Michael said.

"I thought Kate was back from her honeymoon."

"I guess she's not here," Michael said.

"Of course I'll come." She found a tablet of paper in a drawer. "Is there anything I need to be prepared to talk about?"

Michael shook his head.

Just in case, she took her lease binder. "I'm ready."

"How about grabbing lunch after the meeting?" Michael asked.

She didn't have a choice—she had to look at him. He looked tired. His smile didn't reach his eyes, but it rarely did.

"Lunch?" she repeated, afraid she sounded like an idiot.

"I want to apologize for … O'Dair's." Michael looked at Stephen. "To both of you. Thanks for interrupting me."

"No problem." She didn't want to eat alone with Michael, but if Stephen was there … Her fingers floated to her mouth. Before she touched her lips, she tugged her hand back to her side.

"Lunch sounds good." Did she even have money for lunch?

They walked down the hall together. She hoped Stephen didn't mention the meeting with her brother. She didn't want Michael to know she was imposing on Stephen and the family business.

The MacBains were already sitting in the conference room. Timothy paced at the far edge of the room, on the phone, gesturing wildly.

She started for an open seat, but Stephen pointed. "Do you mind if I take that chair?"

She knew Stephen was set in his ways, but conference room seats too? "No problem."

"Don't mind him," Patty said. "I don't know how he developed this weird fetish."

"Mom." Stephen groaned.

Liz moved around the table and took one of the empty chairs, only to find Michael sitting next to her. Now she would be inhaling his cologne all morning.

As she sat, she took a deep breath. Yup.

Mac rapped his knuckles on the table. "We'll start. Timothy's dealing with a problem. Thanks for joining us, Liz."

"Thanks for inviting me." Liz flipped to a clean page on her pad.

"Kate called yesterday," Patty said. "She had some … trouble while they were on their honeymoon. Her OB put her on bed rest."

"Bed rest?" Stephen asked.

Timothy hurried to the table. "What?"

Michael half stood. "Is she okay?"

"She had some spotting." Patty waved him down. "This is all precautionary. Hopefully she'll be back to work soon."

"I'll do whatever I can to help out," Liz said.

"Thank you." Patty pulled her agenda in front of her. "Alex is making sure she stays put."

Stephen snorted. "That's not going to go well."

Mac looked at Liz. "I'd like you to attend the staff meetings until Kate gets the all-clear from her doctor."

"Absolutely."

"Are there any fires in the contract/leasing side of the business?" Mac asked.

"This is a pretty quiet time. I've got all the renewal notices out, and I'm keeping up with any lease requests."

"Good. Let Michael or me know if something changes."

"I will." And Liz would document anything significant for Kate.

Timothy said, "Water main was cut in front of Diamond Lake Mall. Thank the Lord, by the city. They've been doing utility work in the street. Our parking lot is flooded, but no water damage to the spaces—yet."

"Can we keep it that way?" Mac looked at both Timothy and Stephen.

"Fire department's laid down barriers. I sent Abraham over there."

"He'll handle the crisis," Stephen said.

"The Starbucks' manager isn't happy. No one can get into the shop or through the drive-through. I told them to estimate their sale's losses." Timothy looked at Michael. "Can you check with the insurance broker? Let me know what I have to do?"

"I'll call, but this isn't our liability." Michael made a note on his phone. "Although getting the city to cover any of the company's losses could be impossible. The manager should notify their insurance company."

"Act of God?" Liz said, and then covered her mouth.

Startled faces turned her way. Then the group smiled and Stephen laughed.

"The city's risk managers would probably say that." Michael actually chuckled.

"I can work on an email to the tenants," Liz suggested.

"Good," Mac said. "Work with Timothy and Michael on that."

She nodded.

The rest of the agenda was routine. She updated the group on the status of the negotiations of a new lease. Stephen talked about the Swallow's Ridge residential construction and the commercial strip mall out in Woodbury. Patty, the number of cleaning crew jobs open. Maybe her brother could do that if a construction job didn't work out.

Michael updated them on an upcoming software change. Timothy talked about a property they should consider acquiring up in Forest Lake.

There wasn't a lot of extraneous conversation. Each MacBain said their piece and then took notes. Other than Timothy's pen bouncing on the paper in front of him, she was beginning to relax.

"That's all. Liz and Michael," Mac looked at them, "I've got another task for the two of you. Can you stay?"

She nodded.

Michael said, "Of course."

Everyone else filed out of the room. Mac closed his folder. "I'd like to revamp our long-term forecast. I'm concerned our inflators are too high."

"You're right," Liz said. "We changed the cost of capital in the models I use but haven't changed any of the lease renewal assumptions."

Michael rubbed his chin. "We've only been making changes as leases renew."

"I'd like a review of all the assumptions. Bring them in line with the current interest and inflation rates."

Liz couldn't quite keep the smile off her face. "I'd love to."

She couldn't wait to pull apart all the models and see what she could streamline.

The only problem would be working closely with the finance department. She caught her upper lip between her teeth. Michael would assign this to one of his analysts.

Michael made a note on his tablet and looked up. His gaze zoomed in on her lip.

Mac flashed her a smile. "You and Kate are a good team. She made a good hire when she found you."

"Thank you, sir."

"Sir?" Mac pressed a hand on his chest. "You make me feel old."

"Sorry." She swallowed. "Mac."

"Does two weeks sound reasonable?" Mac asked.

She tried to think of all the spreadsheets she would need to review along with her current workload. And drew a blank.

"We'll give it a shot." Michael frowned.

He and his department probably had more work to do than she did. The leases were a big component of MacBain, but they only represented fifty percent of the revenue.

"I was trying to visualize the changes," Liz said. "Two weeks is fine."

"We'll touch base next Monday and see how you're doing."

With that they were dismissed.

She gathered her tablet and phone. Michael sent a text.

As they walked out of the conference room, she asked, "Who do you want me to work with on your team?" She didn't assume the CFO would be involved in something so transaction-based.

"Me." He gave one sharp nod, his dark hair falling across his forehead.

She raised her hand to brush the hair away then faltered. She tucked her own hair back behind her ear.

"We can talk about our approach at lunch after we work on the tenant email."

"Um, won't Stephen be bored?"

"He's heading to Diamond Lake Mall to check on the water damage. Then he has an appointment at Swallow's Ridge. Are you ready to go?"

She would be eating lunch alone with Michael. "Okay."

She'd just have to make sure the only thing between them was business.

"I'M good with the tenant email. Get Timothy's okay and then send it out," Michael said, handing it back to Liz.

"Will do." Liz set the draft on the table.

Michael took a sip of water. He couldn't delay anymore. "I'm sorry about O'Dair's. I … stumbled."

"You don't have to apologize to me," Liz said.

"I think I do. It was … I spiraled after Kate's wedding. Everything got … dark."

Liz stared at him. "You blamed me."

"I'm sorry. You weren't the problem. I was." He straightened his utensils on the table. "My sponsor thought by going to O'Dair's I wanted to be discovered."

She tipped her head and looked thoughtful. "Did you?"

"I might have." He shoved his hair back. "I know Meg goes there and Stephen. I didn't know you did."

"I don't. That was a first for me." She took a sip of her tea. "And how are you now?"

"Over the worst. I've been getting to meetings every night."

"Good." She pulled over her laptop. "We should see what else we can get done before our food comes."

"Got it." Whatever friendship they'd had, was gone. He opened his ten-year projection folder. "On to the forecast. It's been a while since I've looked at this."

Liz flipped open her laptop.

Kate had done most of the work on the last projection. How many years had Michael let his sister flex her MBA skills? She loved to play with forecasts and projections, and he'd let her.

He sighed.

"What?" Liz asked.

"What?"

"You sighed."

"We're both going into this a little blind." He shook his

head. "I didn't have a lot of involvement in the last ten-year projection update."

He pulled out the recap spreadsheet. This time he would be intimately familiar with each component. He wouldn't have Kate's sharp eyes to back him up. Liz was bright, but she didn't have the company history.

"Let's make sure we have all the leases in the models," Liz said.

They compared notes. He jotted down changes for his model. "Wow, we've added twenty new leases since the last time this was run."

"And we haven't even included the McGuire building. Those come online next year."

He made another note.

Liz tapped her fingernail on the edge of her glass of lemonade. "You know I made changes to Kate's base model, so we didn't have to enter the data twice. We need to do that with the ten-year forecast too."

"In two weeks?" Maybe if he was more familiar with the models ...

She rested her forearms on the table. His eyes dropped to the hint of cleavage exposed where the buttons of her pale pink blouse ended, but he forced his gaze back to her face.

"We can do it. And it will make the next pass easier."

And require them to work together.

"Here you go." The waitress held out their plates.

Liz closed her laptop and he set the folder on an empty chair.

She kept her gaze on her food as they ate. Her hand squeezed her fork until her knuckles were white.

"Everything okay?" he asked.

"The forecast will be a lot of work, but that's okay. Your dad was right. This is a quiet time in the leasing department." She smiled. "If two people can be considered a department."

"It is." He dredged a fry through his ketchup and pointed it at her. "I thought maybe you were uncomfortable because I kissed you."

She sat up. "That can't happen again."

"I know." He tried to smile. "Let's just say it was the evening and the moonlight and leave it at that."

"Oh. Oh sure."

He popped the fry in his mouth and kept eating. He liked keeping Liz on her toes.

JORDAN RAN his hand through his hair and almost drifted into the second lane. "Where the hell is this place?"

When Liz had given him the address, his GPS had said the site was almost an hour away. He'd jumped into the shower and hightailed it to his truck, hoping he'd have enough gas to get him to this Swallow's Ridge. What the hell kind of name for a housing development was that?

The streets morphed from asphalt to dirt, and there weren't any street signs. The clock said he needed to be there. Now. Liz would kill him if he was late.

It would be fine if Liz killed him, but he didn't want Rudy taking care of the deed. Even though the air conditioning barely worked and it was pushing ninety on the thermometer, a chill ran down his back, just like the feel of the barrel of a gun on his spine.

Which was why he'd headed out of town Saturday night. He'd taken back roads and crisscrossed the county before heading north to Minneapolis. A trip that should have taken four hours had taken twenty-four. He'd used his last ten dollars to fill up south of the Cities, and he was driving on fumes. He didn't know how he would get back to his sister's place.

Finally he saw framed-in buildings. He picked the building with the most trucks around it and shut off his engine.

He tugged on his shirt. He'd thrown on yesterday's jeans. His sister didn't have a washing machine.

He headed in through an open door.

He just needed another stake to pay off his fucking debt to Rudy. If he could clear a little more cash, he'd catch his streak and ride it to Vegas. It was the crap Iowa casinos holding him down.

He heard voices on the second floor and climbed the open stairway, homing in on the sound.

A group of men gathered round a makeshift table. Blueprints, their edges warn and frayed, were anchored with a rock and two coffee cups.

They must have heard his boots because four heads turned toward the stairs as he hit the top riser.

A man with brown hair and steely eyes moved toward him. "Jordan? Jordan Carlson?"

"That's me. I'm looking for …" He shook his head. "Mac-Bain. I know Liz said his name, but I …" He waved his hand. Nice way to make an impression.

"I'm Stephen MacBain." The man stuck out his hand. "Nice to meet you."

The man was only a couple of inches taller than his six feet, but there was muscle behind his grip.

"Did you have trouble finding us?" Stephen asked.

"Seemed like I ran out of road signs, then I ran out of road."

"Isn't that the truth."

A saw screeched, making conversation impossible.

"Come on." Stephen clapped a hand on his back. "Let's find a place where we can talk."

Jordan followed him downstairs and outside. They headed

across what would be a street and up a set of planks to the skeletal frame of another house.

Stephen sat on a pile of lumber and Jordan sat on a bucket.

"Construction makes for interesting interviews." Stephen dusted off his hands. "We didn't bring in a trailer for this job. Maybe we should have."

"This works for me." Jordan wasn't in this for the long haul.

"So, what are your skills?"

This MacBain fellow was direct. "I'm good with equipment, small engines and big engines. I've worked in an auto repair shop half my life." Any time he needed extra cash. "I can fence, build a barn, reroof a house and milk the cows."

"Liz said about the same thing. And like I told your sister, we don't have any cows. There's the occasional coyote sighting, but I don't think we need to herd them." Stephen raised his eyebrow. "Can you read a blueprint?"

"I can fake my way through it."

Stephen asked about the equipment he'd worked on and what kind of construction he'd done. Jordan answered as truthfully as possible. Everything except Stephen's question about why he'd moved to Minneapolis.

"I like farming, but there's not a lot of satisfaction in waiting for the rain to come or the crops to ripen." He'd wanted to try some of the techniques he'd learned in his two years in college, but Dad hadn't been willing to change.

"I know enough." Stephen took a deep breath in. "Liz is a great addition to MacBain. I think we can use your skills. There's an opening in equipment management; repairs and servicing. How does that sound?"

"Great." Not really, but he had an end goal in mind.

"What do you think about starting tomorrow?" Stephen's gaze hadn't left his face since they'd started this conversation.

"Feel good about it."

Stephen pulled out a business card and wrote down another address. "Why don't you show up around seven?" He grinned. "This address will be easier to find. There are roads, and street signs, and all those modern conveniences."

Seven. Well, at least it was a little later than the day started at the farm. Of course he didn't have any idea where this place was. "I'll be there."

Then he remembered his gas situation.

"I don't suppose you have any gas around here?" He swallowed back his embarrassment, tugging on the collar of his shirt. "I'm driving on fumes and left my credits cards at Liz's place."

"Nothing on site." Stephen pulled a bill out of his wallet. "I can spot you ten bucks."

"Thanks, man. Money's pretty tight in the farming business." Especially since Rudy was breathing down his neck. "I'll get this back to you."

"Nearest station is a little south on the main road."

Jordan nodded. "I saw it. Thanks again."

They stood and shook hands. Then he headed back to his truck.

Was it his imagination or did Stephen's gaze drill a hole in his back.

He didn't care. He had a job. He'd get his stake and tap Liz for more money, although that field was becoming a dust bowl. Then he'd head far away from Rudy and Iowa. Vegas, baby. No one could find him there.

EIGHT

Liz shifted the grocery bag to her hip and unlocked the apartment building's main door. She doubted Jordan had put dinner together. In their family, men worked the fields and women did the gardening and housework.

Tired, she trudged up the stairs. Not only because she'd spent so much time with Michael, but because she was worried about Jordan. She didn't trust her twin.

In front of the door, she took a deep breath. Grasping the knob, it turned under her fingers. Jordan hadn't locked the door.

"Jordan?"

"Yeah?"

"I always keep the door locked." She pushed it shut with her butt, threw the locks and headed to the kitchen.

"Yeah, sure, sure." He followed her into the kitchen and took the bag from her hands. "I was wondering when you would be home. The pizza will be here any minute. We're celebrating."

"You ordered pizza?" Yay, she didn't have to cook. "Does this mean you got the job?"

He grinned, that wonderful infectious smile of his. "I got a job."

She set her purse on the small table and gave him a big hug. "That's great!"

"It's just working in their equipment shop, but it's something." He shrugged.

She smiled as she stepped back. "It's a start."

"Well, everyone can't be in management. Plus, I hardly ever get pizza." He gave her shoulder a little punch. "They won't deliver to the farm."

"I remember." She put the cereal in the cupboard. Then set the milk and eggs in the fridge. "Did anyone reopen the Pizza Palace?"

"No one." He held up the coffee.

She pointed to the cupboard below the coffee maker. "That's too bad."

"Yeah. Oh, the bill's twenty-six bucks."

She froze. The bag she'd been folding dropped to the floor. "But you're buying, right?"

"I'm broke." His face scrunched up. "I owe that MacBain guy ten bucks. I need you to float me some cash so I can get to work tomorrow."

An ache radiated through her body. "I don't have that kind of money. I just brought home no-name cereal and coffee that was on sale, and you want me to splurge on pizza?"

He held up his hands. "But—"

"Look around, Jord. I'm scraping by. Why can't you understand that?"

"But they take credit cards."

She closed her eyes and sank into the kitchen chair. Her brother expected her to keep paying and paying.

"Cancel the order." She felt like she was eighty years old.

The buzzer rang.

Jordan pushed the button. "Yeah?"

A tinny voice came through. "Pizza."

"Come on, Lizzie," Jordan said. "I'm sorry. It won't happen again."

How many times had she heard him say that? She pushed herself out of the chair. Picking up her purse, she said, "Tell him I'm coming."

Each foot felt like it weighed ten pounds as she headed downstairs. And this was only Monday.

MICHAEL CHECKED the time—4:30. Liz should be on her way to his office.

They'd worked together every day this week. He'd spent more time with Liz than he had with his family in the two months.

Liz rapped on the doorframe. "Are you ready?"

"Come on in."

She moved to the conference table, and he had a chance to admire the way her pants molded to her ass.

It was casual Friday, and both he and Liz were in polo shirts and khakis.

"Let's be comfortable." He pointed to the sofa and armchairs. "We've spent too many hours leaning over that table this week."

She stopped and looked at the seating area. Her teeth worried her bottom lip.

Did she think he was going to take her on the sofa? A memory of her soft body against his sent heat through him, and he shut it down. Any sexual thoughts about Liz shamed his memory of Sarah. Maybe he couldn't help responding to Liz, but he would not act on his thoughts.

She settled next to him on the sofa, tucking her foot under her butt. "We made a breakthrough today. Zach and I worked on linking the leasing projections and the ten-year forecast models." Her eyes sparkled as she squeezed his arm. "It worked."

He ignored his body's reaction to her fingers on his bare arm. "That's great."

She opened her laptop. "Now we need to finalize the assumptions."

She handed him a packet of spreadsheets. The first page looked vaguely familiar. "What's this?"

"Something Kate developed, and we refined a couple of months ago. It's our assumption template."

She leaned over the coffee table and laid down a spreadsheet, pointing. "This is the Daschle building. We've got the lease terms for each signed lease." She flipped back a few pages. "And the unoccupied space too."

He perused the first couple of pages. "This rolls up into the building-by-building totals?"

She nodded. "I've expanded all the files out fifteen years. I know it's not what your dad asked for, but it will help in five years."

"That's … brilliant."

"I'm trying to make things consistent and easier. Now all the forecasts are out fifteen years, or they will be once we settle on the assumptions."

She tapped on the keyboard and brought up the same file he was looking at. "We need to finalize the interest rates and inflators. Also, I'd like to set some parameters."

"Parameters?"

"If a lease is expiring, do we assume the lease automatically renews or is there time when it's empty and we have to account for additional remodeling costs?"

She was way ahead of him in thinking through the leases. "What's our current vacancy rate?"

"Ignoring this latest downturn, the vacancy rate has been

low, three to five percent. I'd suggest one model where I use a five percent vacancy, another model where we use a ten percent vacancy. An outlier would be something higher than ten percent."

"If we lost the Sorenson Law firm, what kind of vacancy rate would we have?"

"Twenty-five percent. But we locked in the lease for ten years."

He nodded. "Okay, let's go through what you need estimates on. Start with the best-case scenario."

She worked through each of her assumptions, asking for advice and suggesting solutions. Along with the best-case, they developed a fair and an unfavorable scenario.

The way she concentrated as she entered the information reminded him of Sarah. How focused she'd always been as they'd studied. The way her hair would slide over her cheek. Sarah's hair had been thick, black and straight. Liz's was a blonde with red highlights, and her hair curled around her face.

His favorite pastime had been distracting Sarah, often by kissing her neck as she leaned over her work. And sometimes he would slowly remove her clothes until she could no longer ignore him.

Liz arched her spine, pushing on her lower back. Her breasts thrust out like an offering.

His hand trembled. He needed a drink.

"That should do it for tonight." Liz put everything back in the folder she'd brought and closed the laptop. "I'll load assumptions tomorrow. I'm brain dead right now."

"You're working on Saturday?" he asked.

She shrugged. "I want to ensure we make our deadline. How are you coming on the construction forecasts?"

"Getting through them."

"Why do you think your father wants projections out so far?" Her sharp eyes stared into his.

Dad had been asking for a lot of long-term info lately. Why indeed. "I don't know."

She looked him in the eye. "I hope he's not planning to sell."

He did a double take and almost laughed. "With all of the family in the business? Over our dead bodies!"

She seemed relieved. "Well, I'm heading home."

He checked the clock. "Six? It's already six o'clock?"

He should have noticed the silence outside his office. A vacuum buzzed at the end of the hall.

"We got a lot done without interruptions." She grinned. "My computer is almost out of battery."

"You could have used my charger."

"I knew we were almost done." She pushed on her lower back.

Did she know what happened to his body when she did that?

No. Because this was a business meeting. "I'm sorry I kept you so long. The least I can do is buy you dinner."

She picked up her computer and files, shaking her head. "No thanks."

"I kept you here late on a Friday night." She'd been getting in at seven, if not earlier. "How many hours have you worked this week?"

"A lot." She moved to his door. "I should get home. My brother's staying with me right now."

"I didn't know that." He stood and followed her. "Come on. He's a twin, right? He should be able to fend for himself. Let MacBain take you out for dinner."

～

IT WAS hard for Liz to be around Michael for so many hours and not want more.

She hadn't known that Minerva's would be so … atmospheric. At lunch the restaurant was bright and cheery. Apparently at night they dimmed the lights and brought out candles.

Intimate when she'd hoped for friendly.

Michael looked good in candlelight. His cheekbones stood out in relief. His seven o'clock shadow looked sexy and rumpled. And the sad forlorn look that never left his handsome face made her want to help him smile.

How many times had she wanted to help Jordan feel better?

"Do you know what you want?" Michael closed his menu.

She nodded.

Their server came to the table, a big smile on her face. "What can I get you to drink?"

Michael waited for her. Did she dare order a glass of wine? She deserved it after this week. Michael had told her it was okay, but still.

"Why don't you bring her a glass of Pinot Grigio? That's what you like, right?" he said.

"Yes, thanks."

"I'll have iced tea," he said.

They ordered their meal. After the server left, he said, "How many times do I have to say, you can drink around me."

"I caught you staring into a glass of whiskey not three weeks ago." She exhaled. "And drinking one week ago."

His face froze. "That was …"

She let the silence hang between them.

"That was different. It was the wedding." When he stared into her eyes, his expression was bleak. "When I'm with you, I don't want a drink."

"Don't fool yourself." She shook her head. "I was in the same room."

"But you were dancing with Ashton. Hell no, you were flirting with him."

"Don't make me responsible for your drinking or sobriety." She pushed away from the table. "I can't do this. I won't."

He caught her hand. Warmth curled up her arm and settled into a place where it didn't belong.

She was afraid to stay and afraid to leave.

He wasn't her responsibility.

"Don't leave. I'm sorry. You're not responsible for my actions, and I can't turn this on you and my cousin kissing. I know that. I didn't drink at the reception."

"But you did at O'Dair's."

"I was missing Sarah. It was just …"

His voice was so low she had to lean close to hear him. Close enough to catch a whiff of his cologne mixed with the scent she knew was his alone.

"And has missing her changed? Damn it, you kissed me and then called me her name." She hadn't meant to bring up their kiss.

"I was a mess. That won't happen again."

What wouldn't happen again? Kissing her or calling her Sarah? She refused to ask.

"Please stay." He squeezed her hand, then let go. "I promised MacBain would buy you dinner. You worked hard this week."

There was nothing to keep her here. Nothing but trouble. His eyes peered out from a face so solemn and sad, her knees went weak. She sank onto the chair, no longer able to leave him.

The corners of his mouth lifted. "Thanks."

The server arrived with the drinks, oblivious to the battle just fought.

If it had been a battle, had she lost or strategically retreated?

~

MICHAEL PUSHED AWAY HIS PLATE. The lamb chops had been good but too much food after his salad. He still wasn't used to eating so much. And the rehab nutritionist had said he should eat more vegetables and stay away from sugars.

Apparently Mom was right.

But he didn't crave alcohol for the sugars, or the buzz. Alcohol had been a tool to get to Sarah. If he got really drunk, he would hear her voice.

Liz pushed away her plate.

He was forgetting the sound of Sarah's voice.

He'd promised Sarah he would never forget.

The lavender candle burning on the windowsill didn't mask the pungent smell of Sarah's disease. The bleach undertones couldn't be disguised.

Sarah's mother came into their bedroom with a fresh glass of water. She set it on the end table and stood on the opposite side of the bed from where he sat. "How's my girl? How's my baby?" her mother asked, stroking Sarah's hair.

No response. She hadn't responded for over forty-eight hours.

Michael took her hand, straightening her fingers that had curled into fists. Long, skinny fingers, no longer vibrating with Sarah's animation and joy. Now the veins popped out, and he swore he could count each bone. Not just her fingers, but each vertebra and rib.

Something was missing. He touched her hand and pain smacked into his chest. "Where's her engagement ring?"

Agony created a nest of wrinkles around Sarah's mother's eyes and mouth. "It fell off last night."

She brushed her daughter's hair once more and then moved to the dresser. Opening the jewelry box he'd given Sarah for Christmas when they were in high school, she pulled out the ring. "I put it away so it wouldn't get lost."

Her engagement ring. The one Sarah had pointed out when they'd been seniors in college. They'd been strolling on Michigan Avenue and stopped to look in Tiffany's windows. The ring was decorated with gold roses, her favorite flower. When she'd declared that was her ring, she'd had an enormous smile on her face.

He'd taken a picture, knowing he would return to buy it.

Three years later he'd shown a Tiffany's clerk the picture, and she'd found a ring so similar it might have been the same one.

Sarah's mother held it out to him. He opened his hand automatically, and she set it in his palm. His fingers closed around the ring Sarah had never taken off. Not in the two and half years since he'd proposed on Valentine's Day. Not since he'd gotten down on one knee and said he would love her for the rest of his life.

She'd knelt with him and said, yes. The happiest day of his life.

How could she leave him?

He found a chain in the jewelry box and threaded the ring through it. Then with Sarah's mother's help, he put it around her neck.

He whispered, "I will always love you."

"Are you okay?" Liz's voice broke through the memory. Hauling him back into a world without Sarah. A world where each day was ... empty.

"Sorry, zoned out a little." He blinked his eyes, forcing himself back to the present, the now, the void. "Food coma."

She pointed to a to-go box. "You only ate half your dinner."

He shrugged.

She twirled the stem of her wineglass. She'd only finished half of the wine. "Can I ask you something?"

"Sure." But he wasn't going to answer any questions about Sarah. Those memories were his to keep safe and private.

Her smile was small and forced. She tapped the glass, a tiny tinging noise.

"Yes?"

"Do you really like what you do for a living?"

"Working in the family business?"

"No, not working at MacBain. Do you like being the head of finance?"

"My degree is in accounting with a double major in finance." And he was the firstborn. He'd always known he would join the company.

"I know that, but do you like what you do?" Her eyebrows knit together. "Not working with the company, the company's great. Do you like your role?"

"No one's ever asked me that." He pushed back in his chair and spun his empty water glass. "It's my job."

"I know." She touched his free hand. "But you don't seem passionate about it, not like when you talk about architecture and sculpture. Working with you all week, I know you can do your job, but your eyes don't light up when you talk about work."

"Come on, I'm a guy."

But she was making him think. Passion? The only thing he'd ever been passionate about was Sarah. She'd been the one to make his eyes light up.

And Liz was right. He'd dreamed of designing houses like the one he and Liz had visited. But he would have updated them. Updated prairie school architecture. MacBain Homes.

Designing the homes the company built would have let him make his mark and contribute something of worth to the family. Stephen and Timothy would have built his homes, done them justice.

"You should be passionate about what you do," Liz insisted. "Do you want to be known as someone who was competent in their job?"

That was how she saw him? Competent? He wasn't even sure he was that. *Ouch.*

"Sometimes we do what we have to do." He waved away her statement.

"I've only seen your eyes light up once. Or one day." She

finished her wine and pushed it away. "When you took me through the museum and the house."

"I enjoy what I do," he lied.

Because of Sarah, he'd chosen to give up the idea of designing houses. She'd been his life. Studying, working and living with Sarah ... had been enough. Had been everything.

Look where that left him.

He nodded at the server. "We're ready for our check now."

She pulled it out of the pocket of her apron as she turned away. "Have a nice night."

He tucked his corporate card in the pocket and handed it to the woman before she could leave. He didn't check the detail or the total.

"Are you passionate about what you do?" he asked.

"I am. I love what I do. I love working with Kate." She set her purse on the table. "It's why I don't mind the long hours. It's fun to come up with leases that work for both the company and the leasees." She shrugged. "I like creating present value statements, so sue me."

The server dropped off the charge slip. He signed it, leaving a healthy tip.

"Don't forget your leftovers," Liz said as they stood up.

They headed toward the company's parking ramp. "You don't need to walk me to my car."

He raised an eyebrow and kept walking.

"Come on," she said.

"I am."

"Ha ha." Her heels clicked a little faster.

"You know my mother."

"She's a wonderful woman. But I don't need an escort. Michael, this is ridiculous."

He ignored her protests.

They turned into the ramp and headed to the elevators.

"My mother would chastise me if I let any employee walk into the ramp at this hour alone."

"I feel safe here." She punched the elevator button. The car opened and they stepped in.

Liz had worked late for most of the week. "Did you walk to your car alone all this week?"

It was her turn to be silent.

"You're kidding me? You should have asked me or had security walk you out. That's why they're there."

He waited for her to tell him, yes.

Silence. The car opened on her floor and she stepped out.

"I'm serious, Liz. You worked until nine most nights."

She let her shoulders rise and fall. "I can take care of myself."

Anger welled inside him. "Liz, even I sometimes get security to escort me if I'm here late. A deserted ramp is not a safe place. Not with the trouble that's been happening downtown."

They stopped next to her car. She dug in her purse for her keys.

"You're what, five-foot-two?" he asked.

"Five-foot-three." She pulled out her keys.

Michael decided to make his point. He pushed her against the car. "Five-foot-three. Well, I've got nine inches and seventy pounds on you, babe."

Her eyes flared open. "Don't call me, babe."

She pushed at his chest, but she was too puny to keep him from crowding her against the car.

His body lined up with hers, thigh to thigh, her chest to his.

"Back off." Her voice wobbled.

"Make me." His voice had dropped so he barely recognized it.

She arched back, trying to get leverage. All that did was thrust her chest closer to him. "Michael, don't."

He leaned in, their faces so close his breath made her curls dance. "You said you could get away. You don't need anyone, right?"

He was no longer trying to prove how foolish she was. He wanted to kiss her. He wanted her to wrap the hands pushing him away around his neck.

"Michael," she whispered.

Her hands now rubbed against his nipples. His erection jutted into her stomach.

"Liz." He kissed the soft skin of her neck, under her ear. Her curls teased his cheek. "I want to kiss you. Let me kiss you."

Her fingers dug into his chest.

He needed to kiss her. Needed to taste her lips again. Not in anger like after the wedding, but because they both wanted to touch each other.

She didn't answer. His words hung between them.

What was he doing? She worked for his family. Hell, security was probably watching them right now. He was no better than the asshole she'd worked for before.

Fuck. He took a step back, but her hands stopped him.

"Michael." She stood on her toes.

"Are you sure?" he asked.

"Yes."

He dragged her up so their lips aligned.

Her tongue stroked his, igniting a path to his groin. Her arms wrapped around his body, pulling him so close a molecule couldn't move between their bodies.

His hands cradled her face and he tilted her head.

She tasted sweet, a mix of her wine and the after-dinner mint she'd had on their way out of the restaurant. But she was all Liz. Elizabeth. Lizzie.

She wiggled against him, driving him crazy.

He wanted her naked, wanted her under him, around him.

Her moan drilled into him. His hands slipped down her

shoulders, down her torso and cupped her butt. There wasn't going to be any satisfaction tonight, but he wanted to touch her.

"Michael." She brushed kisses down his throat. "I ..."

He deepened the kiss. Moving in and out of her mouth like he wanted to do with her body.

She clung to his shoulders. He slid his hand up her side and hesitated.

The security guy was getting quite an eyeful.

She solved his dilemma by taking his hand and placing it on her breast. His fingers closed around her curves.

Now he groaned.

His thumb flicked across her erect nipple. He broke the kiss, easing away from her body enough that both of his hands played with her breasts. Her head fell back with a bang against the car door.

He flipped open two buttons on her shirt, exposing the slope of her chest. He kissed her throat and traced his lips down to her exposed breast. He tugged her shirt out of her waistband and snaked his hand under her bra. One flip and the bra released. No more cloth between his hand and her breast.

"I want your nipple in my mouth." His voice cracked. "I want you."

He'd never expected to say those words to another woman. But his body wanted Liz.

There was a squeal of tires above their heads.

"Shit." He'd fucking forgotten they were in a public ramp. "Jesus."

He ripped his hand out from under her shirt. Quickly glancing up at the security camera, he shielded her from view with his body.

She pulled away, trying to re-snap her bra. Her curls were askew, her lips plump from their kisses.

She took in a deep breath then tucked in her shirt. "Umm, wow?"

He tucked a red-blonde curl behind her ear. "Wow." He left his hand cupping her chin. She was so tiny.

A car came around the corner and drove past them. The car tooted as the guy driving past called out his open window, "You go, man."

Liz blushed. The woman who'd let him almost undress her in a parking ramp blushed.

"Please come back to my condo." He kissed her.

She heaved a sigh that pressed her delicious breasts against his chest. He assumed they would be delicious. He hadn't had a chance to taste them.

"I ... I can't." She shook her head. "This isn't right."

"That felt awfully right to me." He was betraying Sarah, but that didn't stop him from wanting Liz.

"I'm sorry." She finished straightening her clothes. "I wanted to kiss you, but there's too much at stake. I need this job."

"Whatever happens between us won't affect your job." He stroked his thumb over her lips. "I wouldn't do that."

"It's not up to you." Her hands twisted the strap of her bag. "I work for your sister. Your parents."

And they'd think he'd moved on when he hadn't. His stomach twisted at his next thought. "Was I pressuring you?"

"No." She stepped away from him and her car. "But you're a temptation."

He closed his eyes. "Liz."

"Good night, Michael."

NINE

LIZ PARKED HER CAR CLOSE TO HER APARTMENT AND LOCKED the door. Kissing Michael had left her ... unsatisfied. Even now she wanted to drive to his condo and take him up on his offer.

Unfortunately her family needed the money she earned, and she couldn't, wouldn't, jeopardize her job for sex.

She glanced at her apartment windows. All the lights were on, even in her bedroom. What was Jordan doing?

She hurried up the stairs. The door was unlocked. Again. Damn it.

"Jordan! You left the door unlocked," she called.

Her bedroom door squeaked, and Jordan came down the hall. "I forgot."

"What were you doing in my bedroom?" She couldn't keep the accusation out of her voice.

"Just looking for a book or something. I'm bored." He didn't look at her. "Why don't you have cable?"

"I can't afford it. And all my books are on the bookcase." She pointed to the living room.

"I found that out. What's for dinner?"

"I sent you a text that I worked through dinner."

"Again?" He pulled out his phone. "Oh."

She got a brief glimpse of his phone. He had tons of messages. *Who was he texting?*

"I need to pay back my boss. I borrowed money from Stephen."

"You what?"

"I told you. When we were waiting for the pizza. I needed gas when I interviewed last week. But I haven't been able to catch you. You're always working."

She was avoiding Jordan. That was sad. He was her twin. They used to be close.

"I don't have much." And her heart ached at the thought of loaning him anything. He never repaid her.

"A couple of hundred should do it. You must have that. Look how many hours you're working."

"I don't get overtime. And I don't have a couple of hundred. Gas doesn't cost that much." She was suddenly nauseous. "You borrowed two hundred dollars from Stephen?"

"No, but I need something to tide me over until payday. How else can I eat lunch while at work?"

"Do what I do. Pack a lunch."

"All the guys in the shop go out to eat."

"And half the people at the office go out to eat, but I can't. I send every spare dollar to Mom and Dad, and you know why." Her family was one bad year away from losing the farm. Without her help, they would have lost the farm two years ago. "Fix your own lunch."

"You don't even have lunch meat."

"I have peanut butter. Suck it up, Jordan."

"Can you spare anything? Come on, sis."

She sighed and opened her purse. She pulled out her emergency forty dollars. "This is all I have until payday so don't ask for more."

"Great." He headed to the door.

"Where are you going?"

"Out. I need something to eat."

She locked the door behind him. Hanging up her coat, she headed in to get a glass of water. And found dirty dishes in the sink.

It looked like he'd already eaten dinner.

∾

FORTY BUCKS? Jordan couldn't build any kind of stake with forty bucks.

He'd checked for things to hock in Liz's apartment. His sister didn't have much. He'd found a ten-dollar bill crunched under the sofa cushions. He doubted it was even Liz's, so he'd claimed it as his own. Now he had fifty bucks on him.

He needed more.

Jordan's phone buzzed. He glanced at the screen. *Rudy.* He shoved it back in his pocket, ignoring the message. Rudy didn't care that he was working to get back the money he owed. Rudy only cared for results.

He checked his truck. No one seemed to have tampered with anything. He sure wished Liz had a garage to park in. He was too exposed on the street.

Once in his truck, he pulled up the address and headed in the right direction. One of the shop guys had known about a poker game. Hopefully he could multiply this fifty into real cash. He had to get Rudy off his ass.

As he drove north, the neighborhoods got dicier and the houses more run down. His GPS said he'd *arrived.* He double-checked the address and walked up the cracked and heaving sidewalk. The porch light let out a weak yellow glow.

Jordan rolled his shoulders and knocked.

"Carlson," Ben, his coworker, said upon opening the door. "Glad you found the house."

"Thanks for inviting me." Jordan kept his jacket on as he walked in. He didn't know what kind of people were in this game. He might need to run.

The buy-in was five bucks. It got him a beer and a seat at the table.

Time to get to work.

LIZ YAWNED as she slipped her bag into her credenza. She'd tossed and turned Friday, Saturday and Sunday, thinking about Michael. But she'd also waited to hear Jordan come home. It had been after two. For the third night running.

When she'd asked about his night, he'd grunted. Nothing new with that. He hated mornings.

She headed straight to the break room, put in a new coffee packet and tapped the button.

"Hey."

Michael.

She cleared her throat. "Good morning."

They stared at each other as the coffee pot chugged away. His blue dress shirt made his eyes brighter. He wore a suit coat but no tie. If it was a photo, the caption would be: *Up and coming executive.*

"How was your weekend?"

"Fine." She covered a yawn with her hand.

"Didn't sleep well?"

"No."

His eyes lit up. "Me neither."

"Oh." She fumbled open the creamer. She didn't like the joy she felt at the idea that he'd lost sleep because of her.

But it could have been sexual frustration. On both their parts.

"How about dinner tonight?" He stood too close.

She slipped back to the coffee pot as it gave its final burps, putting a few steps between her and Michael's heat. "No thanks."

"We have to get through the rest of the forecasts." He pulled a coffee mug from the shelf. "It can be a working dinner."

"Can't we get through the final properties this afternoon?" She filled her mug and then his. "I have to review a couple of leases before we meet."

"I have meetings most of the day." He poured creamer in his coffee. "I can't break free until after four."

"That works." She backed away. "Let me know when you're free. Other than the staff meeting, I don't have any meetings today."

And she had work to finish before she met with Michael. Hopefully she could shore up her resolve to keep everything between them business.

When he called later that afternoon and said he was free, her stomach fluttered. She gathered her laptop and printouts.

Business. Only business.

"We can knock this out in an hour," she said, walking into his office.

"Sure." Michael's expression was remote.

Distance was best for both of them.

She set up at his conference table.

"Do you want something to drink?" he asked.

She jerked her head up. "What?"

His lips formed a straight line. "I don't have anything alcoholic, if that's what you were thinking. Water. Pop. Coffee." He waved his hand at the tray on his table.

"I ... I'm sorry. Water. Water would be great."

He picked up a bottle and twisted off the cap. "I thought you knew me better."

"I do. It was knee-jerk." She plopped into her chair.

He slumped in his, rocking back, and shoved his hair off his face. "Long day."

"Should we do this tomorrow?"

"Let's get it over with." He reached for the packet she'd put together. "Same routine as before. Assumptions first."

She ran through each property and the assumptions she'd made about renewals and turnovers for the strip malls they had left.

When they got to one of the last properties, Michael said, "That location will have a higher vacancy rate."

"Why?"

"A newer strip mall was built about a half a mile away. We'll have to drop our rates to keep our current tenants or endure longer vacancies."

"I should have known that, but I still haven't visited every property." She hated feeling stupid. "Sorry."

He waved it off and leaned a little closer. "Let's see the renewal rates."

They established new assumptions, which she entered into the spreadsheet.

"That should do it for all the strip malls." She uploaded the file to the budgeting system. "I'll send your team a heads-up that we finished."

He nodded. "Thanks."

"I liked working on this." She couldn't gather her materials fast enough, but awkwardness had her fumbling her computer and while she juggled that, her folder slipped out of her arms and papers scattered across the floor.

"Darn it." She crouched, picking up the spreadsheets.

"Hang on." Michael half-crawled under the table, reaching for papers that had sailed to the other side.

They stood at the same time. He ended up behind her. Too close.

She couldn't help it, she jerked away from him.

"I won't throw you on the floor and screw you." He spit the words at her.

She curled her arms around her things. "I know."

"Then what the fuck? I got the message. You're not interested."

"It's not you." She forced herself to hold his stare.

"Right."

"No." She shut her eyes. "It's … a defense mechanism. From when I worked at Colfax. Jerry liked to sneak up on me."

"Damn it." Michael stepped to the other side of the table. "I'm sorry you had to go through that."

"I stopped drinking coffee because he caught me alone too many times in the break room."

His eyes filled with understanding. "I'd like to punch Jerry for what he did to you, and I don't even know the details."

"He's not worth the trouble." And to be honest, some of her reaction was from Michael. Because instead of backing away, she wanted to step toward him.

"Still." He gave her even more space. "Can I carry anything to your office?"

"I've got it."

She hurried out of his office and away from temptation.

AFTER THE STRESS of working with Liz, Michael had to do something. And since a drink sounded mighty good right now, he needed a meeting.

He found one in a nearby church that would start in about twenty minutes. Perfect.

Stephen popped his head in just as he shut down his computer. "Did you get Katie's text?"

"I just finished a meeting and haven't checked. Nothing's happened, has it?"

"No. She wants us to pick up dinner and bring it to her house. She wants work updates."

If he were on medical leave, he wouldn't want to hear anything about work. Hell, when he was in treatment, there'd been radio silence—by design.

But Kate lived for the company.

"Are you in?" Stephen asked.

Dinner with the family instead of going to a meeting … "I guess."

"I'll let her know we'll pick up the food." Stephen sent a text. "Want a ride?"

"That would be great." He used to let Stephen drive so he didn't worry about how much he drank. Now it was habit. Probably one he needed to break.

On the way to Kate and Alex's house, they swung by Kate's favorite Thai place and picked up her order. He dumped the bags in the backseat. "Did you know she had me pay for the food?" he grumbled.

Stephen laughed. "Why do you think I let you go inside? Oldest always pay."

Michael laughed in spite of himself. "Oldest doesn't always pay."

"Hell, charge it to the company."

If all they did was talk about work, he just might.

They pulled into Kate and Alex's driveway. It was still hard to imagine masculine, big-as-a-bear Alex living in this pretty yellow Victorian with a wraparound porch. Michael had expected him to live in an industrial loft, lots of steel and brick.

As they headed up the walk, a rusty Corolla pulled into the drive. Damn it, his sister had invited Liz to dinner.

He should have gone to AA.

"Liz," Stephen called out. "You got the call too?"

"About a half hour ago." Liz locked the car with her key.

As she walked up, she twisted her keys in her hand. "If this is a family thing I can leave."

"I'm sure it's a work thing." Stephen set his hand on Liz's shoulder and guided her to the front door. "Don't abandon us."

She froze and Stephen gave her a small nudge.

Michael jabbed his brother in the back.

Stephen turned and looked at him.

Michael shook his head and held up his hands.

Stephen frowned, then the lights went on. He yanked his hand away. "Sorry."

Liz knocked.

Alex answered the door. "Come on in."

"What's her mood?" Stephen whispered as they walked back with him to the kitchen.

Alex rolled his eyes. "If she wasn't on bed rest, she'd have paced a path in the floors."

"That would be a real pity," Michael said. "The floors are great."

"I heard that," Kate called. "I'm a saint. Easy to live with, right Alex?"

They all entered the kitchen. It had changed since the last time Michael had been here. Where there had been an eating nook, now there was a small sofa and his sister reclined on it with her feet stacked on pillows.

"You're an angel." Alex bent and kissed his sister's cheek.

Both he and Stephen laughed.

"Hey!" Kate complained. "Liz is going to believe your lies."

Liz joined in the laughter.

Michael's tension eased. He couldn't stop grinning at Liz, and she grinned right back at him. And it felt … good.

"Where's Timothy?" Kate asked.

"On his way." Stephen dug in the fridge and pulled out a beer. He handed it to Michael and stopped. "Sorry, man."

"No problem," Michael lied. He wouldn't mind letting the cold brew slide down his throat. But then what would the last few months have been about?

The grin slid off Liz's face.

Was it always going to be one tiny step forward and then a big leap back with her?

He hoisted the food bags onto the golden brown granite island. "Whoever did your renovation did a great job."

"I used Kinketty's."

Stephen and Michael both nodded.

"They're good," Stephen said. "Maybe we should go into the remodeling side of the business instead of only new construction."

"I floated that with Dad once." Michael shook his head. "He wasn't interested."

Kate tried to sit up a little more. "You did? Why didn't I know this?"

"You don't know every conversation Dad and I have."

Liz raised her eyebrows. "You should add remodeling or restorations into the fifteen-year projection."

Michael shook his head.

Alex unloaded the food. "Let's eat while it's hot."

"What's the profit margin on remodeling, Stephen?" Kate asked.

"Since you can never be sure what you encounter behind a wall, it's a little higher, but surprises tend to delay jobs." Stephen tapped his lip. "I wouldn't mind doing more than our own personal home remodeling jobs."

"Eat." Alex handed a plate of food to Kate. "Then you can all talk business."

The rest of them settled on bar stools around the island.

Liz leaned close and whispered, "You should pursue the remodeling and home restoration angle."

"I tried," he said.

"How hard?"

Not very. Because Sarah had just gotten her diagnosis.

"What are you two whispering about?" Kate called from her spot on the sofa.

"All the leases we terminated since you've been gone." Michael dug into his chicken pad thai.

"You'd better not have cancelled any leases," his sister said under her breath.

Liz raised her eyebrow at him, but he didn't enlighten her on the fact that he'd let his discussion with his dad die. That he'd lost all his energy. His fight.

Being around Liz made him want to try again. She inspired him. For some reason he wanted to be a better man.

He should talk to his dad.

TEN

"I'M GLAD YOU INVITED ME," LIZ SAID TO KATE AT THE DOOR. "I like being able to bounce ideas off you in person instead of over Zoom."

"Call me. Any time. Please." Kate wrapped an arm around her tiny belly. "I'm bored."

"Five minutes," Alex put an arm around Kate's shoulder, "then off your feet."

Kate rolled her eyes but snuggled into his chest. "Yes, dear."

Liz smiled. It was lovely to see the way Alex cared for Kate. He may look all gruff and ... huge, but the way he touched Kate made her long for someone for herself.

She glanced at Michael. He, Stephen and Timothy had their heads together.

Michael tipped his head back and laughed. What a rare event.

She headed to her car.

"Liz," Michael called.

After inserting her key, she turned. "Yes?"

"Timothy gave me some updates on the new strip malls. We need to change the models."

"Can you text them to me?" she asked.

"Sure. But I'd like to talk through the possible scenarios with the changes." Michael looked at his brothers. "Could you drop me at my place?"

It was on her way home, but she hesitated.

Michael's expression went cold. "I have meetings all morning, otherwise I would wait until tomorrow."

Liz didn't want to hurt him, but she didn't trust herself around him. "It's fine."

"Stephen," Michael called. "I'll catch a ride with Liz. We can talk through the model changes."

Stephen waved. "Don't let him work you too hard, Liz."

Now it was Liz who wanted to roll her eyes.

Michael gave her the updates as they drove through the neighborhood and headed toward downtown. As he did, his fingers beat a rhythm on his thigh. His foot tapped on the floor of the car.

"Why don't I use the following for the strip malls?" she asked once he'd told her which properties had changes. "Timothy's estimate for the base model. Then three months later and six months later, in case there are construction delays."

"That will work." He kept tapping, and now his head was bobbing. "I'll send you the estimated completion dates."

"I'll input the changes in the morning." She waited for the signal to turn green. "Then we're done with the leasing portion. Again."

"Good. Good."

His nervous ticks were making her shoulders tighten. "What's up?"

"What?" he asked.

"Why are you so ... nervous?" If she'd thought his addiction had been to drugs, she would have believed he needed a fix.

Out of the corner of her eye she watched as he pressed his hands into his legs and took a deep breath.

"I'd planned to catch a meeting tonight, but then Kate called a dinner meeting."

"I could drop you at one." Meetings were important. She wished Jordan still attended.

"Nothing is available right now."

"Don't you have someone to call?"

"My sponsor. I tried."

"That doesn't sound like a great system. Shouldn't you have a backup?"

He shrugged. "It's one of the reasons I asked for a ride. You make things … easier."

"Don't put that on me."

"No. It's … I like being with you."

She glanced at him. "I have a hard time believing that with the way your whole body is in motion."

"I might be a little nervous." She caught his small smile. "Because we're together."

Together. That was dangerous territory in her mind. She didn't respond. She kept driving, finally pulling up in front of his building.

"Miracles do happen. There's a parking spot." She pulled into it. "Will you be okay?"

"Yeah." He checked his phone. "Shit. It's only eight? I was hoping it was closer to ten."

The sun hadn't fully set. She could actually get pretty close to the real time based on the sun. "Nope."

His fingers flexed. "Can you come up?"

"We're keeping this professional, remember?" She was the one who needed the reminder. His aftershave filled her car. And it smelled nice.

"We will. Just talking. That's all I need."

She hesitated, studying him. "I can stay for an hour."

"Thank you."

As they walked toward the door, she asked, "Does exercising help?"

"I worked out this morning."

He entered his security code and headed for the stairs. "Are you okay with four flights?"

She nodded. But by the time they were rounding the corner for the third flight, she was puffing a little. "I think I'm the one who needs to work out more."

He laughed. This time there wasn't an edge to his laughter. "Welcome to my home."

They walked into his unexpectedly modern condominium.

"I figured you lived in a turn-of-the-century house," she said. "Although I knew you were in a condo, so I don't know what I was thinking."

He dropped his keys in a dish in the entry. "I … Sarah picked this place out."

Sarah. The fiancée. Who'd had brain cancer.

"I have iced tea or," he headed to the kitchen and she followed, "milk or apple juice. I might have decaf coffee or tea."

"I'm good with water." She'd had wine at Kate's.

He pulled two glasses out of the cupboard and filled them from a small spout in the sink. "Do you want ice?"

"No. That's fine."

He led her to the main room and took a seat on a leather sofa. Again the place didn't match the Michael who'd taken her to the museum.

On the mantle were pictures. They drew her over. There were pictures with the MacBain family, ones where Michael looked carefree and happy. And pictures of Michael with his arms around a woman with black hair and brown eyes. Lots of pictures of the couple. "Is this Sarah?"

He came up beside her and picked up the photo. "Yes. That's our engagement photo."

"She's beautiful."

He nodded. "She knew exactly what she wanted in life. And she was always positive."

"You look happy." Liz waved her hands at all the pictures on the mantle. "I'm sorry you lost her."

He stared at the photo. She wanted to hug him, but this was his burden to carry.

"Tell me about her." She headed to one side of the sofa.

He released a breath and sat on the opposite side. "She was driven. Some might say pushy. But she wanted to take over her parents' accounting practice. She wanted us to do that together."

"Didn't she understand you would work for your family? Or did that happen later?"

"No. I went to work in the finance department right after graduation." His smile wobbled. "I wasn't interested in public accounting. She was ... disappointed."

"I thought you were a CPA."

"I took both the CPA and CMA." At her frown, he added, "Certified Management Accountant. I always knew I would work with my parents."

"But what about architecture?"

"It's just a strong interest of mine." He drank some water. "When we were freshman, we'd decided on accounting degrees. It allowed us to spend more time together. In hindsight, I guess that was a blessing."

"But you're so passionate about architecture," she blurted out. Holding up a hand, she added, "You don't have to explain."

"No. It's fine. I was passionate about Sarah. She was enough for me."

Liz leaned forward. "What do you think now?"

"I got to be with her." He stared at his hands. "Without Sarah, being CFO is not enough."

She slid closer, wanting to hold and comfort him. Instead she took his hands. "I'm so sorry."

They sat quietly, but underneath the quiet, the connection between them crackled.

This was probably so wrong, but she leaned closer. "Michael?"

His gaze locked on hers. And their connection grew. "Yes?"

"Is it wrong that I want to kiss you?"

"I didn't think you wanted to be near me." His thumb rubbed against her knuckles.

"Because I'm attracted to you." The words were barely a whisper.

He blinked but didn't say anything.

Her timing sucked. They were talking about his dead fiancée, and she confessed her attraction. "I shouldn't have said that."

She started to stand.

"Don't go," he finally said.

"What?" she asked.

"You're amazing." He took her hand and kissed the inside of her wrist. "I want to kiss you too."

Her breath stuck in her throat. No one had ever kissed her hands. Or called her amazing.

There were reasons she'd wanted everything to stay businesslike. Reasons she'd wanted a clear mind. And she couldn't remember any of them. Not with his stormy hazel eyes locked on hers.

With her free hand she swept a curl off his forehead. Then

she touched his cheek. His dark stubble tickled her palm. "I can't stop myself."

She kissed him.

This time she knew which way Michael angled his head. This time she sought out his tongue. And it was better than before. Better than any kiss she'd ever had.

He pulled her onto his lap and she straddled him, getting as close as she could. She leaned in for a kiss but pulled back.

"Liz?" He ran his hand up and down her back. "Is this okay?"

"Are you doing this just to keep from drinking?"

"No." The smile lines around his eyes actually joined his smile.

Relieved, she fell into the kiss. Her fingers tugged on his shirt.

While Michael fumbled with the buttons on his shirt, and shrugged it away, she unbuttoned her blouse. "I want to be skin to skin."

"We're on the same page."

Reverently he ran his hands from her waist to just under her breasts. She wanted his hands to move, to take. But he just stared.

"You're beautiful."

"So are you." She stroked his arms and pecs. Why had she expected him to be … emaciated? He had abs that could be on a billboard.

As she caressed near the waistband on his slacks, he growled. "It's been a long time for me. I don't want this to go too fast. Let me touch you."

He unhooked her bra and cupped her breasts.

She arched into his hands. As he rubbed her nipples, she couldn't hold in a moan. "That's so good."

He pulled her to her knees and swirled his tongue around her breast. Then he taunted her nipple with his teeth.

Her moan was louder this time. She clutched at his head to keep him there, balancing between pain and ecstasy. "Yes."

He pinched one nipple while licking the other. His dark head at her breast was a sight she wanted to memorize.

Heat poured through her.

Michael pulled away and stood with her in his arms.

She wrapped her legs around his waist.

As he carried her down a hallway, he asked, "Are you sure?"

"Yes." She dropped kisses on his cheek and slid to take his ear between her teeth. She loved the way he touched her.

Michael didn't turn on any lights. He set her at the foot of a big bed. Then just stared at her again.

She couldn't wait. Unbuttoning his pants, she grinned. "Happy to see me?"

He grinned back at her.

They helped each other shed their clothes and left them rumpled on the floor. Taking her hand, he led her to the bed and threw back the covers. "I'll be right back."

This was really happening. She bit her lip. She'd made the decision. She'd chosen to be with him. Sitting on the bed, she waited for his return.

In the dim light she spotted a photo on the end table. Sarah smiled out at her.

When Michael came back from the bathroom he must have noticed. He flipped the picture face down. "Sorry."

He dropped condoms on the side of the bed and crawled toward her. A smile creased his face.

"I haven't seen you smile this much."

"I'm ... happy." He grinned. "Happy."

And her heart opened a little more.

Slipping between her thighs, he leaned down and kissed her. And the heat roared back. His hands excited, taunted and controlled her body. She tried to touch him, but he captured her hands above her head. "Let me. Tell me when I do something you like."

And she did. Until finally he slid into her body.

They stopped moving. She wanted more. She wanted all of him.

His hips pulsed. Her body responded. Then it was all glorious friction.

"More," she begged, pulling at his hips.

He gave her more. Her fingers clawed at his back. Being with him this way was heaven.

Her climax barreled through her, setting off a chain reaction in his body.

He collapsed on top on her and she hugged him.

He was sweaty but so was she. It was a good sweat as her mother used to say as they worked around the farm. Oh my, my. It was a good sweat.

"I must be heavy." Michael rolled over and took her with him, so she was on top. "But you're not."

"That was …" She couldn't find the words.

"Amazing? Stupendous? Magnificent?" he asked.

"All that." She rested her head against his chest and listened to his pounding heart.

He kissed the top of her head. "I should clean up."

But they stayed connected, neither of them moving.

Her phone buzzed out in the living room. He eased away and headed to the bathroom.

She pulled on his shirt since it was closest and ran for her phone.

Calls at this time of night were usually bad.

MICHAEL TOSSED the condom and leaned his fists on the counter, staring at his reflection. This wasn't the first time he'd had sex since Sarah died. But it was the first time he'd had sex where it mattered. The first time he'd brought someone to their home. The first time he'd flipped her picture down.

Liz was on the phone in the bedroom. He stopped in the doorway and listened.

"I'm fine. Still out," she said. "I had a business dinner."

She looked at him.

He didn't know what made him do it, but he mouthed, "Stay."

She raked her lower lip with her teeth. "I'll be late."

He sat next to her on the bed and took her free hand.

She turned away a little but leaned into his shoulder. "I can't lend you any more money this week."

He heard a male voice on the other end of her conversation but couldn't make out the words. Her shoulders hunched and her fingers choked her phone.

This must be her brother. Stephen had said something about lending him money when he'd hired him. Maybe the family needed help.

He had plenty of money.

"Do you need money?" he asked after she hung up. "I can help you."

"I'm not borrowing money from you." She stood. "I should go home."

"Stay."

Her gaze locked on his. "I don't know what to do."

"Stay."

"I want to."

"Then do." He pulled her into a hug.

"I'll still need to go home and change for work."

Her head burrowed into his chest. And it was perfect. She was shorter than Sarah had been, but he liked that. Liked the way he could pull her close as if he could protect her.

"Let's go back to bed."

174

ELEVEN

Liz gathered her clothes from the bedroom and living room and took them into the hallway bathroom so she didn't wake Michael.

Last night had been amazing.

Now what did they do? How would they act at the office?

Maybe she was getting ahead of herself. Michael hadn't said anything about wanting to be a couple, but she'd never had a one-night stand.

At least he wasn't her boss. That was a plus. But his parents might think she was a gold digger.

She found paper and a pen and left a note that she'd gone home. Placing it next to the coffee maker, she wished she wore lipstick so she could kiss the paper, but she was a lip gloss gal. Plus, that would be hokey.

She opened Michael's front door and reset the lock. No one was in the hallway. Her car was parked where she'd left it. And no ticket.

At home she tried to quietly open the door. Holy cow, the locks clacked. She got in and relocked everything, then headed into the kitchen to brew coffee.

Dirty dishes filled the sink. Had Jordan had a party? Even now there was a lingering odor of cigarettes.

This was a no smoking building.

She filled and started the coffee maker, then crept past the living room and dropped everything in her bedroom. She gathered her robe and clean underwear. A dresser drawer was partially open. She eased it shut, trying to remember if she'd been in that drawer yesterday and hadn't closed it.

Jordan had better not be going through her things. Not that she could imagine what he'd find. She headed to the bathroom.

The shower felt great, even though the showerhead was a stingy stream of water. She smoothed lotion on the spots where Michael's stubble had scraped. They'd made love twice. A new record for her.

As she toweled off, she couldn't keep the dreamy smile from her face. She wiped a towel through her curls, then left them to dry as she got her coffee.

"Where were you last night?"

She jumped at Jordan's gravelly voice.

"Out."

"With who?"

"Whom. No one you know." She added milk to her coffee, noting they were almost out. "I don't answer to you. You're my brother, not my mother."

"I thought you were at a business meeting." He made quotation marks with his fingers.

"I was."

"So you were with the MacBains?"

"You can keep asking," she said, "but I'm not saying anything more." She took her coffee to her bedroom. "And no smoking in the apartment!" she called.

Damn. Even her brother had narrowed down that she'd been with a MacBain.

How would they keep their relationship, if this was one, to themselves?

～

MICHAEL STILL COULDN'T SHAKE the disappointment he'd felt waking without Liz. She'd left a note in the kitchen, but he'd wanted to wake up next to her.

He eyed the pictures of Sarah scattered around the apartment. He poured his coffee and walked over, touching Sarah's cheek. For two years he'd lived with the reminders of their life together surrounding him. He should tuck them away, but he wasn't ready to let her go.

Liz hadn't said much about the pictures.

He shook his head. He didn't have to decide what to do about Sarah's pictures right now. It was time to get to work and start his meeting-packed day.

Back in the bedroom he picked up the pants Liz had stripped off him. And grinned. Having sex with Liz had been … fun.

That thought got him through his morning routine and into the office. He was in the break room when he caught her floral scent and turned with a smile. "Good morning."

Her cheeks went pink. "Good morning."

He wanted to kiss her. She looked like she wanted to run. "How did you sleep?"

"Fine." She looked around, then whispered, "You shouldn't ask me that."

"That was my best night's sleep in … I can't remember."

Her smile started slow and then softened. "Me too."

"What's your day like?" He had a meeting to get to but didn't want to leave.

"I'm almost done with last night's model changes." Again her cheeks went pink.

"Good. My meetings are with the other department heads. Hopefully I can put this forecast to bed today."

Her eyes widened.

He laughed. "Do you have plans for tonight?"

She shook her head.

He walked toward her. With his voice lowered, he asked, "Dinner?"

"I'd like that."

There was a bounce in his step as he headed back to his office. They had a date. Now he had to find a restaurant. Or maybe they should order in. That would be better.

BECCA HANDED Michael his phone messages. "Can I help with anything?"

"Cancel the rest of my day?"

"Ha ha." Becca pointed at his desk. "Accounting asked if you would sign the check to Erickson Engineering. It's on the top of the pile. Timothy has a meeting with them and wanted to hand them the check."

"Will do." He flipped through his messages, grateful Becca put the critical calls first. There was one from their bank liaison on the top, then a call from his treasury analyst. He'd probably call the analyst first. Kate had left a message. And one from a Jordan Carlson.

He frowned at the name, not recognizing it. There were tons of Carlsons in the area. After all, the Scandinavians said they were the highest population of immigrants in the state.

Wait. Was this Liz's brother?

He called the number on the slip.

"Yes." He heard the hum of an engine in the background.

"Is this Jordan Carlson?"

"Who's asking?"

Rude. "Hey, you called me. This is Michael MacBain."

"Sorry. Thanks for calling me back." The abrupt change to a friendly tone was jarring.

"What's up?"

"I understand you're seeing my sister," Jordan said.

Liz must have talked to her brother this morning because it couldn't have been yesterday. They hadn't been "a thing" yesterday. "Is there something you wanted?"

"I'm dropping off your dad's car at headquarters in the next half hour. I'd like to talk to you."

"Why?"

"I only need fifteen minutes," Jordan said.

He checked his schedule. He could make it work, barely. And he was curious what Liz's brother wanted to talk about. "I'm available at noon."

JORDAN ENDED THE CALL. This would work. It had to.

He'd guessed Lizzie was sleeping with one of the MacBains. Michael had been his first try, and he'd gotten the right brother.

He hailed his boss, Kyle, who was working on a crane motor. "I figured out what was wrong with the head boss's Yukon. It's running clean now. I can drive it to headquarters."

"Great." Kyle wiped his hands on a rag. "I'm glad they found you. You've been a big help."

"Thanks." Tossing the key fob up and down, he walked back to the boss's sweet ride. Hell, he didn't know half the functions on the SUV, but he'd been able to fix it. He was that good.

He wouldn't be working here much longer. If his new plan succeeded, he'd be out of here and on his way to Vegas, baby.

He hadn't been to the MacBain headquarters, but GPS got

him there in ten minutes. He looked at the building. Damn, this family had money. Their wealth needed to be spread around.

After finding the boss's parking spot in the connected ramp, he headed to the first floor receptionist.

"Can I help you?"

"I'm dropping off the boss's car, Mac's car." Even though he had grease under his fingernails, he wanted this woman to think he had a relationship with the MacBains. "Then I'm meeting with Michael, the younger."

"Okay." She called someone. Then directed him to the twentieth floor.

He stepped out of the elevator and had to keep his mouth from dropping open. Plush. The place reeked of money. Everything was wood: the floors, the heavy double doors and the furniture. Even the cubicles and file cases were made of what looked like mahogany.

As he walked in, he tapped the wood. It was solid.

He headed to the next gatekeeper and explained why he was here. This time it was a guy, and he was directed down a hallway. To another gatekeeper. Through another set of double doors he could see into a massive office. A construction model sat on a table.

"I can take Mac's key fob," the older woman said. Her name plate said she was Bernice.

"Of course." He handed it over. "I'm meeting with Michael junior. Can you tell where his office is?"

"Sure." Bernice directed him down another opulent hallway.

He'd been worried his plan wouldn't work, but after seeing all this—he was pleased he'd thought of it.

One more gatekeeper stood in his way.

"Hey, Becca, Jordan Carlson. I have a meeting with Michael junior."

"Let me see if he's free," she said.

He waited. Walked to the window and looked down at the street. Up on the twentieth floor none of the MacBains were in touch with reality. Everything looked pristine. They didn't have to worry about loan sharks finding them. That was only for the lowly slugs that worked for MacBain and earned them all their money.

"He can see you now." Becca stood next to her desk.

Don't let him see me sweat. Jordan walked into another huge office. Not as big as his dad's, Michael senior, but bigger than Liz's living room and kitchen combined.

He pushed back his resentment. He would live like this someday.

Michael leaned over his desk, a desk bigger than Liz's kitchen table, and extended his hand. "It's nice to meet you, Jordan."

His handshake was stronger than Jordan thought it would be. He gave Michael's hand an extra squeeze and pulled back. "Nice to meet the guy sleeping with my sister."

Michael frowned and moved to shut the door. "Listen, this is new for us. We're not spreading it around. Especially not at work."

"Are you ashamed to be seen with her?" Jordan's hands formed fists.

"No! It's just ... new."

"Are you seeing anyone else?" His eyes narrowed. "Are you married, and this is an office fling?"

"No!" Michael shook his head. "Maybe you should talk to Liz if you're worried."

"I don't want her hurt."

"I don't plan on hurting her," Michael finally said after an uncomfortable minute. "Is this why you wanted to meet?"

"Partly." He needed to make Michael feel guilty before he

did the big ask. "Be nice to her. She's barely eking by on what you pay her."

"She doesn't work for me, but MacBain pays excellent wages." Michael frowned. "Is there something else going on?"

"We have to help our parents, and Liz …"

"They own a farm."

"Yeah. It's been a rough couple of years." Jordan cleared his throat. "She's trying to help them get out from under the debt they took on a couple of years ago. Since I'm a laborer, I can't contribute much."

"This is why you wanted to meet? To ask me for a loan?"

Jordan closed his eyes, trying to look remorseful. "Have you seen where she lives and the car she drives? She sends everything to our parents."

"I noticed." Michael tapped his finger on his desk. "But *you* called your sister last night and asked for money."

Jordan swallowed. "I borrowed some cash yesterday to eat lunch and put gas in my truck. I wanted to pay back my boss today."

"How much did you borrow?"

"A twenty," he lied. "But my sister doesn't even have that. Unless we eat oatmeal for the rest of the week."

Michael pulled out his wallet. It was loaded. He handed him a twenty. Damn he should have said more, but he'd had to make it realistic. "Thanks, man. I'll get it back to you after I get paid."

Michael nodded. "How much do your parents owe?"

"Fifty grand. Unfortunately there's a ten grand payment coming up." He was racking up the lies. "I don't suppose Liz could get an advance on her salary?"

Michael's eyebrows came together. "Don't you mean, *you* want an advance?"

"I wish. I don't make that much. Liz is the one who went to college while I stayed home and worked the farm."

Sure he'd gotten in a couple of years of college and then Vo-Tech, but Michael didn't need to know that. In college he'd played Texas Hold'em. And the easy money from his fellow students had changed his career path.

"Ten grand." Michael nodded his head. "I could loan her the money if it helps give your parents relief from their debt."

"Liz is proud. She would kill me if she knew I even told you about the debt." He snapped his fingers. "Wait. I could send the money to our parents. Then our mom and dad can make the payment."

Michael came from behind that big ass desk and stood by the window, looking down at his empire.

Jordan joined him and they stared out the window.

Michael turned. "I don't like going behind Liz's back, but I can do that."

"Great!" Jordan clapped Michael on the back. "Thank you. Liz will be relieved."

"It will take a couple of days to pull together the paperwork and move money around."

"Oh, right." Damn it. He needed to get Rudy his money soon. And what kind of paperwork would be involved? "Thank you so much."

At least he could tell Rudy the money was coming.

LIZ HEADED BACK from the break room. She couldn't stop looking for Michael. She hadn't caught sight of him since this morning. As she turned the corner to her cubical, her brother waited by her desk. "Jordan?"

"Hey, I was looking for you." He hugged her.

"What are you doing here?"

"I fixed the big boss's car and brought it over. I thought we could get some lunch."

"Oh. You should have called. I just finished eating."

Jordan frowned. "I should have called."

"Do you need a ride back? I could probably take a few minutes."

"Nah. I'll call a coworker and they'll pick me up. It's only ten minutes away. Of course I'm just a laborer, and you're here in the ivory castle."

She rolled her eyes.

"Pushing papers."

"I don't want to argue with you." Especially not in the office.

Granted she and Kate had a pretty quiet area of the floor, but you never knew who could walk by.

"See you at home tonight?" he asked.

"I'm not sure."

"Big date?" he teased.

She shrugged.

"I met Michael." Jordan winked at her.

"How?" Whoops, she hadn't meant to sound defensive.

"I have my ways. He seems like a nice guy, but he'd better be nice to my sister."

"You didn't say anything to him, did you?" She couldn't suppress a big yawn.

"Not much sleep last night?" Jordan shook his head. "I'm your big brother, someone has to protect you."

"I can protect myself."

She didn't want Jordan and Michael talking. And she couldn't pin down why. Was it that she didn't trust her brother? Or didn't she want anyone to know she and Michael were dating. She rubbed at the headache building behind her eyes.

"Too late." Jordan snatched a handful of Starburst candies from the bowl on her desk. "See you when you get home."

Too late? Jordan had already said something to Michael? Or too late, Jordan had already done something to protect her. That was a terrifying thought.

She settled behind her desk. Another yawn overtook her. Even after her brother left, her headache didn't ease. A halo formed around the light above her. Damn it.

She pulled out her migraine medication, trying to get ahead of the pain. She hadn't had one in months. Opening the lease she'd been working, wavy lines kept her from reading the document. Pain jabbed into the right side of her head.

She called the front desk. "Hey Jenny, is there an open conference room? One on the interior?"

"Let me check. Yes. The small one, 2002. How long should I book it for?"

"I've got a migraine coming on. I hope I headed it off. Maybe an hour." Please let it stop soon. "If anyone is looking for me, I'll be there."

She wobbled a little as she headed to the conference room. Without turning on the lights, she bumped into the table. Then she lay on the floor in the dark.

She went over what could have triggered it. She'd skipped lunch yesterday because she'd worked through it. She'd had wine last night, but not too much. Stress? When Jordan was around, her stress levels spiked.

She waited out the light show, mesmerized by the zig zag lines. The pain ratcheted up, and she breathed through it.

She kept breathing. Trying to ignore the weirdness of her vision. Closing her eyes didn't stop it. And now she was nauseous. The last thing she wanted was to throw up the sandwich she'd gotten from a vending machine.

Her phone pinged. She tried reading the screen but it was a no go.

The first time this had happened, she'd panicked, afraid she was going blind. But she'd recovered. Unfortunately fifty-percent of the time she got a migraine, she had the crazy auras.

The door opened and light jabbed into her eyeballs.

"Please. Close the door." Her voice sounded weak.

"Liz, are you okay?" Michael knelt next to her and took her hand.

"Migraine."

"You need medication? Can I bring you something?"

"I took it already. I'm waiting for it to work."

"What about a pillow or a cushion. I could get one from my sofa."

She didn't want to imagine the pain of moving her head. "The meds should kick in soon."

He stroked her hair and she whimpered.

Michael pulled his hand away. "Sorry. I don't like seeing you in pain."

"Just—talk to me. It will take my mind off the pain and my loss of vision."

"Loss of vision?"

"I get these patterns and can't see through them."

"I'm sorry." He sat cross-legged on the floor beside her. "Well, let's see. The fifteen-year plan with the three scenarios is done. I'll review with my mom and dad tomorrow, but they already have the summary sheet you suggested."

"Good." It was about all she could say.

"I added a section on restorations starting three years out. Stephen and Timothy helped." He rattled off the assumptions they'd come with up.

"I'm glad." Even though she didn't have the energy to talk, she could hear the enthusiasm in his voice. He should be working on restorations, not numbers. Or maybe both.

"I met your brother." He didn't add anything to the comment.

She nodded, and a stabbing pain had her regretting the movement. "I heard."

"I wouldn't have guessed you were twins."

"Most people wouldn't."

"Timothy said they cleared the final inspection on the Woodbury shops."

"I was working on one of the leases when this happened." She pointed to her head and pain didn't disable her. The auras were fading too.

Michael kept talking, and the auras and pain finally dissipated. She slowly pushed herself up on her elbows and felt … okay. Wiped out but her vision was almost normal and the stabbing pain was now a dull ache.

"Can I help you up?" Michael asked.

"Please."

He stood and gently helped her to her feet. He steadied her as she found her balance.

"Where to?" he asked.

"My office." She hated being weak.

"Maybe you should go home."

"This has happened before." Not too many times working at MacBain. But when she'd worked for Colfax and Jerry kept physically harassing her, she'd had too many.

She wanted to sit gracefully but collapsed into her chair. Blinking didn't focus her vision, but the auras were gone.

Michael knelt next to her desk. "I really think you should go home."

"I have a lease I need to get out."

"And after that you'll let me take you home?" Her vision was clear enough to see the concern in his eyes.

"I'll let you know."

"I was going to see where you wanted to eat tonight. But what about takeout at my place. Then you can sleep and I'll watch over you."

She swallowed against the sudden need to weep. "I'd like that."

~

MICHAEL HATED LEAVING Liz at her desk. He wished he could talk with her doctor. Wanted to know if this was something more serious than migraines.

Sarah's headaches had been a symptom of her brain tumor. One scary night she'd gone blind. He'd carried her to the car and sped to the hospital.

What if Liz had brain cancer, like Sarah? He couldn't live through that again.

He was getting ahead of himself. Most people wouldn't leap from migraine to brain tumors.

But most people hadn't gone through what he had.

He stopped to talk to Claire, his director of budgets and analysis. "Just giving you the heads-up that the models are locked."

"I'm already looking at it."

"Can you start working on the presentation? I'll send you the list of assumptions for each version. How about recapping everything into our quarterly presentation format?"

"I'm on it." She lifted a hand as he left.

In his office he cleared emails that had piled up since he'd been focused on the projection project.

"Can I interrupt?" His mom stood in the doorway.

He stood. "Always."

He hugged her and they sat on the sofa near the windows.

"You're looking good," he said.

His mom had a healthy glow that almost made him forget how gray she'd gone during her surgery and radiation for cancer.

"Thank you." She smiled. "It's nice to have my son give me a compliment."

He kissed her cheek. "I'll remember to give you more."

She brushed back her brown hair and laughed. He'd gotten his hair from her. Although since his was short, there was more curl to it. "You do that."

"I know you never visit me during working hours just to talk, what do you need?" It was a family unspoken rule. They set the example for all their employees.

"I wanted to compliment you on the projections. I was intrigued with the stretch version. Who suggested you add Murphy Maid franchises?" His mother had started Murphy's Maids when she was in college. It was how she and his father had meet. She'd cleaned some of his construction projects. Now it was a key subsidiary of MacBain.

"Who do you think?" he asked.

Together they said, "Kate."

"Do you think she'll slow down when she's a mother?" Michael asked.

"I don't think she'll have a choice. Alex will keep an eye on her." His mom patted his hand. "I really like the idea of franchising. So much that I contacted our attorney. There's an attorney on staff who focuses on franchise agreements. I've set up a Zoom meeting for tomorrow. Do you want to sit in on it?"

"Yes." And wanting to groom a replacement if anything ever happened to him, he asked, "Can I have Claire sit in?"

"Absolutely." She stood. "How about Sunday dinner this weekend?"

"I'd love it." He stood too. Not wanting to keep secrets from his parents, he said, "I'd like Liz Carlson to join us."

His mom grinned. "As a coworker or a date?"

He looked her in the eye. "Date."

"Your dad owes me twenty bucks." His mom did a fist

pump. "I told him there were sparks between the two of you at Kate's wedding."

"You did?"

"Mothers always know. I like her."

"I'll see if she's available."

He and Liz hadn't really talked about keeping everything a secret. But she'd been worried about people knowing at the office.

Crap. He sure hoped he hadn't stepped in it.

TWELVE

"I CAN DRIVE. MY MIGRAINE IS ALL BUT GONE," LIZ EXPLAINED to Michael as they stood in the parking ramp.

"I'd feel better if you let me drive you. I'll take you to your apartment. You could pick up clothes for tomorrow and spend the night at my place."

It was tempting.

"You look wiped out," he added.

"Thanks." Hopefully he would catch the sarcasm.

"Once you eat dinner, you could take a bath and then sleep."

"Just sleep?"

He held up his hand with two fingers pointing up. "Scouts honor."

"Were you a scout?"

He clutched his chest. "Of course."

"I was 4-H, so I don't even know what's covered by your Boy Scout's honor."

"Let me take care of you tonight." He cradled her face in his hand.

She glanced around. They were alone in the ramp, but

there were security cameras. She pulled his hand down but held it. "Okay."

He guided her to his car and opened her door. She was so tired, she didn't complain that she was capable of opening her own door.

As he drove, she said, "I have no clue what the apartment will look like. I can't seem to get Jordan to wash his dishes."

"I get it. I have brothers too."

"And how many of them have maids cleaning up after them?"

He winced. "Probably all of us. I don't know about Stephen. He has strange quirks. He'd be the kind who wouldn't want anyone touching his stuff."

"Yeah, I remember how he wouldn't let me sit in his conference room chair."

"Spend a little more time around him. Even playing games as kids, he always had to have the same piece in Monopoly."

She chuckled.

They didn't discuss anything of substance as he drove. Which was good, her brain couldn't take much more.

"Don't bother finding a parking spot. I can run up." She unsnapped her seatbelt.

"You've met my mother, right?"

He made her laugh again.

He was different from the solemn man she'd first met.

They climbed the stairs together. With each flight, the building got hotter and hotter. She had her keys out, but as usual, Jordan had left the door unlocked.

No one was in the living room, but the TV blared. She could hear the shower running. Shaking her head, she found the remote and turned off the TV. Her arms seemed to weigh twenty pounds each. She sure hoped he would pay half of the utilities since he didn't have any idea how to live economically.

She sighed. "Let me pack some things."

"I'll wait here." Michael kissed her forehead. "What are you hungry for?"

"I'm not sure I can eat much more than soup." She pressed against her stomach.

"I know a place." He opened his phone.

She wanted to get in and out without talking to Jordan, but she also wanted her shampoo and conditioner. And a toothbrush. Make up. She had to wait until he was out of the bathroom. On her way to her bedroom she knocked on the bathroom door.

She found a small duffle to pack her clothes for tomorrow. This was embarrassing. She'd never done something like this before.

She picked out good pants and a shirt that wouldn't wrinkle as she folded them. She took a jacket and set it, hanger and all, on her bag. Then she pulled out a clean sleep T-shirt, underwear, socks and shoes.

When she heard the bathroom door open, she hurried in and gathered what she needed. Packing for a night was embarrassing when you lived with your brother.

Exhaustion almost had her going back to her room and collapsing on the bed. But Michael was waiting.

JORDAN TUGGED the towel he'd wrapped around his waist a little tighter. He wouldn't want to scare his twin, but it was so hot in the apartment, he wasn't ready to put on clothes.

Heading into the kitchen for a drink, he almost bumped into Michael.

"What the …?" He clutched at the towel. "What are you doing here?"

Michael held up his soapy hands. Hell, he was doing the dishes. "I'm waiting for your sister."

"So you decided to do the dishes?" And they were his dishes.

"Liz wasn't happy you'd left such a mess." Michael raised an eyebrow. "I thought I would make her life a little easier."

"It's a pain she can't afford a place with a dishwasher. And an air conditioner." He dug into the fridge. Shit, there was only one beer left. Trying to be a good host, he asked, "Do you want a beer?"

"No, thank you." Michael set the last plate in the drainer. He dried his hands and folded the towel, hanging it on the stove handle.

"I wouldn't figure you for someone who did dishes."

"Why not?" Michael leaned against the small counter, his arms crossed.

Jordan took out the last beer and popped the tab. "You're a MacBain."

"We had chores. One of them was doing dishes. We might have had a dishwasher, but half the time, all the dishes didn't fit." He shook his head. "We weren't allowed to leave dirty dishes in the sink. Whatever didn't fit was washed by hand. You should clean up your own mess."

"I had chores too. On a farm, chores never end." Jordan hated being put on the spot. "Liz helped Mom and I helped Dad."

Michael stared at him.

Jordan took a sip of his beer. The guy made him nervous.

"How's work?" Michael asked.

"There's always something that needs fixing." Jordan let out a sigh. "You have a lot of equipment. Today I worked on a crane. Those things are huge."

That got a smile from Michael. "They are. My brother Timothy loves operating the cranes. Always has."

"I met him. The only family members I haven't met are your dad, mom and sister."

"Kate's on bed rest."

They stood in uncomfortable silence. Jordan took another sip of beer.

Michael looked down the hall. "I did some checking and moved money around. I can free up five thousand by tomorrow."

"Man, that'd be great. Thank you." What about the other five thousand?

"Can you stop at my office?" Michael opened his phone and checked something. "I could be free around lunchtime."

"I'll make it happen. My family will be relieved." Now it was him checking that his sister wasn't listening in. "Just don't tell Liz. She'd be upset."

"I don't want to upset her. She's wiped out from the migraine she got today."

"I thought those had stopped."

Michael studied him. "Has she always had them?"

"I guess they started in our teens. Sometimes she'd go for long stretches without any, but then pow, she'd have a few bad months."

Michael nodded, clearly concerned for Liz. "I'll take care of her tonight. If you want to show your appreciation to your sister for letting you stay here, pick up your mess."

Jordan gave a sharp resentful nod.

They heard footsteps in the hall.

Michael moved to his sister and took the bag and jacket out of her hands. "Ready?"

She nodded and winced. "I almost fell asleep. I could stay here."

Jordan watched the guy step closer and whisper, "I'd like to take care of you."

"I hope you feel better," he called as they left.

His sister had hit the motherlode. This could only mean good things for him.

~

LIZ SHUFFLED next to Michael in his building's parking ramp. He hefted her bag over his shoulder and carried the rest.

In the elevator she slumped against him, and he wrapped his arm around her waist.

"When's the last time you had a migraine?" he asked.

"Maybe two or three months ago."

"What did you do?"

"Kate took me home." Liz tipped her head onto his shoulder. "And picked me up the next day."

"She probably wanted to make sure you got your work done the next day. She's crafty like that."

"She's nice." Liz jabbed her elbow into his belly, but there wasn't any oomph behind it.

He chuckled. "I'm kidding."

She looked up. "It's nice to hear you laugh."

The elevator opened on his floor, and he helped her out. "You make me ... lighter."

Even exhausted, his comment made her worry. She wasn't responsible for his lightness or darkness. She wasn't responsible for keeping him together.

"You're frowning." He opened his door and led her inside. Then he traced her eyebrows with his finger.

"I'm fine."

"I always heard a woman's *fine* was bad." He drew out the vowel in bad, like he was a bleating sheep.

She laughed. "This time I mean it."

"Head into the living room. Sit. Rest."

He carried her things down the hall.

She did what he suggested, then closed her eyes.

She could hear him in the kitchen. Then sensed him in front of her.

"I thought you might like a cup of tea," he said.

She opened her eyes. "I shouldn't."

"It's decaf," he explained. "I realize caffeine can cause migraines."

"That's one of my triggers." She took the mug. "When did you learn that?"

He sat on the coffee table in front of her. "After I left your office. You ... didn't look good. What are your other triggers?"

"Chocolate. Wine." She held up a hand. "Stress."

"Stress from work?"

"Not too often." Changing the subject, she blew on the tea. "What kind is this?"

"Ginger or something. Kate left it here." He sat next to her. "How are you feeling?"

"Washed out." It was the only way to describe it.

"Can you eat anything?"

She waved her hand. "Maybe."

"I know. Crackers." He bounced up. "Let me see what I have."

She sipped the tea, listening as cupboard doors opened and closed.

"Jackpot." He came back with a handful of individually wrapped crackers on a plate.

She pulled one of the cellophane packages open and nibbled.

Between the tea and the crackers, her stomach settled. But Michael sitting on the coffee table watching her had her brushing to see if she had crumbs on her face. "What?"

"When did you last see a doctor?" he asked.

"About my migraines?"

He nodded. His expression was solemn. His body still.

"I see my doctor every year."

"A specialist?"

"When I moved up here, my primary doctor recommended a neurologist."

"And you see the neurologist every year?"

She started to nod, but that made her head throb.

"I just want to make sure it isn't something—more serious."

Now she got it. Sarah. "Like a brain tumor?"

He stared at her. "Like a brain tumor."

"I've had migraines since high school. I see my doctor every year. Nothing has changed." She set her tea down and clasped his hands. "These are not tumor symptoms. I don't have brain cancer."

He exhaled. Moving next to her, he gathered her in for a hug. "Is this okay? Am I hurting you?"

"It's perfect."

She rested her head against his shoulder. He cared. She might be sitting in the middle of all the pictures of his fiancée, but he cared about her.

The security system buzzed. "That should be dinner."

He pulled a throw off the back of the sofa and covered her before letting in the delivery person.

She couldn't sit here. She walked into the kitchen as Michael brought in the food.

"We could eat in the living room," he said.

"I can sit at the table." She smiled. "We weren't allowed to eat anywhere but the table."

"We weren't supposed to. But …"

"You didn't always follow the rules? I don't believe that."

"Well, it was more my younger brothers breaking the rules." He pulled out soup containers. "There's potato and ham, chicken noodle and wild rice and chicken. And bread sticks or …" he rustled the bag "… more crackers."

"Wild rice and chicken sounds good."

She pulled out bowls and spoons. He handed her the container. She poured soup in her bowl. Then she handed him a small ladle she'd found in his silverware drawer.

"Where did you find this?" he asked.

She pointed, her mouth full of the soup.

"Huh. I wonder if my sister or mother brought it. Or maybe Maria." He ladled soup into his bowl. "Speaking of which, would you come with me to family dinner on Sunday?"

Liz choked and dropped her spoon with a clang. "Dinner with your family?"

"My mom asked me this afternoon. And I asked to bring you." He was frowning now. "She likes you."

"You talked about me?" This stress might bring on another migraine. "With your mother?"

"She wasn't surprised when I asked. She thought she'd spotted 'sparks' between us at Kate's wedding."

"But ... your family. They would know that we were ..."

"Dating? Is that the word you're looking for?"

She nodded. "I haven't told anyone. Now my brother knows and your family."

"I doubt my mother is burning up the phone lines." She could hear his irritation.

"I work for your family. What will this look like?"

"That we're attracted to each other?" He opened a package of crackers. He was clutching them so hard they crumbled onto the table. "Did you want to sneak around?"

"I hadn't gotten beyond the fact that we're both attracted to each other." She shut her eyes. "I don't want other MacBain employees thinking I didn't earn my job."

"I don't want to hide the fact that we're in a relationship. You work for Kate, not me." He took her hand. "If people have met you, seen your work, they will know you hold your job because of merit. Screw anyone who thinks otherwise."

"That's easy for you to say."

"You don't think I've had people resent the fact I'm a MacBain?"

"Oh …" She laced her fingers with his. "I didn't think you would understand."

"I do," he said. "But I think it would be worse if we snuck around."

"You're right." She couldn't help smiling. "So you think this is a relationship?"

His fierce expression softened. "Absolutely."

"Good," she whispered. "I can make room in my schedule for Sunday dinner."

"RUDY, I'll have the money in the next couple of days. I'll have some tomorrow." Jordan stretched his neck and vertebras snapped. His cell phone was sweaty in his hand.

Now that he had Michael's promise of half the money today, he'd finally answered Rudy's call.

Jordan planned to make Michael's money multiply. He'd found a poker game. He should be able to double the money fast.

"I don't want to drive to Minneapolis, but to get my money I will," Rudy threatened.

"I can … send you a check."

"No way, my friend." There was a deep inhale on Rudy's side of the phone conversation. The guy was a chain smoker. Wouldn't it be wonderful if he had a heart attack, and Jordan didn't have to pay back the loan?

"Venmo?" Jordan asked.

"Nope." There was a pause. "Maybe I'll come to Minneapolis."

Jordan didn't want Rudy coming up here. "Why don't I drive to Iowa next weekend? I can see my parents and then head to Des Moines to catch up with you?"

"This weekend?"

"I can't make it until next weekend. My boss has me working this weekend," Jordan lied.

"Ahhh, your MacBain boss," Rudy said.

Jordan shivered. How did Rudy know where he worked?

"Nine days from now?" Rudy asked.

"That sounds right." He'd have time to cash Michael's check. Maybe by then Michael would have written a second check. And he'd have time to make some real money. He could finally get away from the nickel ante poker he'd been stuck with since he didn't have squat.

"You'll have the twelve thousand dollars you owe me?"

"I only owe you ten."

"Interest my friend. Interest."

Damn it. "Sure. I'll call when I get to town."

"Don't worry, I'll keep tabs in you." Rudy hung up on him.

THIRTEEN

"Jordan Carlson is here to see you," Becca said from Michael's doorway.

"Send him in."

He pulled out the agreements he'd created. Jordan might be Liz's brother, but he wasn't a fool. He wanted this "by the books."

"Hey, Michael." Jordan hurried into the office. "How's Liz doing?"

"Better." Michael set the documents on the table and shook Jordan's hand. "How bad were the migraines when you were growing up?"

"Pretty bad. It took the docs a while to figure out what was going on." He stood next to Michael's table, his fingers drumming on the wood.

"She was really wiped out." Michael waved at the chair by the table.

Jordan sat, but he frowned as he did.

"Why don't you read through the agreement? Then if you're ready to sign it, I'll write the check."

Michael swung by the door and closed it. He didn't want

Liz discovering her brother borrowing money. It might set off another migraine. He didn't want to cause her more pain or add to her stress.

Jordan flipped through the pages. The promissory note wasn't a long document, but Jordan barely looked like he was reading it.

"Do you have any questions?" Michael asked.

"Where do I sign?"

Michael flipped his copy to the last page and pointed out the red arrow he'd attached that read Sign Here. It was hard to believe Jordan and Liz were twins. Liz was meticulous. Jordan—not.

Michael brought over a pen, and Jordan quickly signed and dated the documents.

"My family will be relieved." Jordan handed Michael the pen.

Michael signed the agreements and handed Jordan the check.

A big grin stretched across Jordan's face. "I can't thank you enough, man."

"I'd do anything to help Liz."

"She might even move out of that tiny apartment." Jordan stood and held out his hand. "Thank you again."

Michael placed one of the agreements into a folder. "Don't forget your copy."

"Sure. Sure." Jordan stuck it under one arm and headed for the door. "Hopefully this will stop Liz's migraines."

Stop her migraines? What did her brother know that he wasn't saying? Was it her parents' financial situation causing Liz's stress?

Michael leaned against his desk, watching Jordan depart. He wanted to tell Liz what he'd done, but she would be upset. She had too much pride. It would have been easier if she'd asked him for help, but at least he could do this through her brother.

And hopefully Liz would never find out.

LIZ SENT out this month's lease renewal reminders. There were only five, and she was early, but she didn't want to miss any deadlines.

She rarely felt this good after a migraine, but Michael had taken care of her. She'd slept more last night than she had in weeks.

There was a rap on her cubical. Michael. He made his shirt and slacks look like *GQ* material.

She couldn't help but grin. "How's your day going?"

"Good. Mom and Dad are very happy with the forecasts."

"What about the restoration idea?"

His smile wavered a little. "They're … thinking about it."

"You'll make it happen."

"I wish I had your confidence." He toyed with the candy dish on her desk but didn't take anything. "Do you want to go for lunch?"

She didn't have extra cash to go out for lunch. And she hadn't brought a lunch because she'd stayed at Michael apartment. But missing meals could trigger another migraine.

"Come on. My treat," he said.

"Okay." She was hungry. "But nothing expensive."

"How about that place in the skyway. The one with the sandwiches and soups."

"Perfect."

He started to take her elbow and stopped.

"Thanks," she whispered as they headed to the elevator.

"Liz. Michael." Patty MacBain waved. "Are you heading to lunch?"

"We are." Michael's smile was so genuine, Liz smiled too.

"Can I join you?" Patty asked.

"Absolutely," Michael said.

"Yes," Liz said at the same time.

They all got on the elevator.

"Did you have a doctor's appointment this morning?" Michael asked.

"Just an eye appointment." Patty rolled her eyes. "I'm getting trifocals. I can't believe it."

Michael laughed.

His mother poked him in the stomach. "No cracks about how old your mother is getting."

"You look great," Liz said.

And Patty did. She'd gained back most of the weight that had come off from her cancer treatments. She hadn't even lost her hair.

"Thank you!" Patty said.

They didn't discuss anything more challenging than the current heatwave. It had been nice not having to sleep in her sweltering apartment last night. Jordan had probably sweated off a few pounds.

"Are you coming for Sunday dinner?" Patty asked as they gathered their garbage.

"Michael invited me," she hedged.

"And you said yes, right?"

"Are you sure you want an outsider at a family dinner?" Liz asked.

"Yes. There is too much testosterone at our dinners." Patty pointed a finger at Michael. "Kate will be coming. She'll have to stay off her feet, but at least she'll be there."

"Do you play basketball?" Michael asked.

"I did in high school." Liz frowned. "Why?"

"We usually play a little one-on-one."

She couldn't stop a blush. Memories of the one-on-one games they'd already played flashed through her head.

He nudged her foot under the table, a knowing look on his face.

"I've played some basketball." She was a better volleyball player, but she was okay with basketball. "I'm pretty good at HORSE."

"That's a little too tame for the MacBains," Patty said.

"You play in the heat?"

"Of course." Michael looked affronted that she'd even questioned it. "You'll have to bring clothes to change into. It'll be fun."

She looked at her fingernails. The manicure she'd given herself a couple of days ago wouldn't hold up.

"Time to head back to the sweatshop. My bosses are slave drivers." Michael gave his mother a one-armed hug.

Liz thought she would put in a good word for him. "What did you think of the idea of expanding into restorations that Michael added to the forecasts?"

"I like it. Diversification of revenue streams is always good. And I like the idea of franchising Murphy's Maids." She nodded at Michael. "The question will be what additional capital and staffing would be needed."

They headed back through the winding skyways. Michael said, "We tried to estimate all possible costs."

"And you did a great job. But we need someone to champion those kinds of changes."

Liz waited for Michael to talk about his passion for restorations. But he didn't say anything. She opened her mouth, but Michael shook his head.

Why wouldn't he want his mother to know how much he cared about this?

Liz didn't get a chance to ask. Patty followed Michael into his office, and she went to her cubicle.

Just as she was settling in, her phone buzzed with a text. Jordan.

Not sure if you'll be home tonight, but I'll be late.

She shivered. What kind of trouble had Jordan found?

≈

JORDAN LUCKED OUT. Michael and he had the same bank. It made accessing the cash easier. The teller couldn't put a hold on the money. Damn bank systems always played everything in their favor. He took out a grand and deposited the rest in his account.

The cash burned a hole in his pocket, but he had to get through his Friday afternoon's work. Maybe tonight would be the night he made enough to blow this town. Maybe tonight he could build enough of a stake to get Rudy off his ass.

That was asking a lot, but he believed in his skills.

His boss, Kyle, came around as he was cleaning up. "You're doing great work, Carlson."

"Thanks." Jordan pulled a couple of paper towels out and dried his hands.

"Next week I'd like you to take a look at another of our cranes. Are you comfortable doing that alone?" Kyle asked.

"Absolutely." He liked figuring out what was wrong.

"I'll let you know what day they want you. Have a good weekend."

"You too." Jordan hoped he wouldn't need to work next week, but it would probably take more than one poker game to get clear of everyone he owed money too.

He checked the game address again. Then headed to the liquor store to buy beer. Tonight was the start of something good.

≈

"I CAN'T KEEP STAYING at your place," Liz said again. She kept her voice low since Michael was standing at her desk.

"Sure you can. Last night you were happy there was air conditioning." Michael tipped his head. "It got to ninety today. How hot do you think your apartment will be tonight?"

Hot.

"Is there some reason you don't want to stay with me?" he asked.

"I …" She couldn't tell him.

"Liz?"

"I feel like your fiancée is watching me." She swallowed. "You laid down the photo next to your bed, but …"

Michael sat in her guest chair. "What you and I have has nothing to do with Sarah." There was a defensive tone to his voice.

Liz didn't believe it, but she wasn't going to call him on it. "Don't you need to attend your meetings?"

"When I'm with you I don't feel the need to drink."

"But that makes me feel responsible for your sobriety." She didn't want that.

"No." He leaned across her desk and took her hand. Even when she looked around, afraid someone would spot them, he held on. "Liz, I'm responsible for my own sobriety. But being with you makes me happy. I don't need to drink when I'm with you. I don't even have the urge. Hell, bring a bottle of wine with you tonight if you want, it won't affect me."

That all sounded good, but she'd lived with Jordan's promises for too long. He'd started gambling back in high school. And he always promised he was done. That he wouldn't do it again.

"Please have dinner with me. It's Friday night. I would like to take you out. Or we can order in. I don't care. I want to be with you."

"You make it hard to say no." She had things she needed to do at her own apartment.

"Then don't." His eyes glittered. "Food and air conditioning. And me. What else would you do tonight?"

"Pay bills." She'd been paid today. This was the time of month she sent money back to her parents. "Balance my checkbook."

"Can't that wait for Saturday?" His thumb stroked her knuckles.

Her body wanted to say yes. "I feel like we're moving too fast."

"We've known each for almost six months."

"But ..."

"I thought after your migraine you'd like another easy night. And it's Friday." He lightly tapped her desk. "Why don't we find someplace to eat between the office and your apartment, then dinner will be ... off your plate."

"That's terrible." But she couldn't help laughing.

They were smiling at each other when Becca poked her head around the corner. "There you are, Michael. Your dad was wondering if you had a minute."

"On my way." After Becca left, he asked, "Is that a workable plan?"

They *were* moving fast.

"Dinner is a workable plan."

JORDAN TOSSED his cards on the table. His luck was shit tonight. He'd gone through the cash he'd taken out and another eight hundred. "I'm out for the night."

The card shark across from him pulled in his chips. "Are you coming tomorrow?"

"Maybe." He didn't want to leave, but his luck wasn't changing. "Same time, same place?"

"Tomorrow is at a different location," the guy said.

Jordan got the address and headed out. Lady Luck had to get on board soon.

At least he'd had enough money to pay some of his credit card bill. He stopped and filled his truck with gas. Plus he'd received his first pay check. Tomorrow night he would make bank.

He had to.

MICHAEL FLIPPED the bacon sizzling on the griddle. Liz had stayed last night. Now she sat at the kitchen counter drinking coffee.

"Dinner was great last night," she said. "Thank you."

"You look like you're feeling better."

"I'm back to ordinary," she said.

Ordinary? "I would never use the word ordinary to describe you."

She took in a deep breath. "You make me feel special."

He dropped the tongs he'd been using and crossed to where she sat on a barstool. Swinging her around, he wrapped his arms around her. "You are special. Very."

His gaze roamed her face. She didn't have on any makeup, and her hair was flat on one side of the head. She was … beautiful. Cupping the back of her head, he kissed her.

Last night he'd tucked away Sarah's picture in the bedroom. Each small loss of Sarah hurt. But Liz had been brave enough to tell him that she was uncomfortable in his and Sarah's home.

Damn. He had to stop thinking that way. His home. It was

his home. Sarah was gone. He hadn't heard her voice since the last time he'd gotten drunk.

The smell of hot bacon pulled him back to the griddle. He flipped everything and turned the heat down.

"Can I do anything?" Liz asked.

Stop pressuring him to give up Sarah. "Do you want to scramble the eggs?"

"Will do." She whisked the eggs and poured them into the hot pan.

He popped down the bread in the toaster and laid the bacon on paper towels. Then he pulled out plates, small bowls, blueberries and silverware.

Liz stirred the eggs. "These are done. And I didn't even have to collect the eggs this morning."

"You do that?"

"Sure. We have chickens. Mom sells the extra eggs." She pulled out a hot pad and set the pan on the counter in front of their plates. Then she topped off their coffee.

"How are the economics of farming?" he asked as they dished out their food.

"The drought last year didn't help."

"Is this year better?" He crumbled bacon on top of his eggs.

She tipped her head, then did the same with her bacon. "Spring was good. Dad said the planting was in almost a week early."

"And have they had enough rain?"

"Better than last year. But they're waiting for rain."

He wanted her to talk about her parents' financial woes, but he didn't want to break Jordan's confidence. "That's too bad."

"They're struggling." She pushed around the eggs on her plate.

He touched her arm. "I didn't mean to make you sad."

"No. I … I've been helping them out. They took on debt a few years ago, and then the weather … well … it didn't help."

"Do you feel like your pay is adequate?" He couldn't help putting on his MacBain hat.

"Oh yes!" She squeezed his arm. "I'm making more than I did at my last job."

"But you have greater responsibilities. You're running the leasing department while Kate is out."

"And I love it. I'm happy." She shrugged. "It would be great to just pay off my parents' debts, but that will take time."

Not as much as she thought. Hopefully Jordan had already sent the first five thousand down to their parents. "What do you want to do today?"

"Pay bills and do laundry."

He gave an exaggerated sigh. "I thought if I got you in my clutches, you'd spend the day with me."

"How about dinner?" she said. "You've been feeding me. I'll cook for you."

"Are you any good?"

"You'll find out." She looked at his balcony. "You have a grill?"

"I'm male. Of course."

She smiled at him. "I've missed grilling."

"You can use mine anytime."

They finished breakfast and cleaned up the dishes. Liz repacked her duffle with her dirty clothes. "I should go."

"You'll stay tonight, right? And spend Sunday with me?" He hated how needy he sounded.

"Yes."

"And if you wanted to plan clothes for Monday, you could spend Sunday night too." He took her hand. "I've got plenty of closet space. You could leave whatever you want here."

She chewed her lip. "I'll think about it."

It wasn't a commitment, but it was a start.

He walked her to her car. Kissed her goodbye.

She brushed one more kiss on his lips. "I'll be back around five?"

"Earlier is fine. Noon is fine." Not leaving was fine.

"I'll call before I leave so I know you're home."

He waited on the sidewalk and waved as she left.

Back in his apartment, he stared at Sarah's pictures.

It was time.

He wrapped each photo in newspaper and stacked them on his coffee table. Then he moved into the master bedroom. Wrapping the picture, he added it to his pile.

There was an ache in his chest as he opened the closet door. Sarah's mother had removed most of her clothes. He hugged her favorite dress. He used to be able to catch her scent. Each piece of clothing he picked up, he sniffed, but nothing remained.

He sank to the bed, holding one of her sweaters. What would Liz think if she opened a bathroom drawer and found Sarah's things? He needed to clean out the bathroom too.

Each item he packed was like tearing out a piece of his flesh. He folded and placed Sarah's things on the bed. Then did the same in the bathroom.

Tears stung his eyes.

He had to do this. He had to move on.

Before he could change his mind, he grabbed his keys and took the stairs to his car. Then he headed to the nearest liquor store.

"Haven't seen you in a while," the owner called out. "We're doing a Scotch tasting in the back. You should try some out."

"A little too early for me." Temptation was around every corner. He'd been a frequent customer at the store. It was the closest liquor store to his place. "I'm hoping to take some boxes off your hands."

"Not a problem. Give me a minute." The owner finished ringing up a customer. "Come on back."

Michael followed him, passing by the people sniffing and sipping scotch. The smell was like a big warm hug, one he wanted to embrace.

"How many do you need?"

"Three or four." He inhaled. Damn he wanted to sniff a glass of Scotch. Not sip. Sniff.

Maybe he should buy a bottle of wine for Liz. She liked a drink. She shouldn't suffer because he was an alcoholic.

The owner handed out four boxes.

"Can you pick out a nice red wine for me?" he asked.

"Will do." The owner did and then rang him up. "Don't be a stranger now."

There was a feeling of rightness as he stuck the bottle under his arm and headed out the door.

God, he wanted a drink.

LIZ FOUND a parking spot in front of Michael's building. She pulled out the bags she'd brought and locked her car. Maybe when she'd gone to the grocery store she'd bought too much, but Michael had fed her so many times, and she wanted to return the favor.

She hiked a tote onto each shoulder and found the button for his apartment.

"Yes?" Michael's deep voice filled the entry.

"I'm here."

"I'm glad."

A shot of warmth went through her. She should be protecting herself, her heart, but Michael was destroying all her barriers.

The door buzzed and she headed to the elevator.

Michael waited outside his door, wearing cargo shorts and a golf shirt. He looked good. Hurrying to her side, he took her totes. "What is all this?"

"Dinner." She gave him what she hoped was a sexy smile. "And breakfast."

"Wow."

In the kitchen they unpacked what she'd brought. When she opened the fridge, there was a bottle of wine lying on the shelf.

Everything in her body stilled. She slipped it out. "Michael?"

Smiling, he turned with a potato in each hand. "Yes?"

She held up the bottle.

His smile disappeared. "I thought you'd like a glass of wine with dinner."

"I don't want to make anything hard on you."

He laughed. "Are you sure?"

Her mouth dropped open.

"I'm fine with you having a glass of wine around me." He moved across the room and took the bottle out of her hand. "I bought it for you."

"Thank you. I don't need to drink."

He shrugged. "Then it will be here when you want it."

Since she'd bought steaks, the red wine would be a good pairing. "I don't want to set your progress back."

"My poison of choice was whiskey." He set the wine on the counter and ran his hands up and down her arms. "Wine wasn't my thing."

But it was alcohol. And it hadn't been here before. "You went to a liquor store to get this?"

Michael kissed her. "I needed boxes."

She let herself be hugged and even hugged him back. But Jordan's voice ran through her head.

He was fine. He could control his addiction.

≈

THE WINE HAD BEEN A MISTAKE. Michael helped Liz in the kitchen and lit the grill when she'd asked.

She hadn't even recognized he'd packed up Sarah. Put her stuff and her pictures into his closet. It was like she couldn't see past the damn bottle.

He shut the sliding door a little too hard as he came back in.

Liz's head snapped up.

"It's cooled down enough that we could eat outside," he suggested.

"That would be nice."

"Listen, if the wine bothers you, toss the damn stuff."

"I … I'm sorry." She rubbed her face. "We have addiction in my family. I don't know what line is too far to cross."

"You offered to make dinner. So I wanted to do something nice for you."

She came over and wrapped her arms around his waist. "I'm sorry. It's a touchy thing for me. My family has been hurt before by someone who … who couldn't …"

He stroked her back. "I won't hurt you."

They kissed. And it was the same jolt that took him by surprise every time he touched her.

When they pulled apart, they were both a little breathless.

"I don't suppose we can put dinner on hold?" he asked.

"No." She smoothed a hand over his chest. "But I can't wait for tonight."

Thank goodness they were back on an even keel.

"Let me know when you want me to throw anything on the grill."

"If it's warm, you can put the potatoes on." She handed him the foil-wrapped spuds.

He weighed the potatoes in his hands. "This is probably

enough for a family of four."

When he came back in, she was shredding carrots into the salad.

"I should have worked out today," he said.

Her hair was in a ponytail, and he kissed her neck, inhaling her floral scent.

She leaned into him. "What did you do today?"

"Did some cleaning. Oh." Reaching into his pocket, he pulled out a key. "I had an extra key made for you."

"A key?" She turned around and they were chest to chest.

He held it out. "I want you to feel at home here. This will get you into the security door and the apartment."

"Oh, Michael." She sighed.

"Oh, Michael, good? Or oh, Michael, you idiot?"

She took the key and tucked it in the pocket of her shorts. "Oh, Michael, good. You're …"

"Amazing?" He kissed her cheek. "Sexy?" He kissed her nose. "A god?"

She laughed. "All of the above. Except the god part. I just don't know when I would use your key."

"Today. Any day. You have an open invitation. I missed you."

She stood on tiptoe and kissed him. "I missed you too."

They fell into a tender kiss. Her tongue stroked his, and her hands roamed his back and burrowed into his hair.

He lifted her onto the counter. The salad bowl squealed as he slid it out of the way.

"You're too short, or I'm too tall." But right now she was the perfect height. He stepped between her legs. "Perfect."

"I thought we were waiting until after dinner."

"Hang on."

He ran out to the patio. Flipping off the grill, his feet pounded as he ran back to Liz. "Now we don't have to worry about anything overcooking."

He stepped back between her legs and kissed her.

"You cook here."

"I have ..." he pulled off her T-shirt "... disinfecting ..." flipped open her bra and covered one of her tight nipples with his mouth "... wipes."

Liz held him to her breasts. He had just enough space to take her nipples between his teeth one at a time.

She groaned, her hips curving into his erection.

He kissed his way to the waistband of her shorts and made short work of the button and zipper before she squirmed out of them. He stepped back and stared.

Liz was naked. On his counter. And hot.

He kissed his way down her thighs.

"Michael." She squirmed again and told him where she wanted his mouth.

He finally complied, kissing her intimately.

"Michael." Her head fell back. Her hips rose and fell as his tongue played over her.

When her motions grew choppy, he curled a finger, then two, inside her and continued to work her clit.

"Michael!" she cried as she began to orgasm.

Her body squeezed around his fingers. He moved in and out until the contractions stopped. Then he stretched along the counter for his wallet, pulled out a condom and dropped his shorts.

Even as she was still gasping from her climax, he plunged into her. His thumb found the tight bundle of nerves and he rubbed and stroked. With his other arm he tugged her closer.

She tightened her legs around his waist, her gaze locked on his. "Yes ... yes."

He wanted to make this last. Make her come again and again. But his orgasm thundered through him. Now all he wanted was for her to come again before he finished.

Her pelvis twisted. "Harder."

"You. Got. It." He could barely choke out the words.

Her eyes closed. Her head dropped back. Then the exquisite waves of her orgasm ignited his. He slid deeper and held on as they came together.

Their breathing heaved. He gasped, "Damn."

"Yeah." She flopped back on the counter.

His legs were wobbly, but he was still standing. He collapsed and her belly cushioned his head.

She wrapped her arms around him. "That was amazing. I'll never look at your counter the same way again …"

"Without thinking about making love?" he asked.

"Ummm, sure."

"Say it."

"Are you sure this wasn't just sex?"

He sat her up and looked into her eyes. "That, my dear, wasn't sex. That was love."

He gave her a smacking kiss, pulled out, located his shorts and headed to the bedroom.

Let her think about that for a while.

LOVE. Liz stared at Michael as he set the steaks on the grill.

She tossed the last ingredients into the salad and set it on the table. Away from the counter.

It was like Michael wanted her off balance.

"Potatoes are almost done." He wrapped an arm around her waist and pulled her close. "I think we found a new technique to bake them. Start them on the grill. Bake fifteen minutes. Turn off grill. Make love and let them rest. Then restart grill. We should write a cookbook."

"Right." But she couldn't help laughing.

He turned her around and kissed her. When they finally

separated, he studied her closely as he asked, "Would you like a glass of that wine while the meat cooks?"

She looked him straight in the eye and said, "Sure."

He smiled and let her go.

While he dealt with the cork, she put butter and sour cream on the table. Then she set the dressing she'd made next to the salad. "Everything's ready here."

He handed her a glass. "Patio?"

"That sounds nice."

She followed him through the living room, glanced at the mantle and stopped.

He was opening the patio door when he noticed she wasn't behind him.

"Michael, when you said you'd cleaned today …"

"I did what you asked."

She couldn't read his expression.

"You took Sarah's pictures down." She shook her head.

"They made you uncomfortable." He shrugged like it wasn't a big deal. "I packed away her stuff too."

"That's huge. I didn't expect that. I thought, maybe the one in the bedroom." She couldn't stand halfway across the room and talk about something so significant.

Setting her glass on the coffee table, she moved in front of him and took his hands. "She was an important part of your life. I appreciate what you did. I do. But you can't make someone you loved … disappear. I don't want you to resent me."

He stared over her shoulder. "I didn't want you to be uncomfortable in my home."

She tapped his chin so he'd look her in the eye. "Is it too much for you?"

His shoulders relaxed. "Without you, I might not have taken down her pictures and packed away her things, but I'm … okay."

"If you aren't, you need to let me know." His statement about love had been confusing enough. Now this. "We have time to figure it out."

His phone buzzed in his pocket. "The steaks. Come out for a few minutes."

She picked up her wine and followed him.

Sitting on a patio in the city was not something she'd done before. The terrace wasn't very wide, but there was enough room for his grill, a small table with four chairs, and two lounge chairs.

She settled in one of the loungers.

The grill cover clanged as he pulled it open. There was the sizzle of the meat on the hot grates as he flipped them, then she caught the scent.

"It smells great," she said. Just like a Sunday at home.

Except this was Saturday in the city. And they hadn't raised the beef.

He closed the grill and reset his phone timer. Then he took the seat next to her. "It does smell good."

"How long were you and Sarah together?"

He didn't say anything for a minute, maybe two.

"We were friends since first grade and started dating when we were sophomores. Her parents did accounting work for my mother before Murphy's Maids merged with MacBain. And we all lived in the same suburb."

"Edina?"

He nodded again. "It was a great place to grow up. Now I'm hearing complaints that people are tearing down the homes built in the fifties and sixties and building McMansions. Pretty much the lot only consists of house. It's not happening in my parents' neighborhood, but there has been quite a bit of renovations in the neighborhood I grew up in."

He stretched his hand out and laced their fingers together.

"What was farm life like?"

"I was outside—a lot. And we had chores. They were fairly traditional, but that didn't stop my dad from having me help with the corn harvests or bale hay. That's pretty thankless." She smiled. "I showed cows, and one year I talked my dad into letting me get goats. That backfired because not only did I have to feed them every day, I had to milk them too. A neighbor bought the milk and made cheese."

"I grew up cleaning construction sites and being a slave for the crews. Those were pretty good times too."

"Any word on the restoration branch you added to the fifteen-year model?" She squeezed his fingers.

He slid around in his seat and his knees rested against her chair. "Nothing."

"Did you tell your parents you wanted to be involved with that branch?"

"No. I want the idea to succeed on its own merits, not as a … a pity assignment."

"Your parents wouldn't manage the business based on emotion." She shifted so they faced each other, legs touching. "But it might weigh on the positive side if you said you wanted to be hands-on."

He was saved from responding by his timer. "Okay," he said, standing. "Five minutes to rest and then we eat."

She sipped her wine. Her first sip. She was always conscious that alcohol was Michael's addiction.

Before she jumped up to help Michael with the door, she sent Jordan a message.

Hope you're having a good day. I'm staying with Michael tonight.

As she opened the door for Michael and their food, her phone pinged.

Don't do anything I wouldn't do! LOL I'll be out tonight too.

Jordan now had a paycheck. Would he keep his promise not to gamble?

For his parents' and her sake, she hoped he did.

FOURTEEN

Jordan waited for the flop. He'd gone all in. This could make his night.

And the flop was garbage. He tossed his card to the table. "Without bad luck, I wouldn't have any luck."

Fuck. He was down another two grand.

He headed to the bathroom. The game was in a warehouse. And that was just what the bathroom looked like: a warehouse washroom no one ever cleaned. The toilet at one time might have been white, or a light yellow. But he didn't look too closely. At least there was soap and paper towels. He could stand dirty, but after he dried his hands, he used a paper towel to open the door. Why risk sepsis?

He checked his watch. Seven o'clock. He'd been at this since eleven this morning. And he didn't have anything to show for it. Rudy expected he would be bringing his money in less than a week.

"You okay, Carlson?" one of the players asked.

"Just taking a break." What the hell could he do? He still had some of the money Michael had lent him, but he'd lost three grand already. Maybe he should find a bar and buy a bunch of pull tabs. He'd have as much of a chance of recouping his losses as playing with these guys.

He could almost feel Rudy's hot breath on his neck. He could fail to drive back to Iowa next weekend, but Rudy would find him. Or one of Rudy's minions. And with his luck, he'd find Liz. Or worse, his parents.

He could try online sports bets, but he hadn't had a lot of success in the past.

So it was back into the game. He had to win. There was too much at stake to lose.

"I DON'T KNOW if my mom told anyone we were dating." Michael tried to keep his voice as even as possible. He put on his blinker and turned onto his parents' street. "You've been nervous ever since we woke up. My family is not going to be upset. As a matter of fact, my brothers will probably kiss you. Mom's been pressuring all of us to bring dates to Sunday dinners. My brothers will be ecstatic they aren't on the hot seat anymore."

"I'm worried they'll judge me." Liz's hands twisted in her lap. "I really want to go somewhere with the company. When Kate moves to another position, I want her job. But I don't want anyone to think I'm using you to get there."

"You mean, you aren't a gold digger?" He laughed. "Since I don't have all that much gold, I don't think anyone will think that."

She bopped him with her fist.

He held her left hand. "You know everyone, including Kate, will be over the moon." He winced.

"What? You winced. What about Kate?" Hysteria made her voice almost higher than a cat's screech. Not that he would tell her.

"Well …" He rolled his shoulders. "When you first started working with Kate she warned all of us that we couldn't hit on you."

"Oh." Liz slid back into the passenger seat. "I did tell her why I left Colfax."

"That may have played into why she yelled at us. But I think it was because you're so beautiful. Stephen made some comments."

"What?" she asked.

He only caught a glimpse of her shocked face before he turned his attention back to driving.

"My brother mentioned how beautiful you are." He drove up the driveway. Looked like everyone was already here. "I kept my thoughts to myself, but I thought you were beautiful too. *Are* beautiful."

He shut off the car. Turning, he smiled. If he had known talking about Kate's warning would stop Liz worrying about dinner, he would have said something earlier. "Ready?"

"No."

"Let's go." He got out of the car and moved to open her door, but she was already standing, taking in the entrance of the house.

"I know I've been here before, but this is amazing."

"It's home." He glanced at the gray-beige stone facade. The remainder of the three-story house was tan brick. Stone pillars flanked the massive red double doors. He'd always loved this house.

"How long have they lived here?" she asked.

He held the door for her. "Since I was in middle school. We lived about a mile away before. We didn't even have to change schools."

He dropped their bags on the floor with the other gym bags. "Are you sure you're ready for MacBain basketball?"

"I'm not ready for any of this."

He wasn't either. Not that he would tell Liz.

He'd never brought anyone but Sarah. It had only ever been Sarah. He almost stumbled from the sorrow that swept over him.

"Are you okay?" Liz asked.

"Of course." He shook off his pain and listened, trying to identify where everyone was gathered.

He ducked his head into the formal living room. No one. Then headed to the family room. The atrium doors to the terrace were open, the sheers fluttering in a breeze. He heard laughter outside. "Come on. Sounds like we found everyone."

He slid the screen open. The conversations stopped.

His mother got to Liz first and gave her a hug. "Welcome. I'm glad you're here."

"Thank you for having me."

His dad was up next. He pulled her into a hug too. "Hey, Liz."

Michael watched as she barely got over that shock, then Stephen came next, holding out his arms.

Michael stepped in between them and wrapped an arm around her waist. "Just say hi."

"Hi." Stephen chuckled as he headed back to his seat.

"Hey, Liz," Timothy said.

"Thank you all for having me." Liz went to where Kate lay on a lounge chair. "How are you doing?"

"Feeling ridiculous." She patted her small belly. "And Alex hovers too much."

Liz knelt next to the chair, and Michael couldn't hear the rest of what they said, but Liz seemed to relax and then actually laughed.

"Thanks for taking the pressure off me," Stephen said.

Timothy nodded. "Me too."

"Do you really think Mom won't be hounding you guys to find someone?" Michael asked.

His brothers groaned.

"You're right," Stephen said in a low voice. "Ever since her cancer scare, she wants to see everyone settled."

Alex came out from the house. His gaze shot to Kate. He nodded, then joined Michael and his brothers.

Michael shook his hand. "Everything still okay with Kate?"

"Yes, but I may need to lash her to the bed."

Timothy held up his hands. "Too much info, bro."

They laughed.

"What part of bed rest doesn't she get?" Alex asked.

"Is the baby doing okay?" Michael asked.

Something sparked in his eyes, but then it was gone. "Yes."

He must have read Alex's expression wrong.

His parents had disappeared into the house and now came out with trays loaded with flutes and champagne on ice.

His mouth watered even though he wasn't into champagne.

Mom set her tray down and picked up two of the flutes, already filled. "For Kate and Michael."

Nothing like being singled out. He took the champagne flute and unclenched his teeth. "Thanks, Mom."

Dad filled the other flutes and they were distributed.

Alex moved to Kate's side and Liz came back to Michael.

"Is this a family tradition?" Liz asked.

"No."

Alex sat next to Kate and wrapped an arm around her. His fiercely independent sister rested her head on her husband's shoulder. Michael never would have paired him with Kate. But they worked.

"What's up with the champagne?" Timothy asked.

"Your sister's request," Mom said.

Kate cleared her throat. "Alex and I have been holding back some news."

It couldn't be about the baby. His sister being pregnant was obvious to everyone.

"It's a … complication. And why I was put on bed rest after the spotting." Kate took a deep breath. "Well anyway. We waited to make sure they were both doing all right."

"They?" Michael asked.

"Both?" his mother asked.

"Yes." Kate grinned. "We're having twins."

Mom shouted, "Twins?"

Kate and Alex smiled at each other and nodded.

"Twins. Double the blessings." His mom raised her glass. "To their health and happiness."

Everyone raised their glasses and repeated the toast.

And for Michael it wasn't so bad drinking sparkling apple juice when it was such great news.

Then his mom and dad hugged his sister.

He leaned into Liz. "Kate's taken the focus away from us."

"I'm glad I was here." A tear slipped from her eye. "Kate and Alex are having twins. That's amazing."

"You might get that promotion you want a lot faster than you ever expected."

A thunderstorm formed in her eyes. "That's not why I'm happy."

He kissed her forehead. "I know."

They joined the rest of the family to congratulate the couple.

"This is a fantastic day." His mom had her hands clasped in front of her chest. "I wish we had more than steak and potatoes to serve. This calls for something fancier."

"I have a new way to cook potatoes on the grill," Michael said.

"Don't you dare," Liz warned.

But his mother wasn't listening. She crouched next to Kate's chair with stars in her eyes.

Timothy leaned in. "With this news and the fact you're

dating again, the pressure is off Stephen and me for a long time."

Michael laced his fingers with Liz's. "Glad to be of service."

~

EVEN THOUGH LIZ was sweaty from the basketball game, Kate pulled her down for a quick hug.

"Congratulations on having twins." Liz sat on the end of the lounge chair.

"Thanks, I think." Kate touched her stomach. "Just so they stick in there for a while."

"I hope they do. And thanks for calling fouls on all your family," Liz added.

Kate's blatant favoritism had helped Liz's team win.

Kate grinned. "Now that was my pleasure. They're cheap players."

"I heard a rumor you're the worst," Liz said.

Kate laughed, then glanced to where her brothers stood talking.

"I'm really happy you and Michael are dating. He's ... lighter. You're good for him."

"I was worried you would think the worst of me," Liz confessed.

"I don't understand."

"That you would think I was dating him to move up at MacBain."

Kate actually laughed. "Why would you pick the most difficult, grumpy brother to climb the ladder? No. I've seen the sparks before."

"That's what your mother said." It was embarrassing to think she was so transparent.

"And thank you for all the work on the forecasting."

Liz grinned. "It was a lot of work."

"I'll bet. I've looked through everything." Kate frowned. "Why is there a proposal for a restoration division?"

"Michael's idea."

When Kate still looked puzzled, Liz explained, "He loves restorations. It's … his eyes light up when he talks about old homes. Especially the Prairie School style."

"He does?" Kate glanced at Michael. "He's never said anything."

"Talk to him about it sometime."

"I never knew."

That was on Michael for never speaking up.

"Take care of yourself and those babies," Liz said. "I can't wait until you're back in the office."

Liz went over to thank Michael's parents. And then there was a chorus of goodbyes as they headed out.

"So, was all your worry worth it?" Michael asked.

"Your family was lovely. I should have known." She tugged at the neck of her T-shirt. "Your family's reputation and integrity were a big part of the reason I'd applied for the job with Kate."

"That's nice to hear." He set his hand on the small of her back. And his warmth was comforting.

Michael held her door and she slid into the car.

As he started the engine, she asked, "How was being around your family and the wine and beer?"

She didn't want to bring him down, but she was concerned.

"It doesn't bother me." He sat quietly for a few minutes. "I wasn't drinking for drinking's sake. I drank because when I would hit a certain … level … Sarah would talk to me."

"Oh." Her breath caught in her chest. This was about Sarah. "That's …"

Silence filled the car.

"I know," he finally said. "Crazy. Maybe I was a little crazy. I swear she would talk to me. But it took a lot of alcohol."

"Have you ever told anyone?" He couldn't have only shared this with her.

"No." He pulled his hand away and adjusted the rearview mirror.

She folded her hands in her lap. "Do you think you should tell your family at least?"

"Nope."

"Your sponsor?"

"Give it a rest, Liz."

She stiffened. Her phone buzzed in her purse. Jordan. At least that would keep her from having to stare at Michael's clenched jaw.

R you coming home?

Soon, she texted back.

Were you paid?

"Shit."

"What's wrong?" Michael asked.

Damn, she hadn't meant to say that aloud. "My brother."

"What's he want?"

"I assume money."

"Money, but ..." Michael didn't finish his sentence.

"He always wants money," she said bitterly. "He promised me he wouldn't gamble."

"He ... gambles?" His fingers squeezed the steering wheel.

"It's why I worry about ..." She looked at him. "He's caused so many problems for our family."

Michael pulled into the parking lot of a coffee shop. "I'm sorry."

"It's not your problem." Still, it was nice that Michel was sympathetic.

"No. I screwed up." He put the car in park. "I believed your brother."

"What are you talking about?"

He turned to her. "You know when he was in the office, dropping off my dad's SUV?"

"Yes?" She dreaded what Michael would tell her.

"He stopped in. Said he was worried about you. How you took care of the family. You were always sending money to your parents. You were always broke."

She knew where this was going. "He hit you up for money?"

He nodded.

"How much?" She could barely get the words out over the lump in her throat.

He waved off her question.

"Tell me. How much did you give him?"

"He said your parents needed ten thousand for their next payment."

She covered her face. There wasn't any way she could pay Michael back. "Ten thousand. I wish that was all my parents owed. Because of my brother."

"I didn't give him the whole amount."

"How much?"

"Five."

"Five hundred?" she asked.

"Thousand."

She rubbed the headache forming behind her eyes. "I'll figure out how to pay you back."

He shook his head. "I should have talked to you. I shouldn't have believed him when he wanted to keep this from you."

"Yes. You should have." Her stomach churned. "How could you lend him that much money without talking to me?"

"Because I wanted to help you out. He said you were sending everything you could to your parents."

"I am." She wrapped her arms around her waist. "Now I have to pay you back too. Because he won't."

"I don't want your money."

Her shock was disappearing. Anger was taking over. "How could you do something so stupid?"

"I was trying to help you."

"In treatment they called this enabling, right?"

He gave a sharp nod.

And she couldn't help that he was getting mad too.

"That's what you did. Enabled a gambler." She pressed her temples. "I need to find out what he's done with the money."

"I'll take you to your apartment."

She shook her head, her ponytail whipping across her face. "Just take me to my car. I'll talk to my brother."

"Liz."

"This is my problem. Not yours."

He'd already made a difficult situation … impossible.

MICHAEL WATCHED LIZ DRIVE OFF. She hadn't even kissed him.

Hell, he'd been trying to help her. Why was he the bad guy?

But he couldn't let Liz confront her brother alone. As much as she didn't want him around, he'd caused this.

Michael got back in his car and drove to her apartment.

If he were honest about the loan, he'd wanted to play hero for Liz. There had been so few opportunities in his life to play that role.

He hadn't saved Sarah. As much as he'd tried. He could only help her eat or massage oil in her dry cracked skin after her radiation treatments. But he couldn't save her. Hell, when she'd ended up in a wheelchair, she didn't want to be pushed. She wanted an electric one so she could be independent.

Liz and Sarah were a lot alike that way.

At her apartment, he circled the block looking for a parking spot.

Since there wasn't a security system to keep him out, he walked in. Liz probably wouldn't have let him in. He took the steps two at a time. When he hit the second-floor landing, he heard the argument between Liz and her brother. He hesitated. She'd been clear she didn't want him around.

Fuck it. He was here. He'd created this problem.

He knocked on the door.

Liz pulled it open and shook her head. "What?"

He would ignore her tone. "I'm here to help."

"This is a family matter."

"When I lent your brother money, it became my matter." He stepped into the apartment. "Besides, I heard your argument down on the second floor."

She dropped her head against the door.

Jordan stood in the middle of the living room, his arms crossed over his chest. "You told her about the loan."

"Is that a problem?"

"She's all freaked out about it."

"Where's the money, Jordan?" Liz asked. "The money you got from Michael. The man I … was dating?"

What did she mean *was*?

"I … I sent it to Mom and Dad."

"Let's see if they have it yet." She pulled out her phone and made a big deal of scrolling through her contacts. As she pressed *Call*, Jordan snatched her phone out of her hand and hit *End*.

"Stop," he said. "They don't have it yet."

"Show me your bank balance, Jordan." Liz took her phone back and tucked it in her pocket.

"It's gone." Jordan thrust his fingers into his hair.

Liz's legs just let go. Michael caught her before she hit the floor. Guiding her to an armchair, he stood over her, glaring at her brother.

"You've been gambling." Liz's voice shook.

"I had to. I had to get a stake to pay back what I owe."

"Mom and Dad already paid back your debt."

Jordan pressed his lips together, like he was trying to hold back from saying something.

"Do you owe more than what your parents took on as debt?" Michael asked.

"This doesn't concern you," Jordan snapped.

"It does when you conned me into loaning you my money and convinced me not to tell Liz," Michael shot back.

"Where's the money?" Liz asked.

"I'll get it back. My luck will change." Jordan pounded his fist into his hand.

Liz shook her head. "How can you say that? Did you lose all the money Michael lent you? All f-five thousand dollars?" She choked on the amount.

Jordan shifted his feet. "There's some left."

"How much?" Michael didn't think Liz could talk through the tears streaming down her face. He squeezed her shoulder.

She shrugged off his hand.

Jordan crumpled onto the love seat, his head in his hands. "Maybe five hundred."

"Does that include your paycheck?" Liz asked.

Jordan raised one shoulder and let it drop back. "Yeah."

"You promised Mom and Dad. You promised me you were done."

"I ... Rudy ... I owe him."

Michael had no idea who Rudy was, but this didn't sound good.

"You're dealing with Rudy again?" Liz got up and stood

over her brother with her hands on her hips. If she could, Michael had no doubt she'd be shooting fire out of her eyes. "How much do you owe?"

At least she'd stopped crying.

Jordan mumbled something.

"What?" Liz demanded.

"Twelve."

Liz gasped. "Thousand?"

Jordan nodded. "You have to help me."

"Mom and Dad helped you before. I've helped you." Liz paced the small room, ending in front of her brother. "This is the real reason you came here. You're hiding from Rudy."

Michael couldn't figure out how to help Liz or her brother. He was helpless.

Was this how his sister and brothers had felt when he was drinking?

"I need more money to get clear." Jordan put his hands together and turned to Michael. "If you could give me the other five grand, I'll make everything back."

"Do you think I'm an idiot?" Michael asked.

Liz shot him a look that said she thought he was.

"Fool me once, Jordan," Michael said. "I'm not going behind your sister's back again."

Tears filled Liz's eyes. She mouthed, "Thank you."

Michael took a deep breath. "I know what it's like to be powerless against an addiction. You need help, man."

"You're up in the ivory tower with all the money you want." Jordan shook his head. "You have no idea what I'm going through."

"You're wrong," Liz said. "Michael knows more than anyone."

Jordan glared at him. "He and his family have everything."

"And he and his family have worked hard for what they have."

Liz was defending him.

236

He did have a lot. Everything but Sarah. All his connections and family money hadn't saved her.

"You're … selfish." Liz pointed at her brother. "We keep rescuing you, and you keep making the same mistake over and over."

"I …"

When he'd been drinking, Michael had used all the same excuses. Just one more, for Sarah. Always for Sarah.

But news flash. It hadn't been for Sarah. It had been because the pain had been too much. The fact that he couldn't save the person he loved.

He hadn't saved Sarah.

But maybe he could help Jordan. "MacBain has great mental health benefits. You need to talk to HR. You need help."

Liz nodded. "Thank you."

"I can't do that. Rudy wants his money—soon."

The guy looked afraid. Maybe he'd hit rock bottom.

"How soon?" Liz asked.

"Next weekend." Jordan scrubbed a hand across his face. "I have to bring it to him."

Now it was Michael who was pacing. "What will happen when you don't have the money?"

"Rudy had him beaten up the last time he didn't pay up." Liz let out a shaky breath. "He was in the hospital for a week. In a cast for six with a broken arm. That's when my parents paid his last debt."

Jordan chewed on his lip. "I'm trying to make things right."

"Working to earn the money will make things right. Not risking the money to double it, trying to take the easy way out." Liz sank into the chair again. "You always take the easy route, and that makes things harder for everyone who loves you."

"What can I do?"" Michael asked.

Jordan's eyes lit up. "Can you—"

Michael held up his hand. "I'm not lending you money."

"Fuck." Jordan closed his eyes. "Rudy's going to kill me."

"You have to decide you'll stop gambling." Pain filled Liz's voice. "I'm not letting Mom or Dad take another mortgage out on the farm to help you out of this. You'll have ask Rudy for more time. And earn your money by working."

"It'll take forever." Jordan rubbed his arm and actually looked afraid.

Michael wondered if that was the arm that had been broken. He steeled himself to not feel sorry for the guy and not offer to clear his debts.

"There are Gamblers Anonymous programs, right?" Michael asked.

Liz nodded. "But he lied about going to those."

"I'll have HR get in touch with you about programs," Michael said. "But, man, you have to take the first step. And you have to mean it."

"This was your last chance, Jordan," Liz said. "You screw up again and you're out of here."

Michael wondered if by loaning money to Jordan, he'd screwed up and used his only chance with her.

LIZ HATED Michael witnessing her brother's weaknesses. This had been the family's secret for so long she wasn't used to talking about it with anyone.

Michael stepped outside her apartment door. "I'll check with HR unless you want to."

"Should Jordan do it?" She shivered, even though it was steamy in the hallway.

"I'll have them send the information to Jordan," Michael said. "Then it's up to him to take the next step."

She nodded, exhausted.

Michael framed her face with his hands. "Are we okay?"

She stepped back and his hands slipped away. "I can't think past what Jordan did."

He tried to hug her, but she held up her hands. "I can't do this Michael."

"Liz, please."

"I can't think." She held her head. "Just go home."

"I don't want to lose you," he said. "I think I'm—"

She shook her head. "Don't. Don't say any more."

"Don't tell you the truth?"

"I can't deal with all of this. I need to call my parents." Then think about what happened next. "I need to concentrate on my family. Rudy beat him up before. What will he do now?"

Michael nodded slowly. "I'm sorry I screwed up with your brother, but don't give up on us. Let me help."

"It's not your problem." She couldn't rely on him. "I ... I don't trust you, Michael."

"Liz, please." He waited.

"You gave money to my brother without talking to me." She shook her head. "I can't be with someone I don't trust."

"Give me a chance. Please."

She couldn't talk over the lump in her throat.

He turned and walked down the stairs.

Pain ripped through her. She hurried into the apartment and ran to her bedroom before collapsing on her bed.

She was an idiot. She'd fallen in love with Michael.

FIFTEEN

MICHAEL GAVE UP ON SLEEP. HE BREWED COFFEE, NOT THAT IT would be good for his churning stomach.

He had things to do today.

It was the second anniversary of Sarah's death.

He should hit the building's gym, but he didn't have the energy. Instead he took his coffee out to the balcony and leaned on the half wall, staring at the people already stirring even though the sun was just coming up.

Two years. It seemed like a lifetime and also a blink of the eye. He couldn't remember her scent. Or the feel of her skin. He was mixing up Sarah and Liz.

After Sarah's funeral, he'd visited her grave every day. He would talk to her, tell her how much she was missed, and then go buy a bottle.

Eventually he just bought the bottle, knowing he could get closer to Sarah the more he drank.

Even now he could taste the bite of whiskey.

When it was time he pulled on clothes, not paying attention to what he found in his closet. Then he drove to the florist.

"Welcome," the owner said. "It's been a while since you've been here."

"I know."

"Do you want your usual?" she asked.

"Please."

He waited as the owner pulled together the bouquet of peach roses and pale alstroemeria. Sarah's bridal bouquet flowers. The wedding they'd never had.

After paying he drove to the cemetery and followed the familiar drive to where she rested. He parked behind an SUV.

Climbing the hill, he shook his head. He should have waited a little longer.

"Mrs. Dolman," he said to Sarah's mother. She sat at the foot of Sarah's grave.

"Michael."

He placed his flowers at the base of the granite headstone. Resting his hand on the stone, he wished there was some warmth, some indication that Sarah's spirit was still here.

It was cold.

"You don't come around much anymore," Mrs. Dolman said.

"Not as much."

"I'm here every day." Her fingers curled into fists.

"I know. I share your sorrow."

"Do you?" She stood and glared at him. "It feels like you've forgotten how much she loved you. How she had your future planned out."

"I haven't forgotten anything. I loved her."

"You have forgotten her! You're using the past tense."

"I …" Had he? "I will always love her."

But the love had dimmed as he'd fallen for Liz. Did he have to set aside his love for Sarah to be with Liz? Not that Liz wanted to be with him. He'd fucked that up.

"Who will remember her after I'm gone?" Mrs. Dolman

swiped at the tears on her face. "Even her father can't bring himself to visit."

"I'll always remember her."

Their goodbyes were uncomfortable. He stayed for a few moments but couldn't think of anything to say to Sarah. He didn't think she would want to know about Liz. And she'd always seen MacBain as a rival.

Even though Sarah had tried to persuade him to work with her parents, his place was in the family business. That was work. Sarah had been his everything.

Back in his car he hung his head. He was losing her.

He drove out of the cemetery, his thoughts spinning. Sarah had been his anchor for so many years.

He turned into the parking lot and stopped his car.

Shit. He'd driven to the liquor store he used to come to after visiting Sarah.

If there was any day he could drink it was on the anniversary of Sarah's death. He could have one drink to dull this pain.

First he'd lost Sarah and now Liz.

He'd tried to talk to Liz last night. She didn't answer his call or texts.

He'd lost her too.

Inside, his eyes locked on the whiskey display. He'd bought plenty of bottles here. He could handle one drink. Right?

There was one way to find out.

He stood in front of the whiskey section. He could try it. He could test this new theory.

Just one drink and no more.

He picked a bottle of fifteen-year-old Redbreast and headed to the checkout counter.

One drink.

In the car, each turn was on autopilot. Each signal something to wait through. Sometimes he wondered if his whole life had been spent waiting. Waiting for answers. Waiting for results. Waiting to get home so he could use the whiskey to numb the pain and memories that flooded through him.

That was all he needed, the numbness of one drink.

He waited for the parking garage doors to open. Waited for the elevator. And then waited as he unlocked the door. Tossing the keys into the small bowl his mother had bought him, he pulled off the brown bag and cracked the seal on the bottle.

A glass. He couldn't drink from the bottle. He needed a glass. And ice.

He dug into his freezer, searching for his whiskey stones. Wouldn't want to dilute the drink.

But they were missing. He tossed in one stingy ice cube and poured his drink.

"To you, Sarah." He sniffed and let the sharp aroma fill his nose. The ice cube rattled as he swirled the glass. Setting the edge of the glass to his lips, he waited. Then let the liquor fill his mouth. It burned. It soothed. It mellowed as it numbed his tongue.

Swallowing, he closed his eyes. The sting in his throat a reminder of all he'd tried to block out. His pain. Sarah's death. His regret that he hadn't forced her to go to the doctor sooner. That he hadn't gone with her and insisted she get an MRI. They might have caught the tumor earlier. Might have saved her life.

Now he'd screwed up with Liz.

He never got it right.

He took another sip. Swallowed. Let the rush relax his muscles. The tension in his shoulders eased.

He topped off his glass. He was fine. He could stop after this drink.

Then he took the glass into his living room, grabbing the bottle as he left.

LIZ FOUND out Michael had taken the day off.

She'd ignored his call and texts last nights. Now he wasn't answering hers. Maybe she could catch him at home. She'd overreacted yesterday. They needed to talk.

The key he'd given her burned in her hand. She should give it back.

She headed for the security door.

There was no need to use the key to get into the building. Someone held the door for her.

If Michael wasn't here, she would head home. Not that she wanted to face Jordan. All she and her brother did was fight.

She knocked, not loudly, because if he was asleep she didn't want to wake him. He'd looked tired last night. After waiting, she unlocked the door.

It was quiet. His keys were in the entry table bowl.

She kicked off her shoes and dropped her purse on the table. Maybe she shouldn't be here.

But she was here now. She headed for the hallway to the bedroom. Instead she found him in the living room.

"Michael." Her jaw dropped.

He was sprawled on the sofa. Asleep.

Or passed out.

A glass sat on the coffee table. But it was the half empty whiskey bottle sitting next to it that had her knees giving out.

She dropped into the nearest chair and covered her face with her hands.

She held back a sob.

"Sarah?" Michael muttered. "Talk to me."

She stared at him for a moment, shaking her head. Her eyes were dry. She pushed out of the chair and headed into the kitchen. Finding a piece of paper and a pen, she wrote –

We're through

And left the key on the note.

MICHAEL ROLLED OVER. And fell on the floor. "Damn it."

He clambered to his feet.

The evidence was there. The whiskey bottle. The drool on the pillow. The massive headache pounding behind his eyes. His upset stomach.

And this time when he'd achieved the edge of drunkenness, he hadn't found Sarah. She was gone.

He took the bottle into the kitchen and went straight to the sink. There he dumped the remains. Obviously he couldn't have *just one.* He wasn't that strong.

As he dumped the empty into the recycling bin, he spotted a note on the counter. With a key.

Only his family had keys. And Liz.

"Shit."

He spun the note around, but he could read it. Liz's handwriting. *We're through.*

She must have come in yesterday. And found him.

He dug his phone out of his pocket and went to wake it up. No juice.

After setting it in the charger, he waited. He had to talk to her.

Finally there was enough battery to open the phone. He found her number and put it on speaker, so he could keep charging the phone.

It rang once, then a second time. Then it went to voice mail.

"Liz, I'm sorry. That won't ever happen again. It was … I can explain. Call me. Please. I … I …"

He looked down at his crumpled clothes, his hands shaking. "Call me."

He stared at the phone, hoping it would ring. That she would forgive him. And everything would be all right.

He went to get aspirin from the cabinet and took four with a couple of glasses of water.

He made another call. This time to his sponsor. "I screwed up."

≈

MICHAEL HADN'T SHOWN up at work on Tuesday. Liz tried not to look for him, but it was obvious he wasn't in because his office was dark.

Maybe he was back in treatment.

She checked her notes on the terms the tenant requested and input them into the lease spreadsheet. The tenant was asking for additional concessions, but if she adjusted the final two years lease amounts, they would still achieve their required ROI.

She should be clearing this with Michael, but he wasn't here.

Was he still drunk? Had he finished the bottle? Maybe she should tell one of his brothers or his parents.

She had enough on her plate without adding an alcoholic.

Maybe she needed to look for another job. That was the only way she could survive what she felt for Michael.

She tapped her fingers.

Even though she didn't want to bother Kate, her boss had said she was bored. Liz created a quick email explaining her proposed lease terms and sent it along with the ROI information.

For the rest of the day she argued with herself about whether she should talk to a MacBain about Michael. And never did.

~

MICHAEL WAS WIRED. Too little sleep. Too much coffee. But by Wednesday morning he was ready to face work, and ready to admit to his parents he'd been stupid.

He'd spent most of Tuesday with his sponsor and then had attended a meeting at night. Day one on his sobriety path. Again. It was day two and he would not drink today. Maybe this third time would be the charm.

He'd gone through all the excuses. The anniversary of Sarah's death, her mother's accusations and him driving to the liquor store on automatic pilot.

And losing Liz.

But he was the one who'd walked in the liquor store door. He was the one who'd bought the bottle and taken that first drink. He'd been the fool to think he could only have one.

He'd truly lost Liz. He would talk to her. See if by apologizing they could get back to where they had been.

He wanted her in his life. She made things better. He was a happier man when she was around. As much as he'd loved Sarah, she wasn't here. Memories of her weren't enough for the rest of his life.

Liz inspired him to want more from life. Because of her, he wanted more than to just survive each day. He wanted to restore older homes *and* restore their relationship.

He wanted, no needed, her in his life.

His assistant corralled him as he walked in his office.

"Glad to see you back." She handed him two folders. "Accounting needs these checks signed. And Timothy needs you to review this contract by ten."

So much for checking in with Liz.

~

‹

LIZ KNEW Michael was in the building, but she'd avoided him all morning. There had been one close call. She'd gone to the break room for a cup of tea and ended up ducking into the bathroom after hearing his footsteps. Weird that she could pick them out from all the people in the building.

"Liz."

She didn't want to look up but she did. Michael stood in her cubicle doorway.

"Michael."

He sat in her visitor chair.

Too bad she hadn't thought to get rid of the damn thing.

"I'm sorry. That won't happen again."

"Good for you." She looked back at her computer. "I'm sure your family will be happy."

She twisted her fingers together, then hid them in her lap.

"It was a mistake."

"You forget, I've heard these lines before. My brother is always sorry. Always done with gambling."

Michael shoved his fingers through his hair. "I'm not your brother."

"Maybe I'm drawn to vulnerable men." She traced a pattern on her desktop. "But I can't do it anymore. I don't believe you can stop drinking."

"I can!"

"You called me Sarah."

He shoved back in the chair. "I what?"

"You called me Sarah."

"It was the anniversary of her death," he said quietly.

"I'm sorry." She picked up her pen and turned the page in her planner, not looking at him. "You can't use her death as an excuse to drink."

Still sitting, he leaned over her desk. "I spent yesterday with my sponsor and then went to a meeting last night. I'm living my program. I slipped. Once."

"You drank at O'Dair's."

"Twice. But I'm done."

"I'm glad you're getting the help you need." And it was breaking her heart.

"I don't want to lose you." He slowly stood and turned to leave. At the door he said over his shoulder. "I want to be with you."

How she wished that was true. "Don't lie to yourself. You want to be with Sarah."

SIXTEEN

On Wednesday Jordan left for work early, just to escape Liz. He was heading out to the crane they'd wanted him to fix on site. What a relief.

His sister had watched him like a hawk last night. There hadn't been any way to get to the poker game, not that he had enough of a stake to make it worthwhile.

He supposed he could head to one of the casinos and play the slots, build up his cash. Maybe he would do that after work.

He'd find out which casino was the closest. But Liz couldn't know. She would kick him out of her apartment.

He was still angry at Michael. He needed the other five grand. If he could ride one lucky streak he could dig himself out of the hole he was in.

He headed to the Woodbury construction site. It was so far east he swore he almost crossed into Wisconsin. It was nice to be out of the shop and nice that his supervisor had assigned this one to him. At the gate, he waited for the foreman to let him in. A man came out of the construction trailer and waved.

"Carlson?"

"That's me."

"I'm Trent. Glad to see you."

Once the gate opened, he drove as close as he could get to the mobile crane.

He may resent the fact that Liz had finished college, but he'd been happier in technical college versus listening to professors drone on and on. He liked working with his hands and he was good. The more computerized the equipment became, the more fun it was to figure out the problems.

This crane was the oldest one he'd seen on the MacBain properties. Even from the ground, he could see the rust.

Trent walked up as Jordan opened his truck door. "Sure hope you can get us back on line soon. We'll have a small crew here today, but I need my crane."

"This one's pretty old."

"The company pulled it out of retirement." Trent handed Jordan a key. "If you can nurse it back to health, we could get this structure up."

"Tell me the symptoms."

"It's off balance. We dropped a load and almost had a couple of injuries."

"Okay. Anything else?"

"We had a broken chain link and thought that was the problem, but it's still not working."

"I'll see what I can do. Do you have the maintenance records?"

The foreman handed him a worn book.

Damn, the crane was fifteen years old. Too bad there weren't any parts he could sell for cash, but the thing was too old.

He stood under the massive crane. Time to work his magic.

～

MICHAEL KNOCKED on her cubicle doorway. "How are you?"

She'd be better if he would leave her alone. "I'm good."

He looked around for her visitor's chair.

It was gone. After his last visit, she'd taken it to an empty cubical.

He ended up leaning against the doorframe. "I talked to Ed in HR. I thought maybe Jordan would accept help a little easier if it's from another man. Sorry I didn't get to it until today."

"That was thoughtful of you." Her brother's weakness embarrassed her.

"Ed will contact Jordan."

"And this is all confidential?"

"Of course. I thought maybe Jordan's supervisor should know, but Ed said no. It's just me, you, Ed and Jordan. And now I'm out of it."

"Thank you." They stared at each other.

"I meant what I said." He walked to her desk and leaned on his hands. "I won't drink again."

"Good for you."

"Can you do lunch today?" he asked.

"I have a meeting with a prospective tenant for Water's Edge."

"Dinner?" he asked.

"No."

"What do I have to do to convince you I'm a good bet?" he asked.

"I'm sorry." Her heart cracked. "There isn't anything."

JORDAN STEADILY CHECKED ALL the parts of the crane. He did basic maintenance as he worked. He re-lubricated the wire ropes as he rewound them. It would have been too easy to find the problem there. The boom on the crane had been fine too. The chain looked okay now.

So what was wrong?

He changed the filters. They were a little clogged but not enough to create the problems they'd had.

"Carlson," Trent called to him.

Jordan stuck his head out of the engine. "What's up?"

"I need to pull this crew and head to another building. Timothy needs us for some work."

"Okay."

"I'll leave the gate unlocked. If I'm not back when you leave, put the padlock back on."

Jordan saluted. "Will do."

He sat back and thought through what else he could check. He'd already replaced some rusted bolts.

"You're a hard man to find, Carlson."

Fuck.

Standing on the ground was Rudy and his muscle, Kalen. *How the hell did he find me here?*

Jordan, from his spot on the engine, looked down to see if Trent was still in the parking lot, but he was out of luck.

"Hey, Rudy. What are you doing here?" *Shit. Shit. Shit.* Jordan stayed on the crane. No way was he climbing down.

"Since you needed to work last weekend, I thought I would come get my money." Rudy set his hand on the tread.

Boy, wouldn't Jordan like to turn on the tread and scare the shit out of Rudy.

"My girl is shopping at the Mall of America. She sure loves that place," Rudy added.

"Glad she could get some shopping in."

"Where's my money, Carlson?"

"I don't have it on me. Do you think I'm crazy?"

"No. I don't think you're crazy. I think you're a liar."

"What?" If Jordan could get his phone out, maybe he could call someone—anyone. Even the police. They probably wouldn't help him, but sirens might make Rudy run. "You're calling me a liar?"

"I know you lost money this weekend. Six thousand? Is that what you lost?"

Damn it. Rudy must have had someone in one of the games. "My luck was running cold."

Kalen pointed a crowbar at him.

"My business shouldn't be based on your luck, should it?" Rudy climbed on the tread.

Jordan could jump over the side of the crane and run. Somehow get away. "I'm not trying to stiff you."

"No? But I don't have my money."

Jordan stumbled backwards as Rudy climbed higher.

"Come on down from there. We gotta talk."

Jordan tossed the wrench he'd been holding at Rudy. Rudy stumbled, slipping to the ground.

Jordan hurdled over the opposite side of the crane and ran. There wasn't much cover, but the crane was a great obstacle.

He had to get to his truck.

Rudy swore.

Jordan heard Kalen's footsteps getting closer. He just had to get in and start his truck. Get away.

He threw open the door and vaulted face-first into the seat. The crowbar caught him behind his right knee. The pain didn't register for a moment, then it streaked through his leg. He fell onto the seat, but not for long.

He was yanked out of his truck and hit the ground. Rocks cut his face as Kalen dragged him away from his truck. He kicked, tried to get free. But his right leg wouldn't work.

Snatching a handful of dirt and stones, he rolled, throwing them in Kalen's face.

That got him a kick in his chest. Something snapped inside. Pain ricocheted from his chest to his leg and back again.

"You shouldn't have run." Rudy hovered over him. "You shouldn't have lost the money you were going to pay me. I don't want to do it, but I gotta teach you a lesson. Again."

Rudy kicked him. Jordan got his arms around his head before Rudy's boot connected, but it didn't do much good.

He curled in a ball as punches and kicks tore him apart. He wasn't going to survive this beat down. Everything hurt. Blood gushed from cuts. He couldn't move.

And he didn't care.

Darkness finally blanketed the agony.

MICHAEL ANSWERED HIS PHONE. "What's up Timothy?"

"There was a problem at the Woodbury project."

"Something I need to call the insurance company on?" That was usually why Timothy would call him.

"Maybe, I don't know. It was Jordan Carlson. At least we think it is. He's hurt. Bad. Trent found him."

Michael was already moving. "What was he doing out there?"

"Working on the crane. That old one."

"Did it fall on him?"

"No. It looks like he was beaten up."

Shit. "Where is he now?"

"I got here as the ambulance was leaving." Timothy words rushed together. "There was so much blood. Man. I don't know how he'll survive this."

"Which hospital?" He needed to get Liz.

"Regions. I'll meet you there."

Regions. It was in Saint Paul. Not too far away. And it was a Level 1 trauma hospital. One of the best.

"Liz," he called as he came around the corner.

She wasn't at her desk.

He checked the time. Two in the afternoon. Was she still with the potential tenant?

Michael ran to the receptionist. "Jenny, is Liz back from her outside meeting?"

"I haven't seen her, but I just got back."

He pulled out his phone and called.

"Hi," Liz said.

The reception sucked, everything crackled. "Where are you?" he asked.

"I can barely hear you. I'm … into … parking ramp."

"Hang on. Stay where you are." He turned to Jenny. "Let Becca know I left. And Liz won't be back. It's an emergency."

He ran to the elevator and punched the button.

"What level are you parked on?" He could drive her car. Then he wouldn't have to go to his condo and get his own.

"What?" Liz asked.

But he was in the elevator. No service.

Once he was in the lobby, he hurried to the parking staircase, asking again. "What level are you parked on."

"Three. —wrong?"

He burst through the security door and headed down. Three. He sure hoped he'd heard her correctly.

As he ran out the door, he called, "Liz!"

His voice echoed in the concrete cavern.

"Liz!"

He scanned the floor, not sure if he should head up or down. But she moved into the aisle and waved.

He ran. "I'm driving your car."

"Why? What's wrong?"

He guided her to the passenger seat. "I'll tell you as we drive."

As he slid into the car, she said, "You're scaring me."

He searched for the buttons to move the seat back and realized it was manual. "It's Jordan."

"What?" She pressed her fingers to her mouth.

"Timothy called. The foreman found him at the Woodbury project. They think he was beaten up."

"Not again." Liz clutched her hands around her stomach and rocked.

"I know where they're taking him. He's already in the ambulance."

He tapped his parking card on the reader and drummed his fingers on the steering wheel as the arm slowly rose.

"This is my fault," she moaned. "I should have found a way to get him the money."

"We don't know what happened yet. Don't jump to conclusions."

Michael turned onto the street and headed east. He needed to get on I-94. The hospital was right off the interstate. "I shouldn't have given him the money. I should have wired it to wherever it needed to go."

"I should have watched him closer. Instead I …"

He filled in the blank. "You were with me."

They waited through each signal until he merged onto the freeway. He punched the fan for the air conditioning, but it just blew hot air at them.

"It doesn't work. Just like my life."

"Hang in there." He could sweat and he was. "Air conditioning doesn't matter right now. Your brother does."

"Where are we going?" she asked.

"Regions. It's a great trauma center. Downtown Saint Paul." He'd rushed Sarah there once.

"Trauma. That's not good." She bit her lip. "Was he conscious?"

"I don't know. Timothy saw him briefly as they loaded him into the ambulance."

257

"My parents. I should call my parents."

He put a hand on her arm. "Why don't we see what's what before you do?"

"My parents will have a long drive. I should …"

"Wait."

He found the exit and followed the hospital emergency signs. "I'll drop you off and find parking."

She caught his hand. "I don't want to be alone."

At least that was something.

He found a parking spot and they ran to the emergency entrance.

The door slid open, and the antiseptic smell of a hospital took him back to all of Sarah's ER and hospital stays.

The memories crashed through him. They'd had such a nice day exploring Stillwater. Then she'd started throwing up blood. He'd rushed her here. Another time he'd followed the ambulance to a different hospital after she'd passed out.

"I'm looking for Jordan Carlson. He came in by ambulance." Liz clutched Michael's hand, bringing him back to the immediate crisis.

The woman typed on her computer. "Okay. Will you both be waiting?"

They nodded.

"Driver's licenses."

They handed them over. The receptionist scanned them, then typed some more. A printer spit out name tags.

"Wear these. Someone will call you."

They headed to the waiting room. The chairs were the same uncomfortable plastic molded things.

There were only a few people waiting. And one person held a bloody towel around his hand.

He hated the waiting. Too many memories. "Do you want something to drink?"

"No."

He couldn't sit still. He paced.

Liz sat curled up with her thoughts.

He wanted to tell her Jordan would be all right. But he knew better than anyone that things didn't always work out. Even when you loved someone with all your heart.

Timothy arrived and stopped at the receptionist, pointing to where he and Liz waited. Michael walked over. "Anything new?"

"Trent is talking to the police. He feels awful. I pulled the crew and since Jordan was still working, he left the gate unlocked. This happened on our property."

The receptionist handed Timothy his license and a name tag.

Timothy asked, "Do you know anything?"

"Not yet."

They joined Liz in the waiting area. Timothy gave her a hug.

Michael sat next to her, and his brother sat across from them. He took her hand and asked, "How are you holding up?"

"Not good. I should call my parents. This is taking too long."

"How far away are they?" Timothy asked.

"About four, four and half hours."

Timothy looked at him. "I'll call Blake and see if he's able to pick them up."

"Good idea." He should have thought of that. Being in the hospital was messing with his ability to think. And damn, he wanted a drink. He'd lied to himself all through treatment, thinking he wasn't really an alcoholic. That he'd only gotten drunk for Sarah. Lies.

He was an alcoholic.

Liz dug in her bag but stopped when a man called, "The Carlson family?"

"Here." Liz rushed to where the man stood in the doorway. Michael and his brother followed.

"How is he?" Liz asked. "How's Jordan?"

"He's … stable."

Michael didn't like the guy's hesitancy.

"Can I see him?" Liz asked.

"He's in radiology right now. I can let two of you back to wait in his room."

Timothy stepped back. "I'll call Blake and wait out here."

As the man led them back, he said, "I'm Greg."

The hallway didn't look familiar. But when it opened up to the rooms, Michael almost turned right to where Sarah's room had been.

Instead Greg led them left.

"Did he recover consciousness?" Michael asked.

"Not yet. That's probably good right now."

Liz gasped. "How bad is he?"

"That's what we're figuring out."

Nonanswers. Medical staff must learn that in their training. Greg led them to a room. The garbage can overflowed with bloody pads and large bandages. Was all that from Jordan?

"It will be a while. He's scheduled for a lot of pictures."

"Is there somewhere to get water?" Michael asked, staring at the garbage can.

"Just out the door and to the right." Greg must have seen him staring. He pulled out the garbage bag. "I'll get this out of here."

Liz turned into his shoulder, a small sob breaking free.

He hugged her. Let her cry. "He's where he needs to be. Trust that the doctors will do whatever needs doing."

It was lame. He couldn't reassure her that everything would be all right because they didn't know anything.

"I'll call my parents now."

"Tell them we're working on sending a plane for them," he said.

Michael texted Timothy. *Let me know what Blake says.*

As she found her phone, he headed out the door. This was too familiar. Too much. He pulled out money and bought two bottles of water. Then he leaned his head on the glass and breathed.

How long had Sarah been in this ER before being admitted? Hours? A day? His sense of time back then had been warped. They'd waited on her oncologist and additional tests. All the while she'd been throwing up until the medication they'd given her started working.

He brought the water back to the room.

"I'll let you know as soon as I have any information." Liz paused. "I love you too."

"Are you okay?" he asked, cracking the cap and handing her a bottle.

She shook her head. "My parents are in shock. I'm in shock."

"I'll go see what Timothy has found out." Because he couldn't stay in this room.

He headed to the waiting area. Déjà vu. He remembered the nightmare of moving between Sarah's room and the waiting room. Updating everyone and sending texts.

Timothy looked up from his phone. "Any news?"

"No. What do you know about the plane?"

"Blake can get to the Des Moines airport by five," Timothy said. "Let me send you the message of where they should meet him."

"Good. Liz talked to her parents. They know Jordan is in the hospital. We haven't seen him yet."

"Mom and Dad will pick his parents up at the airport. They're lending them one of their cars. They also booked a room at the closest hotel."

"Thanks for calling them."

"They were glad I did." Timothy patted his shoulder. "How are you holding up?"

Couldn't pull much over on his brother. "I'm here to help Liz."

"I'm still wishing I'd asked her out first. I like her."

"Too late." Although Liz had broken up with him.

Michael didn't want to go back to the room, but he did. The room seemed to have shrunk in the last fifteen minutes. Liz looked up. Her face was a study in fear.

"Can your parents get to the Des Moines airport by five?" he asked.

She checked her watch. "I'm sure they can."

"Okay, the pilot's name is Blake. I'll forward where they should meet him. My parents will pick them up at the airport. They've already booked a hotel and are lending them a car."

"What?" Liz asked.

He repeated what he'd said.

"They didn't have to do all that." She wiped at the tears on her face.

He pulled her out of her chair and hugged her. "He was hurt on our property. They would do this for any employee, but especially for your brother."

She sniffed. "I'm getting your shirt wet."

He reached over and pulled out a few tissues. They were rough but would do the job.

She mopped her face and sat.

He forwarded the message about Blake to her and heard Liz's phone ping.

She shared it with her parents, and then called. "Hi, Mom. I sent you a message on where to meet the pilot." Then she explained the next steps. "I love you. It's going to be … okay."

After she ended the call, she sat with her eyes closed.

He couldn't stand the waiting. The sitting. So he paced.

At one point Liz opened her eyes and watched him. Then her mouth dropped open. "Did you spend much time in emergency rooms with Sarah?"

He nodded. It was a jerky bob, like he couldn't quite control his muscles. "We were actually across the hall."

She stood and put her hand on his back, forcing him to stop moving. "You don't have to stay. I can handle this until my parents arrive."

"No." He blew out a breath. "I want to help you through this. It's ... there's so much ... waiting."

She rubbed his back. "If you need to take a walk, go."

Here she was comforting him during her own family crisis. She had such a big heart. No wonder he was falling in ...

He wasn't just falling in love with her. He loved her.

With Liz, there was comfort. Not the desperation to love, the panic he'd felt over Sarah.

Hugging her, he said, "What can I do for you?"

"Hold my hand. That's what I need."

"Always." He pulled the extra chair closer to hers. Lacing their fingers together, he sat.

LIZ COULD FEEL the tension in Michael's body just holding his hand. Every few minutes, his fingers flexed. His leg bounced up and down as if he were Timothy.

But he was here by her side. That counted.

She needed him. Maybe it wasn't fair because she'd broken up with him, but she didn't want to be alone.

Greg pushed through the door, guiding a bed into the room.

Both she and Michael stood, backing out of the way.

"Oh God." Bandages covered half of Jordan's face and chest. Dried blood was everywhere.

Michael put an arm around her, but even his face had gone pale.

"Don't panic," Greg said as he and another person moved IV bags and other equipment into place. "When I get a chance, I'll clean him up. But it was important to find out what was broken."

"You still don't know?" Liz whispered.

"They're reading the X-rays and MRIs now. They did an ultrasound too." Greg locked the bed in place.

"Did he wake up?" Michael asked.

"The tech said he moaned as he was being moved. They're sure he has broken ribs. But we'll figure out what else is damaged with all the pictures."

"Oh, Jordan." Liz moved closer, examined his hand for injury and then held it. "Mom and Dad are on their way."

Michael sat in the corner. Stress radiated off him in waves.

"Michael?"

His head jerked up. "What can I do for you? More water. Food?"

She shook her head. "You don't need to be here."

He hurried to her side and set his hands on her shoulders. "I can handle it."

"You don't have to."

"It's bringing back memories, but I'll be fine." He was battling demons for her. Just the thought he would do that broke her heart a little more.

"Thank you."

"Why don't I get you something to eat," he repeated. "You need to keep up your strength. Your parents won't be here for hours. I know a place that makes great sandwiches."

He should get out of the hospital. "That would be nice. Maybe turkey or chicken."

He let out a shaky breath. "I'll check with Timothy and see what he wants."

"Thank you."

He kissed the top of her head and headed out of the room almost at a run.

Her heart went out to him.

"Wake up so I can yell at you," she muttered, brushing back Jordan's blood-encrusted hair. "I love you."

MICHAEL RUSHED through the automatic doors and drank in the hot summer air. It was the first deep breath he'd drawn since they'd walked through the hospital doors.

Thank God he wasn't in the building anymore. The walls had begun to close in on him. He didn't want to fail Liz, but he was glad to be outside.

He got in Liz's car and headed to the store he remembered.

It didn't take long to go the short distance. Since the small parking lot was full, he circled the block, finally wedging the car into a spot. At least he'd escaped the hospital's antiseptic smell of illness.

He held the door as another man walked out with a bottle in his hands. Of Redbreast.

He'd been drinking back then. To wash away the inevitable. To help him sleep, though that hadn't worked. But drinking had numbed his brain. His overindulging hadn't begun until after she'd died.

Shit. He'd forgotten this was a liquor store and deli.

He ignored the alcohol displays and headed to the counter and ordered.

He kept his gaze locked on the food. He could do this.

But he hurried out of the store. He backed through the door and into the heat. It was as if the temperature had gone up ten degrees since he'd walked into the deli.

Using his arm, he wiped the sweat from his forehead. It

would be cooler in the hospital. That was the only thing he could say for the institution.

You couldn't tell what the weather was like outside once you were locked inside.

LIZ'S PHONE BUZZED. Her mother.

We're boarding the plane. Any news?

Liz typed: *Still unconscious. He has broken ribs, a broken nose and a fractured forearm. Probably a concussion.*

Liz debated whether to send this news via text, but it was the truth. She would want to know. Taking a breath, she hit Send.

She waited for a response. And waited. Maybe Mom had already shut her phone off. Then it pinged.

We'll be there soon.

Liz typed: *Luv U*

She headed out of the room and found Greg. "Is there any way I could clean up some of the blood? My parents are on their way, and I don't want them to see him like this."

"I'm releasing another patient, then I'll get that done. Give me five minutes."

"Thank you." Back in Jordan's room, she peered out the window at green grass and flowers. There wasn't a cloud in the sky.

It should be rainy and gloomy.

"Hey Jordan," she said. "Mom and Dad are on their way. Can you believe the MacBains are sending a plane for them? And Patty and Mac will pick them up at the airport. I didn't realize there was private airport so close to downtown Saint Paul. It's apparently across the Mississippi River."

He didn't make a sound.

"Michael is picking up sandwiches. If you wake up, I'll give you half of mine. I'll bet you're hungry."

She had no idea if that was true or if he could eat. She couldn't remember if Jordan had thrown up when he'd had a concussion playing basketball. All she remembered was he'd moaned a lot. And the egg on the back of his head where he'd hit the floor had been huge.

But she couldn't see any egg.

Greg pushed into the room with a rolling table. "Okay. Let's clean you up, Jordan. We want you looking good for your parents."

Greg watched to see if there was any movement from Jordan. Nothing.

He filled a small tub with warm water and handed Liz gloves and a small towel. "Be as gentle as you can. We'll start on his face. I'll take the injured side."

They worked together. Greg held a one-sided conversation with her brother, asking whether the water was too cold or too hot and telling him what was happening. Then he launched into the prospects of the Twins.

"He's not into baseball," she whispered.

"That's okay. I am." Greg smiled at her.

"I think the last time he had a concussion was when he played basketball in high school."

"I played too." Greg took the conversational football and ran with it.

That was fine with Liz. Because as the water grew dirtier with each cleansing of the towels, her heart grew heavier. Who had done this to Jordan?

Rudy had been responsible for Jordan's last beating but Jordan refused to tell the authorities. And he'd sworn her to secrecy. The sheriff's department hadn't been able to do anything.

"Was this old trouble or new?" she whispered after Greg left.

Jordan didn't move. Didn't answer her.

Would there be more consequences for her family? They couldn't take another financial hit, they would lose the farm. And she couldn't do more than what she was.

Now she needed to pay Michael back the money he'd lent her brother. Five thousand dollars.

Maybe she could sell her car and take the bus. Although she wasn't sure her car was worth five thousand dollars.

She was opening the Blue Book app when Michael entered.

"Any news?" he asked, handing her a long sandwich.

"The doctor stopped by. He has a broken arm, a broken nose and probably a concussion. Oh and broken ribs. They haven't set anything yet."

"Ouch." He pulled a chair next to her and pulled out another sandwich.

"I won't eat all this."

"Give it a try. You need to keep up your strength." He took a bite of his sandwich, and they ate in silence. Or what silence they could have sitting in a busy emergency room. Even now there were loud voices in the hallway. A woman in uniform ran toward the angry voices.

"Wonder if we should lock the door?" Michael asked.

She winced. "You're joking, right?"

"Sort of." He moved to the door and looked out. "Whoever was yelling is now in custody."

As he sat, he added, "Your parents are in the air."

"Mom texted me."

"It shouldn't be too long. I know you'll be relieved to see them."

She nodded. "This isn't the way I wanted to have my parents visit."

He hugged her. "I'm sorry you're going through this," he said. "Waiting is the hardest."

She clung to him. "I hate this."

He rubbed her back as she sobbed.

"Let it out."

"I can't." She gulped. "I have to be strong for everyone."

"Not for me."

MICHAEL REMEMBERED TRYING to be strong for everyone. Trying to be positive even when Sarah's doctors warned them she wasn't benefiting from her treatments.

He held Liz as his past and present crashed together.

"Thank you," Liz said.

He pulled a couple of tissues for her, and she wiped her face.

"Why don't I give Timothy an update? And I'll check your parents' ETA."

"That would be great." She set her foot on the edge of the chair and wrapped her arms around her leg.

"Everything will be fine," he said as he left.

How sad was that platitude? Everything wasn't fine. Her brother had been beaten on MacBain property.

When he entered the waiting room, Timothy was on the phone. He waited. God, he hated waiting.

Timothy hung up. "How's Jordan?"

"No change." Michael told him about what damage they knew. "Are there any clues at the construction site?"

"Nothing was stolen. We don't think it was thieves."

Michael hesitated before he said, "Jordan gambles. He'd promised Liz that he wouldn't, but ..."

"That's not good." Timothy scratched his chin. "I'll check with his supervisor again, see if he knows anything about that."

"Have you heard from Mom and Dad?" Michael asked.

"They're waiting at the airport. They'll call once they're in the car."

Waiting.

"How's Liz holding up?" Timothy asked.

"She's had a couple of breakdowns, but that's expected. It's hard because Jordan hasn't recovered consciousness. And it doesn't feel like the doctors are doing anything."

Timothy stared him in the eye. "How are you?"

"I'm … dealing."

He looked longingly at the exit. Then headed to Jordan's bedside.

LIZ LEANED against the wall outside of Jordan's room. She'd given him privacy as the doctor examined him.

As she'd left, she'd glanced at his chest. There was a bruise forming in the shape of the toe of a boot.

Jordan was right. His gambling was going to kill him.

As kids, they'd been best friends. They'd done everything together. They'd even saved a small puppy abandoned in their field, bottle feeding it under Mom's supervision. Heidi had been the family dog for twelve years. And she and Jordan had stuck up for each other. If anyone teased or bullied them, they'd had each other's backs. They were the Carlson twins.

How could she have prevented this? She wasn't rich enough to endlessly support her twin's gambling.

Michael moved next to her and pulled her into a side hug. "Did something happen?"

"His doctor is examining him." She turned her face into Michael's shoulder. "I wish I could have done more for him. Was this my fault?"

"No. This isn't your fault. You did everything you could to

help him." He tipped her face toward him and looked her in the eye. "We don't know if this was someone trying to steal from MacBain or there to attack your brother."

"Oh. I assumed …" She'd assumed this was about Jordan's gambling.

"Timothy's checking out all angles and the police are involved," Michael said.

She rested her head on his bicep. "Could Jordan be arrested?"

"I don't think so, but whoever did this to him should be."

"There's a bruise on his chest that looks like the toe of a boot." She shook her head. "How can a person do that to someone?"

"I don't understand how anyone can do that to another person."

The doctor held open the door. "You can come back in."

She walked to the door but turned when Michael didn't follow her.

He stared at the doctor, his face pale and drawn.

"Michael?" she asked.

He jerked. Then slowly followed her through the door.

They stood together.

"We're admitting your brother," the doctor said. "We've splinted his arm for now, and he's scheduled for surgery."

"Surgery?" Liz asked.

"He has four broken ribs and possible internal organ damage. The surgeon will assess if anything else needs to be repaired."

"Is there any risk to the operation?" Michael asked.

"There's always risk of complications from anesthesia and surgery. But there is severe risk if a fragment punctures his aorta or lung."

"Of course." Liz stood a little straighter. "Is there something I need to sign?"

"Greg's gathering the paperwork." The doctor frowned at Michael. "You look familiar. Have we met?"

Michael nodded. "You treated my fiancée."

The doctor tipped his head. "Glioblastoma."

"Yes."

The doctor looked between Liz and Michael. "How …"

Michael closed his eyes. "She died two years ago."

The doctor closed his eyes. "I'm sorry for your loss."

"Thank you."

He patted Michael's shoulder as he left the room.

Liz took Michael's hand. But he didn't look like he was here.

Greg came in with the paperwork and gave a better explanation of the complications and risks. She signed everything.

Michael's phone buzzed. He checked the screen. "I'll be right back."

After he left there was a knock on the door and a police officer stuck his head in. "I'm looking for a Jordan Carlson."

Liz signaled him to step back, and they moved into the hallway outside the room. "That's my brother."

"I'm Officer Adams. I'd like to see what he remembers."

"He hasn't recovered consciousness yet." She swallowed back her fear. "They're operating soon on his broken ribs."

"Were you there when he was attacked?"

"No."

The officer dug in his pocket for a business card. "I'll ask the hospital staff to notify me when he's conscious, and I'll ask the same of you."

"Okay." She stuck the card in her pocket.

As the officer left, she spotted Michael coming down the hall. And her parents.

She ran. "Mom. Dad."

They hugged, crying, as they held each other.

"Where's Jordan?" Mom asked as they finally stepped back.

"He's scheduled for surgery." Liz led them to his room. "I signed the release."

Before pushing the door open, she warned, "He's a mess."

She let her parents go in, explaining no more than two at a time, and turned to Michael. He hadn't moved from the hallway. "I know this is hard on you. I can see you're … stuck in the past."

He nodded, covering up a yawn.

"You're exhausted. Take a break. Go home. Go to a meeting. Take a nap." She pointed to the door. "Go do what you need to do to find your balance."

"You keep me balanced." He pulled her close and she let him. "I'll sit with you, bring you food and hold you when you need to be held."

Oh God. The love she'd tried to push away filled her. "Thank you."

SEVENTEEN

LIZ CHECKED THE CLOCK. JORDAN HAD BEEN IN SURGERY FOR not quite an hour. Michael had gone for more food. Her parents hadn't eaten dinner yet.

He'd looked relieved as he'd walked out of the waiting room.

Patty brought over a basket of water, energy bars and fruit. "I know Michael is picking up dinner, but you should eat or drink something, honey."

Liz took an apple, then rolled it in her hands. MacBains filled the surgical waiting room: Mac, Patty and Timothy.

Stephen had taken her parents to the hotel the MacBains had booked to get rid of the luggage, but they should be back any minute. "Your family has been wonderful, but you don't need to stay."

"I'm right where I should be. If Kate weren't on bed rest she'd be here too. She sends her love."

Liz tried to hold back the tears. This was too much. "Your family is wonderful."

Patty set down the basket and sat next to Liz, pulling her into her arms. "We know what it's like to have to wait for answers. Now you get those tears out before your parents come back."

Liz let everything go. The fear, the worry slipped away with her tears. Finally her sobbing slowed.

"Better?" Patty asked.

She nodded. "I'm so embarrassed."

"You have no reason to be." Patty pulled a small package of tissues out of the basket and handed them to her.

"You thought of everything." Liz laughed.

"Not my first rodeo." Patty patted her hand.

"Michael said Sarah was in the ER here."

Patty nodded.

"The ER doctor was the same man who treated Sarah." Liz drummed her fingers and finally asked, "What was Sarah like?"

"I know Michael loved her and so did our family." Patty paused, before saying, "They did everything together. It was never just Michael, it was always Michael and Sarah."

"Losing her must have been such a blow," Liz said.

Patty nodded. "They were so happy, and then she was diagnosed. She didn't like that he wouldn't work at her parents' firm, but Michael wanted to work with us."

"Do you worry about his drinking?" Maybe she shouldn't be asking his mother that.

"Yes, especially after last week. But he actually seems better than after he came out of treatment. More committed to staying sober. You've helped him."

"I don't know about that." Apparently his family didn't know they'd broken up.

"After Sarah died, he pulled away from the family." Patty held up a hand. "You've helped bring him back. But he's hard to read."

"I know what you mean."

"Why don't you splash water on you face."

Liz headed to the bathroom and did just that. Her eyes were still red, but she looked a little better as she headed into the hall.

The elevator dinged and her parents and Stephen stepped out.

"Any word?" her dad asked.

"Nothing yet."

Back in the waiting room, she tried to eat the apple she'd left on the table.

"I brought Monopoly," Patty said.

"A game?" her mother asked.

"We found it made the time pass faster."

Liz didn't want to play, but if it would take her parents' minds off Jordan she would.

They crowded chairs around a table, and the MacBains reached for their favorite pieces.

"I guess I'll be the thimble," Liz said.

"I haven't played this since the twins were young," her dad said.

"This is kind of our thing," Stephen said. "But watch out, my dad always trades for Mediterranean and Baltic. Don't let him buy that from you."

"So noted," Liz said, waving Mediterranean.

"Hey," Mac said, "I'll make a good offer for it."

Liz checked her phone.

There was a text from Kate wishing Jordan good luck, but nothing else.

Where was Michael?

∾

SOMEONE SHOOK LIZ'S SHOULDER. "Honey, wake up. The doctor is here."

Michael was back.

Stretching as she stood, she went and joined her parents.

"We've repaired all the fractures. Your son now has new plates and bolts. They shouldn't give him any trouble. There were lacerations from the bone fragments we repaired. He's not awake yet, but that's because of his head trauma."

"Can you guess when he'll wake up?" her dad asked, putting an arm around her mom's waist.

Her mother did the same to her.

"That's a question for the neurology team," the doctor said. "But things look good in his chest. And we casted his broken arm."

Liz set her head on her mother's shoulder. "This is good, right?"

"This is good." The doctor smiled. "Now he needs to heal. He'll be in recovery for another hour and then moved to ICU. One of my team will let you know when you can see him."

She hugged her parents. "One hurdle cleared."

Patty and the rest of the MacBains stood. "We're glad he made it through the surgery."

"Thank you for flying us here," Mom said. "And staying during his surgery, and everything else you've done."

Mac waved his hand. "Jordan works for us. He was hurt on our property. And Liz and Michael …"

"Are dating," Patty added.

"Only because I didn't ask you out first." Timothy threw an arm around her shoulders.

"Hands off," Michael said to his brother.

News flash. They weren't dating anymore.

She would explain to her parents when they were alone.

Her mom smiled at her, but her father stared at Michael.

"Call me if there's anything you or your family needs," Mac said.

She nodded, hoping her dad wouldn't say anything embarrassing to Michael.

"Liz, you should get some rest," her mother said, elbowing her father. "Your dad and I have it from here."

Her dad mumbled something but all she caught was "rest."

"Call me if anything changes," she said to her parents.

"We will."

Hugs were exchanged. Patty and her mother spoke privately in low voices.

"I'll bring the car around," Michael volunteered as they walked outside.

It was hard to believe it was still light outside. But it was almost nine at night. The heat took her breath away, but she didn't want to wait inside. "I'll walk with you. I feel like I've been inside the hospital for a week."

He stopped and touched her cheek.

They stared at each other. If he took a step closer, they could kiss. Or she could take that step.

She did take a step—backwards. Her emotions were all over the place. Wishing he'd kissed her and wishing she didn't feel her heart break every time she looked at him.

He unlocked her door.

As he drove, they sat in silence. There was soft music playing on the radio. The sun set as they drove west. She closed her eyes and let the hum of the tires and the music lull her to sleep.

"Hey."

She blinked. They were in a parking garage. "Where are we?"

"My place." He crouched on her side of the car with the passenger door open. "You can stay here tonight."

"Michael."

He held up his hands. "You can sleep in my bed or in the guest bedroom. But it's hot outside, and I thought you would get a better night's sleep here."

"Why are you being so kind? I broke up with you."

"For one thing, I have an understanding of what you're going through."

"And …?"

"We can leave it at that." He held out his hand and she took it.

"I don't have anything to change into," she said.

"I'll find something."

They took the elevator to his floor. She dreaded walking into his place, afraid she would find bottles lying around. She wanted him to have slayed his demons but didn't trust that he could.

The living room was clean. So was the kitchen.

"Why don't you take a bath and then hop into bed? I remember hating the smell of the hospital clinging to me." He handed her a bottle of water from the fridge. "I'll get you something to sleep in."

He walked past her.

She put out her hand and caught his arm. "Why are you doing this?"

He took both her hands and kissed them. "Because I love you."

"What?"

"I love you." When she didn't say anything, he sighed and headed down the hall. "I'll get you some clothes and start the bath. If you want me to, I'll wash the clothes you're wearing."

"Thank you."

But he was gone.

MICHAEL TOSSED her clothes in with his and added detergent.

What should he do now? The water was still running in the

bathroom. He checked for messages on his phone. Nothing. Which was probably good.

He was tempted to check Liz's phone, but he didn't have that right. He didn't have any rights. He was a guy in love who'd screwed up and feared she would never forgive him.

He turned on the TV and found the Twins game. It had been a long time since their kiss cam kiss.

He'd learned a lot about himself from being with Liz. He'd learned that he could love again. He'd learned he could live a sober life. And she'd encouraged him to take a risk on his dream of restoring houses.

He would convince his parents MacBain should have a restoration line. He'd move out of finance just to be in charge of that group. And wouldn't it be fun to get his hands on a property.

He glanced around the condo. This concrete and warehouse look wasn't his style. It was all Sarah. When they were together, he hadn't cared. Being with her was everything.

But she was gone.

He and his sponsor had talked about him having a hobby. He was going to find a place to restore. He had the resources to make it happen.

It would keep his mind off losing Liz. And drinking.

He heard doors close and then everything was quiet by the bedrooms. The washer buzzed, and he transferred everything to the dryer.

It was time to go to sleep. He wanted to hold Liz tonight, but …

An end table light was on in his bedroom. That was nice of her.

Then he spotted Liz in his bed.

His heart thumped a little harder.

He moved to her side of the bed and sat. Her eyes fluttered

280

open. "Do you want me to sleep in the guest bedroom?" he asked.

"I … if you don't want me here, I'll move." Her face went pink. "I … I don't want to be alone tonight."

He stroked back her hair. "I was just thinking how much I wanted to hold you tonight."

She cuddled into his hand. "Thank you."

He got ready for bed and threw on a pair of gym shorts.

Shutting off the light, he slid between the cool sheets. When he lifted his arm, she curled into his chest.

Heaven.

He kissed her cheek. "Get some sleep, love."

EIGHTEEN

"More coffee?" Michael asked her.

She held her hand over her mug, her mouth full of cereal.

Neither of them had broached the subject of last night's sleeping arrangements. And she'd slept. When she woke up, his arm was around her. She'd been curled into his chest.

"Any news on Jordan?" Michael asked.

"He's still in a coma." She tapped her fingers against the counter. "I'll drive over there after this."

"I'll go with you."

He was killing her.

"I'd like it if you were there," she admitted.

"Then that's what we'll do." He moved next to her and swung her stool around. Holding her face between his hands, he said, "There is nothing more important than you. I love you."

She stared into his eyes.

There were no guarantees in life. She loved Michael. He said he loved her.

Everything he'd done yesterday showed her he cared. She clutched his wrists, and then leaned forward.

"Thank you," he groaned and met her halfway.

His kiss was so tender, tears filled her eyes. She wrapped her arms around his neck. Being with him made her heart feel like it was bursting with joy.

"Liz," he murmured, kissing away her tears. Michael pulled her off the stool and hugged her. "I love you."

"I love you too," she whispered into his chest.

"You do?"

She nodded. "I do. I love you."

He searched her face. "But can you trust me?"

"I'm trying."

They held each other.

"We should head to the hospital and give my parents a break." She didn't want to let go. She didn't want reality to wreck the peace she found in Michael's arms.

Together they cleared the dishes. She pulled on the clothes she'd worn yesterday. At least they were clean. Holding his hand, they headed to his car.

"I almost don't want to go in," she confessed as Michael turned the car east to Saint Paul. "What if ..."

"This might be rock bottom for Jordan. I know I had to go through the worst." He squeezed her hand. "But I've come back from the darkness. And you were waiting for me."

"Oh Michael, don't make me cry." She swiped a hand on her cheeks. "For Jordan's sake, I hope you're right."

He kissed her knuckles. "Maybe he'll find someone as wonderful as you are."

"No one's ever made me feel this special."

"You are special."

She let his love wrap around her. The silence was comforting. But too soon he was parking in the hospital ramp.

They got Jordan's room number from the receptionist and found the ICU. It was probably against the rules, but they both went into his room.

"Mom, Dad." Liz hugged her parents. Then she studied Jordan.

His bruises were darker today. Maybe it was how pale his skin was, but Jordan had a black eye along with bruises covering his face. There were IVs hanging with fluids going into his body and tubes coming out of his body.

"You're a mess, my brother." She kissed his forehead.

"I think he squeezed my hand," her dad said. "The doctors are optimistic."

"I hope so." It was hard looking at her twin lying so still.

"Did you get any breakfast?" Michael asked them.

"I ran down to the cafeteria and brought a tray back up," her dad said.

"I could bring you something if you're still hungry," Michael offered.

"Oh no," her mom said. "We've also been snacking on the things your mother put together."

Michael talked with her father while Liz watched Jordan. She wanted him to move, to say something.

But he just lay there.

"Since you've been here all night, why don't you run over to the hotel? Liz and I will stay with him," Michael said.

"I don't know." Mom stroked Jordan's hand.

"Take a little break," Liz said. "We'll be right here. If something happens, I'll call."

It didn't take much more convincing to get them to leave.

"We'll be back soon." Dad gave her hug.

She watched her parents walk down to the elevators and turned back to Michael. "I know how I hate to see Jordan in the hospital, what must it be like as parents?"

"Hard. Very hard." His smile from this morning was gone. Just like yesterday. "Let's hope this is the last time they see something like this."

"Did you ever think of what it must have been like for your

parents?" she asked, then regretted her question. "You don't have to answer that."

"Not when I was drinking." He moved a chair next to the one she was sitting in and took her hand. "I only thought about my own pain. But when I was in the hospital and in treatment I worried about my family."

"I always thought this kind of sorrow was only for people who had financial problems. Not for a family like yours." She shook her head. "That was stupid of me."

"Everyone struggles with something," he said. "Mom was just finishing up her cancer treatments when I hit rock bottom. I'm glad my actions didn't affect her recovery."

She hoped Michael had hit rock bottom because she wanted to be with him, and if he couldn't stay sober, she would have to make a choice.

"I want to tell you something." He swiveled his legs around so their knees touched. "I don't compare you to Sarah, I don't. But I want you to know that what we have together, how you make me feel is ... different."

It was hard to hear Michael talk about loving someone else. "Different?"

"Different. Better. Because I don't want to give up my dreams to be with you ... somehow being with you makes me want to follow my dreams." He gave her a quick kiss. "I love that you inspire me. I want to do that for you."

And there went the tears again. She dashed them away. "I'm sorry I'm so emotional."

"I love that you are."

"You'd better treat her right," Jordan grumbled.

Liz jumped up. "Jordan!"

"I'll find his nurse." Michael stood.

Jordan's eyes were shut, but his mouth twitched. "Do you have to do this in my ... Where the hell am I?"

"The hospital. You were beaten up." She took his left hand. It didn't have a cast on that arm, but there was an IV.

"That I can feel." He shifted his body and moaned.

"Don't." She gently pressed on his shoulder. "You had surgery yesterday."

"What happened?"

"You don't remember?"

"I …"

"From what Timothy knew, you were fixing a crane."

"Right. The crane." He opened his eyes, but then slammed them shut. "Can you turn off the overhead light?"

She moved to the switches and found the right one. "The police want to talk to you."

Jordan's gaze searched the room. "I'm not sure what I can tell them."

"Maybe you'll remember more," she said.

Michael came in with a nurse trailing behind him. "Good to see you're awake, Jordan."

"It's good to be awake, but damn it hurts."

"I'll see what I can do about pain management now that you're conscious." The nurse checked his vitals. Blood pressure, temperature and oxygenation.

"Should we step out?" Liz asked.

"You're good," the nurse said. "I've notified his doctors."

Liz sent a text to her parents, telling them the good news.

Michael wrapped his arms around her waist. "I'm glad you were here."

"I'm glad you're here with me," she whispered. There was a weight off her shoulders she hadn't realized had been there.

Hospital staff hustled in and out of his room. A new IV was connected, one where he could control the pain meds. When his neurologist visited, Liz and Michael stepped out of the room.

"This is good." Michael rubbed on the frown line between

her eyes as they waited in the hallway. "I sent my family a note that he was awake."

She took in a deep breath. "Do you believe that he doesn't remember what happened? Is … he lying about not knowing what happened?"

"I could talk to him," Michael volunteered.

"Would you? I know he thinks I nag him." She curled into his arms.

"Let me try. All he can do is ignore me."

Her parents rushed out of the elevator and joined them in the hallway.

"He's really awake?" Mom asked.

"Yes. He's in with his neurologist."

Now it was Mom's tears that flowed.

"What does he remember?" Dad asked.

"Not much," Michael said. "Just working on the crane."

"So we don't know whether this is because of his gambling." Her mother covered her mouth with her hand. She shot a glance at Michael.

"Michael knows about Jordan's addiction." Liz looked between her parents. "He'd like to talk to Jordan. Would that be okay before you see him?"

"What about?"

"I'm an alcoholic." Michael straightened. "I know a little of what he's going through. How hard it is to fight your demons."

Her parents exchanged a silent conversation. Then Mom said, "Yes. Please."

Liz looked at him. "You're amazing."

"No. But I'm glad you think so."

MICHAEL TRIED to remember what had gotten through to him when he'd been in treatment. Not much. The impact on his family, yes. Kate had come for one horrific family session and described how she'd found him passed out on the bathroom floor, his head bleeding.

The embarrassment had been awful.

If being beaten and immobilized in a hospital bed surrounded by his family and his boss's family didn't do it, what *would* get Jordan to admit he was helpless against his gambling?

The doctor came out and talked to the Carlsons.

Michael kissed Liz's cheek and headed into Jordan's room.

"Hey," Michael said. "How are you feeling?"

"A little floaty. But the pain is gone."

"Good." The chair squealed a little as Michael pulled it to the side of Jordan's bed. "You know I've been in your place."

"You were beaten up?"

"No. I've been where you are. Lying to my family. Doing stupid things. For me it was just one more drink."

Jordan frowned. "You're an alcoholic?"

"Yes. I had all the excuses lined up. Why I drank. Why I didn't stop."

"So, you still drink?"

"No. My sister found me passed out in my bathroom. I'd hit my head." Michael raised an eyebrow. "I even played the *I don't remember card* when I came to in the hospital."

Jordan stared at the cast on his arm.

"Have you ever gone to Gambling Anonymous?" Michael asked.

Jordan shrugged.

"About a week ago I decided I could have one drink." Michael stood and paced the small room. Your sister found me passed out. I almost lost her because I thought I could have *one drink*."

"You seem on the same page now."

"I love her. I screwed up and she dumped me. But I'm keeping my promise to never drink again."

"That sounds … hard."

"Not if I take it one day at a time. And I will because I never want to disappoint her or my family again." He pointed at Jordan. "Do you like disappointing your family?"

Jordan swallowed. "No. But I have to get the money I owe Rudy."

"Rudy." Michael circled his finger at Jordan. "Did he have anything to do with this?"

Jordan raised both hands, winced and set the one with the cast back on his lap. "Yeah."

"So you lied when you said you didn't remember."

"Sort of. It's coming back to me. But it was Rudy."

"Then tell the police."

"I don't know what he'll do to me if I do."

"You need to make the right choice. For your family. And for you." Michael stopped at the edge of the bed. "Get treatment or go to meetings. Because your actions are hurting your family."

Jordan didn't say anything.

"I'll call Ed in HR again. It's confidential. But you have to take the first step."

"You don't know what it's like to ride a winning streak."

"You think that's not the same feeling as that first swallow of whiskey? But I'm not willing to pay the price. Because the price would be losing your sister, and I've done that once. I don't want to live without her. And I don't want to live without my family. Think about that. What it would be like to lose your family."

Maybe something would sink in.

All three Carlsons looked up when he opened the door.

"You're right, Liz. He remembers more than he's willing to say."

289

She closed her eyes.

"I told him I would call HR again. But he has to take the step to get help."

"Thank you." Liz wrapped her arms around his waist.

He smiled at the group. "Can I get anyone coffee or something to eat?"

He got their coffee orders. When the family went into Jordan's room, Michael called Ed and explained the situation.

"I'll call his hospital room and see if he wants help," Ed said.

"Perfect." Michael looked through the door at the family gathered around Jordan's bed. He sure hoped Jordan would take this chance. But no one could force him to change.

LIZ FOUND Michael sitting in the waiting room. "I don't know what you said, but Jordan is willing to look at treatment for his addiction."

"Good. Ed's going to call him." He handed her a latte.

She stared at him.

He wiped his mouth. "Do I have something on my face?"

"No." She touched his cheek. "I'm memorizing this moment. The moment that I gave my heart—and trust—to you."

"You trust me?" His voice cracked.

"With all my heart."

He pulled her onto his lap. And she didn't care if anyone walked in on them.

"I'll try to never disappoint you." He kissed her, a soft, sweet kiss.

She clung to him. "You're my rock."

"What do you think about moving into my condo?" he asked.

She laughed. "I would like that."

He dropped his forehead to hers. "I should warn you. Yesterday I decided I want to find a house that needs restoring. I like my condo, but I plan to … live my passion."

"I love that idea. And I'd love to help. I have two hands available for you."

He captured her hands. "Perfect. Because I want to be with you—always."

Her heart filled with love. "Always."

EPILOGUE

TWIN'S OPENER

Michael took Liz's hand as they trailed behind the rest of the MacBain employees to the opening game of the Twins. At least this April day was nice. He'd worried it might snow. But the sun was shining, and the weather forecasters said it might get to the high 60s.

He'd spent a lot of time talking to the Twins support staff in the last few weeks.

"Jordan's coming to the game." Liz swung his hand.

"Good."

"Hey, you two, hurry up." Kate waved them forward.

"How are those babies?" Liz asked.

"Crawling. Who would guess they could get into so much trouble? And Zander is pulling himself up on the tables."

Alex nodded. "I'm worried he'll learn how to climb out of his crib."

"Who's taking care of them today?" Kate was back at the office, but she worked from home about half the time.

"Alex's mom. I think she wants to see what musical instrument they'll play. She's hoping for another prodigy or two."

"Didn't you tell them MacBains are athletes?" Michael asked.

"Why should I break her heart?" Kate wrapped an arm around her brother's waist and whispered, "Is everything working out?"

"Under control."

"What are you two whispering about?" Liz asked.

"Kate doesn't like the paint colors on our Victorian," Michael lied.

They'd done it. Bought a place and were restoring it together.

"You're wrong, Kate. The colors are perfect," Liz said.

They entered the stadium and moved with the crowd to the concierge level. People were already drinking and eating.

"Are you okay?" Liz asked Michael.

"I'm with you, so everything is perfect."

"Do you remember the kiss cam?" she asked as they found seats.

"My favorite memory."

The Twins took an early lead, but Michael wasn't really into the game.

"Hi, sis." Jordan sat in a seat behind them and rubbed his knuckles against the top of her ball cap.

"Hey!" Liz readjusted her cap. "How are you? I haven't seen you in a while."

"I'm good." He leaned closer. "I got promoted to supervisor. Today."

"Good for you."

"So they finally announced it?" Michel said. "Congratulations."

"You knew?" Liz said.

"I know all," Michael answered.

His parents moved up and down the stairs, talking to staff and meeting their families.

Mom hugged Jordan. For some reason they'd connected, and Jordan was now an honorary member of the MacBain clan, ending up at most family gatherings.

"I get my eight-month honor next week," Jordan said to Liz and Michael. "I was hoping you could join the celebration."

"Yes." Liz squeezed her brother's knee. "I'm so proud of you."

"I'd be honored," Michael said.

"I'll shoot you the info." Jordan nodded at a female employee. "See you later."

"Is that one of your cousins?" Liz asked. "I think I met her at Kate's wedding."

"Courtney. She's one of the good ones." He tipped his head. "Are she and Jordan together?"

"I don't know," Liz said.

Michael chuckled. "I don't care."

"Hey, they're doing the kiss cam." Liz pointed at the screen. "I remember how embarrassing that was."

"Well …" Michael dug for the box in his pocket. When the screen focused on him and Liz, he flipped the box open. "Liz, will you marry me?"

On the screen flashed the words *Will You Marry Me?*

"Michael." Her hands covered her face.

"Is that a no?" He couldn't believe it would be. They talked about the future all the time.

"It's a yes, you fool!" She pulled him toward her, planting a huge kiss on his lips.

Applause broke out around them.

He didn't care about the camera or the applause or the crowd. He just cared that he would spend the rest of his life with this incredible woman.

"I love you." He wanted to pick her up and swing her around, but the aisle was too small.

Liz stuck out her hand and he slipped the ring on. She held it up, and when he looked up they were still on camera.

He mouthed, "She. Said. Yes."

Then he hugged her to his side. Right where he wanted her.

ACKNOWLEDGMENTS

I'm lucky to have amazing people help me in my writing. First and foremost my critique partners: Ann Hinnenkamp, Leanne Taveggia, Cat Schield and Lizbeth Selvig. And of course my editors Victoria Curran and Judy Roth. Your advice is so appreciated.

I'm blessed to have the Dreamweavers in my life. They are such an inspiration.

And of course my family — because they are everything to me.

And to my readers—thank you. If you enjoyed Liz and Michael's story, please consider leaving a review at your favorite bookseller or book club website.

WANT MORE OF THE MACBAINS?

Turn the page for the opening of MAID FOR SUCCESS - Book 1 in THE MacBains.

MAID FOR SUCCESS

THE BELL ON THE DOOR CLANGED AS ALEX PULLED IT OPEN AND stepped inside. He took a deep breath and scanned the coffee shop. *Good.* Frederick wasn't here yet.

He ordered and took his coffee to a minuscule table, wedging his legs into the small space. He took his first sip and winced. Even the milk he'd added didn't soften the bitter taste. The only positive to his drink—it was hot.

The shop must have changed their supplier since he and Frederick had met here last. Back when he'd made music. Back when life had been easy.

Before.

The bell on the door clanged again, a dissonant grating sound. Frederick came in, saw Alex and waved as he headed to the counter.

Alex traced patterns in the tabletop. He didn't want to disappoint his friend. He didn't want to live through the next thirty minutes of confession time. Only priests should hear confessions.

"Alex." Frederick smiled, holding out his hand.

"Frederick." Alex stood, banging his thighs into the table. "Good to see you," he lied.

"How are you? It's been ages since we talked." Frederick took off his suit jacket and pulled a packet of papers from the inside pocket.

Alex swallowed. It was the contract he'd signed with the Saint Paul Chamber Orchestra almost eighteen months ago. Frederick let it drop to the table, and it thumped down like a big fat elephant.

"I'm fine." *Not really.* "Let's skip the small talk. It's not done."

His friend tasted his coffee and closed his eyes. "This is the best coffee in town."

Alex took a sip, forcing himself to swallow. Nope. Still bitter. "I don't know if the sonata will ever be done."

Sympathy filled Frederick's eyes. "What I've heard is wonderful."

"Yeah." He'd completed one movement before the magic had died. "I keep trying. It's just …"

All he'd written lately were commercial jingles. At least he tried. He hadn't finished any.

"How long has it been since your divorce was final?" Frederick asked.

"About a year." Fourteen months, twenty days, two hours and a handful of minutes.

A small smile creased his friend's face. "That long."

Frederick's smile evaporated. Able to control a full orchestra with a searing glare, his expression turned serious. "The orchestra took a risk when they commissioned the sonata."

"I know." Alex's jaw ached from clenching his teeth.

"You need to work. You're too brilliant to let a failed marriage ruin your career."

"I'm trying." Alex's ex-wife had not only destroyed their

marriage and the life they'd created, but her actions had sucked out every note and ounce of his creativity.

"I can buy you three more months, but that's it. I'm sorry." Compassion filled Frederick's voice. "That's as long as I can keep the board of directors off your back."

Alex clenched his mug. He'd never let anyone down before, not when it came to his music.

When he'd taken the grant, ideas had poured out of him. He'd barely slept, needing to get the notes written. His music had been joy-filled.

After his world imploded, he'd had trouble writing meaningless dribble.

"Thanks for getting me the extra time." Alex looked into his friend's eyes.

"I'll send the contract update to Aubrey," Frederick said.

"Sure." Maybe his business manager would stop leaving reminder messages about the deadline for a month or two.

"I'll get it done." The lie was as bitter in his mouth as the cold coffee he swallowed.

"YOU WANT ME TO CLEAN ... be a maid?" Kate cringed at the slight screech in her voice. She pushed down the panic trying to burst out.

Her mother's eyes flashed, a clear warning Kate was on a tightrope without a net. "Is cleaning beneath you?"

"I didn't mean it that way." She would never insult the company her mother had started. "But ... I have an MBA." Kate pressed her palms against the conference table that dominated a corner of Dad's office. "My salary is four times what we pay the cleaning crew. Our profit margin will take a hit."

"Katie." Her father leaned a hip against the granite top of his desk. "All your brothers did the same."

She was twenty-nine. When would her family call her Kate, not *Katie*? "My brothers *never* cleaned houses. Hell, they never picked up their rooms."

"Language," her mother said sharply.

Her oldest brother, Michael, snorted and slumped deeper in his chair. She wanted to wipe the smug expression off his face. Why was Michael even in this meeting? Probably to witness her humiliation and report back to their two younger siblings.

Michael grinned. "I worked construction."

"In high school." She forced her lips into a neutral position, trying to keep from frowning. Why would her parents want her working as a company maid? As an account executive, she wined and dined clients. Her role didn't include cleaning their dinner plates.

"Your mother and I have already discussed this." Her father stalked over to the window, staring down on Minneapolis from his twentieth floor office. "If you expect another promotion, you need a better understanding of every branch of the company. That means not only dealing with the leasing clients, but also the Murphy's Maids clients."

"But …" Kate raised her hands in the air, pleading. "No one else cleaned. There must be another role I could perform. I don't have to scrub floors to understand what a maid does."

"Are you better than your mother?" Her father's voice boomed out.

Uh-oh. The volume of his voice might break his office windows.

"Your mother started Murphy's Maids when she was nineteen," Dad continued. "She worked nonstop *and* graduated with honors."

He moved behind Mom and rubbed her shoulders. She flashed him a grin that excluded Kate and her brother.

Her parents were exceptional. They'd built their own businesses. But shouldn't she be launching off their shoulders and not repeating their efforts?

"Are you better than your mother?" her father asked again.

"No. That's not what I'm saying, it's just …"

Mother turned and faced her. "What are you saying?"

"I want what's best for MacBain." Kate inhaled. Something was wrong with the building's HVAC. She couldn't get enough oxygen and her head was wonky. "Is my cleaning what's best for MacBain?"

"Yes," her parents said.

She would do anything for the family business, but cleaning didn't make sense. Not every potential CEO had to get their hands dirty.

She was good at her job. But she wanted more. More of everything. When her father retired, she wanted his position.

She loved her brothers, but they didn't have the training to run the family business. Every college course, article, and seminar she'd taken attended or read were part of her bigger plan. When her father retired, she wanted to lead MacBain Enterprises.

But her father still hadn't acknowledged her as his successor. Her hands clenched into fists. She might have to crawl over her brothers' bodies to get there.

What a lovely image, all three lying in a pile as she stepped over them in a new pair of Louboutin high heels. It would have to be Louboutin; the blood wouldn't show on the red soles. She'd seen the perfect pair in Saks last week. Too bad they cost $900. And they sure wouldn't be practical if her parents forced her to clean.

"I know you're tough, Katie MacBain," her father said. "But I'm not having you swing a hammer on any of Stephen or Timothy's projects."

If she did work as a laborer, she'd figure out ways to do the job more effectively. She looked at her manicure to keep from glaring at her family.

"I've brought in new tenants in a failing economy," she said. "I'm good at what I do."

"Yes, you are." Her mother's dark brown eyebrows drew together.

"Who will handle my workload?" She had to get out of this. "I'm in the middle of negotiations with both Sorenson Law and Telling Chemicals. They're asking for massive concessions. I need to concentrate so they don't ruin the profitability of the Daschle Building."

Michael stretched out his legs. "What about that assistant you *had* to have. When does she start?"

Katie's shoulders stiffened. She'd pushed for additional help over Michael's vehement objections. Was he retaliating because Mom and Dad had finally agreed to her proposal? "She starts Monday."

"Waste of money," Michael mumbled. "Typical Katie."

Why wouldn't her family call her Kate? *Katie* was a little girl with pigtails. She tucked a wayward strand of her auburn hair behind her ear. *Kate* was a professional.

God, what she wouldn't give to have been the firstborn. Instead Michael had the honor. She was the only daughter. When the two youngest had come along, she'd been stuck babysitting.

"It will only be one job," her mother said. "You should be able to work your schedule around the cleaning, especially now that you have an assistant."

"Katie, if you want to get ahead, you need a strong foundation." Her father looked pointedly at his desk.

The desk she wanted to fill.

"You've done time in marketing, sales and public relations, but we realized you haven't had any *hands-on* experience in the company." Her mother stood next to Dad and leaned against the window. A united front.

"But cleaning?"

"Yes." Her mother didn't leave any room to argue.

"You'll have a week to orient your assistant before you start working for Murphy's. You can manage your department and learn the cleaning side of the business. It's only one job a week, but he's an important client. Probably only four hours twice a week."

"You'll still handle the lease renewals," Dad added. "Plus, I remember how slowly the negotiations for Sorenson Law firm progressed five years ago. Their office manager vets everything with the partners. Besides, their lease still has six months to run."

When her father's voice took on that head-of-the-MacBain-clan tone, there was no arguing.

"How long will I have to do this?" Kate asked.

Her mother tipped her head, her brown hair swinging to her shoulder. "As long as we say you do."

Kate had one last weapon in her arsenal. "Dad, two nights ago you complained I was still working at seven-thirty. You said I couldn't focus all my energy on the company. This will make it worse."

"On top of new experience, we're hoping you'll learn balance and how to delegate," Mom said.

God, did they have to act like a tag team?

"But … cleaning?"

"Katie, this may be a family business, but you're still an employee. If you don't like my management style," her father pointed to the door, "you can always leave."

How could they do this to her? "I want what's best for the company."

If by working at Murphy's Maids she was closer to being named her father's successor, she'd suck up her resentment. "If you think cleaning is the best use of my talents, then that's what I'll do."

Her parents nodded at her. She and Michael pushed away from the table. Her brother started to walk past her. "Kiddo, you need to tame that mouth of yours."

She whipped an elbow into his abs. "Don't call me, kiddo."

KATE MANHANDLED the van's reluctant gearshift into drive. It was mortifying driving the bright green Murphy's Maid van. She missed her BMW, but the cleaning equipment wouldn't fit in her car, not without ruining the leather interior.

She'd tried to convince Lois, her Murphy's Maid supervisor, to let her clean one of their office-building complexes—at night. No go. She was working in the residential cleaning group. Housecleaning!

Well, how tough could housecleaning be? She'd endured a two-hour training video. And she'd helped Lois clean a house the day before.

She wouldn't need her strategic leadership course to figure out the best way of removing the ring around a bathtub. And she'd bet her iPad that Lois couldn't run a project probability analysis.

Kate glanced at her phone's GPS, making sure she was on the right street. Did Murphy's provide smart phones to the cleaners? It would save time and money.

If her directions were accurate, she'd found the right neighborhood. Large older homes were set back on their lots. Trees lined the quiet street, their leaves a freshly unfurled bright green. The color would deepen as spring turned to summer. *Hopefully she wouldn't still be cleaning in summer.*

Passing bright blobs of yellow forsythia, flashes of red and yellow tulips, and jonquils ... or daffodils ... she didn't know the difference, Kate finally pulled to the curb in front of a lovely yellow three-story house with white trim and black shutters. A wide porch held a couple of rattan chairs. Even *she*, an apartment dweller, could tell the gray porch begged for flowerpots.

Kate wrestled the cleaning equipment and supply carrier onto the sidewalk. The buckets were the same lime green as the van. So was the hideous polo shirt she'd tucked into her oldest blue jeans. The vacuum cleaner banged her leg as she dragged everything up the sidewalk.

Mr. Adamski. Kate sure hoped this client was a kindly, tidy old gentleman.

Lois had warned her. "He's not happy Martha's gone. Unfortunately it's been almost two months since Martha retired, so the place might be dirty."

Then Lois had handed her a five-page list of written instructions on how and what to clean in the Adamski house. Christ. Kate was anal retentive, but she hadn't left five pages of instructions for Elizabeth, her freshly hired employee.

Since she was thinking about her new assistant, she set the equipment down and called. "Hi Liz, how's it going?"

"Nothing I can't handle yet. I've answered most of the questions thrown at me. The one I couldn't answer, I got your brother's help."

She didn't want her brothers bugging Liz. "Which brother?"

"Michael. Doesn't smile much, does he?"

"No." Her brother was too serious. "Call if you have any questions. I can't imagine cleaning is very challenging." Kate shivered. "I'll need mental stimulation."

"Will do. But don't worry. I know your filing system and have access to all the active leases." Liz laughed. "I think I can manage on my own for the next four or five hours. I'll see you this afternoon, right?"

"Yes." Kate sighed. Four hours of scrubbing and vacuuming sounded like a lifetime.

"Don't worry. I won't sign any new leases while you're gone."

Kate laughed as she stuffed her phone into her back pocket. With a big sigh, she climbed the porch steps. Sure, her mother had started this way, but her mother had cleaned houses while attending night school. As demand grew, she'd hired other students looking for work. Then she'd expanded into cleaning office buildings. Since the college students she'd hired attended school during the day and could clean at night, it was a perfect fit. Lois said they still got fifty percent of their new hires from the nearby colleges.

Maybe Murphy's should establish a work/study program with local colleges. She set everything down again and pulled out her phone, making a note to research setting up a program.

At the door she wound her hair into a bun and wrapped a scrunchie around it. She pushed the bell and smiled when it played a tune. It reminded her of some commercial, but she couldn't recall what product.

The door opened.

She looked up, still smiling. "Hi. I'm Kate from Murphy's Maids."

The man blocking the entrance reminded her of a bear. And he wasn't old. He wasn't much older than she was.

His shoulders filled the doorway and looked twice as wide as his waist. Everything about him was dark. Dark hair, dark eyes, and a dark scowl on his face. "You're twenty minutes late."

She straightened. "I'm sorry." It wasn't like they were negotiating a multi-million-dollar lease.

He didn't move.

She chewed her lip.

His bushy eyebrows pinched together so tight it almost

looked like he had a unibrow. He was taller than her brothers, and they were all over six feet.

She stared into his brown eyes, snapping with anger. "Are you letting me in?"

"I'm thinking."

God. Her brothers would tease her endlessly if she failed this job. And Dad and Mom. Shoot. She couldn't let that happen. She couldn't disappoint them. She wanted that CEO position. She tapped her foot against the wooden floor of the porch. She had to clean this guy's house.

She touched his arm. "Please don't get me fired. This is my first day on the job." She let her gaze drop but looked up at him through her half-closed eyelashes. Let this work. Failure was not an option.

His craggy face softened. When he wasn't frowning, he was … good-looking.

"I can't be waiting for you every week. You need to be punctual. Martha was never late."

Martha must have been part saint. "It won't happen again. I promise."

"It better not."

The client was a real grump.

He stepped aside and she hauled in the cleaning supply bucket. He grabbed the vacuum. Maybe he'd help clean too.

"Martha knew how I wanted everything," he muttered, glancing over his shoulder. "And one of my first requirements of your company was punctuality. Please remember that."

They moved through the hallway. She loved the wood floors. They were probably maple, but the stain was light and kept the hallway from feeling closed in.

"Here's the kitchen." He set the vacuum down with a thump.

Judging by the white cabinets and golden brown granite counters, the space had been remodeled. Then she took in the stain rings, lumps of food stuck to the counter, and the dishes overflowing the sink. The whole room left a general impression of dustiness. She caught of whiff of something foul, but then all she smelled was coffee. Wonderful.

Adamski poured a cup from the pot. Huh. She didn't know his first name and he hadn't offered her a cup.

Of course she hadn't given him her last name. Her cheeks grew warm. She didn't want anyone knowing what she was doing.

She waited for him to offer her a cup. Nothing. She tapped her fingers against her leg.

"Did you talk to Martha?" he asked.

She pulled out the five-page list Lois had given her. She hadn't read it yet. "I have her instructions."

"Good. I'll leave you to it. I have to work." He pivoted and headed out the door, surprisingly graceful for such a tall man.

Unfolding the list, she read.

Mr. Adamski is very particular about the service he receives.

Be on time. He only wants cleaners in the house from 10 until 2 on Tuesdays and Wednesdays.

Kate planned to propose a schedule change where she would work eight hours in one day. Then she would only miss a day out of her week. And she wouldn't have to change into regular clothes after she'd done her penance.

Most important rule—Never disturb him while he's working.

Mr. Adamski and I developed a routine satisfactory to him. Clean in the following order:

Kitchen—do dishes.

Clean all surfaces.

Clean inside microwave.

Every other week, wipe down cupboards.

Once a month clean out fridge.

He's okay if you throw away dated food.

This sounded like four hours of work right there. And there

were five pages of instructions. Maybe she should expect more of her own Murphy's house cleaners.

With a deep sigh, she began with the dishes. A week's worth of pans and plates filled the sink. She swallowed at the sight of dried spaghetti sauce and gross baked-on brown goop in a pan. Snapping on Murphy's Maids green gloves, she filled the sink with steaming water. She might need a power washer to clean the place.

Kate scraped, rinsed and filled the dishwasher. She scrubbed at the countertop until her arm ached and sweat dripped into her ear. She'd only been working thirty minutes, and she already needed a shower.

Once the counters and sinks gleamed, she stretched out her sore back. She deserved a reward.

The coffee aroma lured her to the pot. She poured a cup and found sugar in the cupboard. She sipped, closing her eyes. The man made better coffee than the shop in her office building. "Great coffee," she murmured.

"It should be. I have it shipped in special."

She jumped and almost dropped the mug. Mr. Adamski stood behind her. A smile creased his face, a dimple winking out of one cheek. God, she loved dimples.

Everything on him was large … his nose, his cheekbones and even the dent in his chin. Rarely did a man tower over her five-foot-eight inches, but Adamski did. Warmth curled through her body. This guy was cute.

She shook her head; she wasn't here to flirt. She was here to prove to her parents that she could handle everything they dished out.

"I'm sorry, the coffee smelled delicious." And she believed in rewarding her efforts. Adamski should be admiring his empty sinks and clean counters.

The muscles in his face relaxed. "Don't worry about it." He poured himself another cup. "I keep the coffee going all day. If you need to make a pot, the coffee and filters are here."

He opened the cupboard above the coffeemaker. At least that was organized.

She'd always resented making coffee at the office. Mostly because she swore her brothers never bothered. They waited for a staff member to make a fresh pot, and nobody called them on their laziness. But for coffee this good, she'd make a pot.

"So, you just started with Murphy's Maids?" He leaned against the counter.

She wiped the inside of the microwave. She might need to take a chisel to the dried-on food. Hefting out the glass tray, she set it gently in the sink. "First day by myself."

She scrubbed, standing on her toes, putting muscle into scraping off what looked like more red sauce. How much spaghetti and pizza did this guy eat?

She looked at him. His eyes were the same color as his rich dark coffee.

He topped off his cup. "Are you finding everything?"

She'd only done the dishes, and it had taken half an hour. Frowning, she sniffed. Why hadn't the faint foul smell in the kitchen disappeared? "I'm good."

She tilted her head. "Cleaning would be easier if you rinsed your dishes after you ate. Then I wouldn't have to chisel and chip at the dishes and pans. I almost threw a pot away."

He took a step back. "Martha never said anything."

Maybe she'd overstepped her role, but really. Saint Martha might have wanted to get in as many hours as possible working here, but not her. She wanted to get back to her real job. She bit her lip.

His gaze zoomed in on her mouth. "I'll rinse my dishes from now on."

"Good." She wanted him to leave. Let her finish her

penance. Wow. She needed to strip off her sweatshirt. The room had gotten really warm.

"I'll let you get back to it." His hands waved around the kitchen. "Oh, I use the filtered water for the coffee." He pointed to a spigot on the sink.

"Thanks." She swallowed and watched him leave. For a big man, he had a very nice butt. Very nice.

She wished they'd met at a bar. They might have dated for a week or two. Maybe she'd have slept with him, at least until she'd gotten this attraction out of her system. She didn't date a guy for much longer than a month or two.

Until her parents admitted she was the right person to guide the future of MacBain, nothing would distract her.

So, she scrubbed. When Adamski's home sparkled like the Hope Diamond, he would rave to her parents, and they would free her from cleaning.

Because the alternative was too awful to consider. If Adamski complained about her work, her parents would write her off, and her brothers would tease her until the end of time. And Michael would be named CEO of MacBain Enterprises.

ALEX STRIPPED off his headphones and powered off his keyboard. He took a sip of coffee, grimacing as the cold liquid slid down his throat.

Crap. Now he couldn't even write jingles. What else could go wrong?

He wasn't hurting for money. His songwriting paid for a near-perfect life. Or at least half the life he'd planned. Meredith and his dreams of a family had been the other half.

Those dreams had crumbled around him. Meredith had made a fool of him and now he could barely sit at the keyboard where he'd composed so many songs—for her.

He closed his eyes and let his chest rise and fall in deep breaths. He'd jokingly promised an award-winning jingle for Gabe. Gabe had stuck by him through last year's hell. Friends stuck together.

So, he would finish this jingle. Then he would battle the sonata.

Unstructured phrases haunted his nights, but as soon as he started working on the melody and counterpoints, everything vanished. Maybe if he finished the sonata, he could move on. Tuck away his grief.

Alex tapped his fingers against the soundless keys. He needed inspiration to create this jingle for a retail lighting store. *Maybe they'd settle for "Twinkle, Twinkle Little Star."*

Slipping the headphones back on, he flipped the switch on his electric piano. The melody should be light and bright.

He pictured a little girl with Kate's auburn curls and bright green eyes, gave her a dimple. Sure, he hated his own dimples, but a little girl would look right with a dimple gracing the corner of her smile.

The notes flowed. For the first time in months, music poured from him like liquid gold. He could hear it all: the violins, the horns and the harp. He made a quick note: *add bells or xylophone.*

The words followed. He infused the music with images of light and hope. Always set against a backdrop of a bright-eyed, one-year-old girl with copper-colored curls. Touching the record button, he played the tune one more time. Then he laid down the lyrics.

His gravelly baritone growled out the words. The ad agency wouldn't use his voice, but at least Gabe's client would get an idea of what he was after.

He played it back. Added harmonies, tweaked. His hands shook as he pushed the play button.

The song sounded like he'd imagined. Like the sun rising

on a brand-new day. A day filled with hope. Alex let out a massive sigh that ruffled the composition paper on the stand.

He'd broken through. He'd finished a composition. Almost eighteen months of creative drought and all he'd needed was a new cleaner stalking through his door. A good-looking woman with fiery green eyes who told him to rinse his plates.

He tossed his headphones on the console and rolled his chair back from the keyboard.

A vacuum buzzed above his head. Kate with her full, plump lips was in his bedroom. Her lips made him think of what a mouth like hers could do to a man who hadn't had sex in … too long.

Sure, he'd checked out her ass. Hell, he wasn't dead. Over the last few months, his libido had come back to life. Ripped, torn designer jeans had encased her nicely rounded cheeks. But she was his house cleaner for God's sake.

She was tall. He was a big man, and the next time he slept with a woman, he wanted someone in his arms that wouldn't break. Meredith had been—fragile, model-thin. He'd always worried he might hurt her.

Kate. He liked her name. Her gaze crackled with intensity. He could fall for a woman like Kate.

What the hell was a bright young woman doing cleaning houses?

THE MAN WAS A PIG. Kate threw another pile of laundry into the hamper. Didn't he pick up after himself?

She stripped the sheets off his bed. He probably hadn't changed the bed since Martha retired. She wished she'd kept the rubber gloves on.

The hamper overflowed as she carted it downstairs. He must work out a lot. Most of the dirty clothes were T-shirts and sweatpants. She pushed opened the laundry room door and snapped her head back. A foul odor wafted from the space, like something had died. *God, what was it?*

It had to be the smell she caught while in the kitchen.

Another pile of clothes overflowed the table next to the washer. That couldn't be the source, could it?

One of her high school chores had been doing her family's laundry. Her brothers' sports clothes had been the worst, especially Stephen's hockey uniforms, but never this bad. She gulped in a breath and the smell stung the back of her throat.

Rolling her eyes, she pulled her gloves back on and sorted his clothes. There must be a thousand athletic socks.

Family sock-matching Sunday nights had been the worst. She and her brothers had to finish before they could watch TV. Most of the socks had been her brothers, but she'd been forced to match too. Life as the only girl in the MacBain family had been unfair. Who in their right mind wanted kids?

Apparently Adamski liked silk boxers. Mostly black, very nice, but she ran across a series of holiday boxers. Santa Clauses, pumpkins, four-leaf clovers and hearts, numerous heart-covered boxers. Girlfriend?

At least she hadn't found any women's underwear. And she hadn't found evidence of a woman living in the house. No clothes in the closet, no makeup in the bathroom. No condom wrappers in the garbage. Yuck.

With the clothes sorted, she opened the washer. "God!"

Kate jerked her head away, but not before her eyes watered from the stench. The lid slammed shut with a clang.

Shit. Had something died in there? She tried to breathe through her mouth, but the taste had the coffee she'd drunk threatening to come up.

Her brief glimpse into the depths of the washer had shown sheets, towels and moldy socks. Cringing, she backed out of the door and down the hallway into the kitchen.

This was the seventh level of hell!

Kate slapped her hands on the counter and pulled in deep breaths. The smell wouldn't go away. Spores of death probably filled her nose. She would end up with consumption, coughing and weak in bed. Her family would cry by her bedside, sorry for the way they'd treated her. Sorry they hadn't cherished the too few moments they'd had with her before she died.

"I want my office. My *clean* office. Where someone else removes the garbage and vacuums the floors." She wanted to work at a job that mattered. "I hate this."

She snatched her coffee mug off the counter and sniffed. Even the heady, rich aroma couldn't clear away the stink.

What she wouldn't give to pull the whole mess out of the washer, find where Adamski was hiding, and throw everything in his lap. If it had been her brothers' mess, she would have done just that.

Grabbing a garbage bag and wishing she had a facemask, she returned to the laundry. With a deep breath, she rushed in.

Throwing open the washing machine's lid, she frantically stuffed the contents of the machine into the bag. The fabric squished and slid through her gloved hands, covered with slime. Something green came up with the clothes. It looked like a piece of meat. She gagged.

Hurry. Hurry.

She leaned over and chased the last mildew-speckled sock around the inside of the machine. *The smell. Oh God.*

She stuffed the final sock in the bag and yanked the draw strings shut. She refused to breathe until she reached the kitchen.

Gasping, she rushed to the back door off the kitchen. Wrenching it open, she stuck her head out and drew in deep gulps of fresh cool air. Even with the bag closed, the stench escaped.

"What the hell?" Adamski's deep voice made the door clutched in her fingers vibrate. "What is that smell?"

She gasped in fresh air again. Would she ever get rid of the taste in her mouth?

"What's wrong?"

He was so close, her eardrums hurt from his shouting.

"I ..."

"Sweet Jesus, what is that?"

Fingers bit into her arm. He pulled her into the room and the door closed.

She fought back with an elbow to his stomach. She needed fresh air. "Don't!"

She shrugged him away and bumped open the door. She gulped in air laced with the scent of flowering trees.

"Did something die?" he asked.

"Your laundry." She grabbed the bag and then heaved it onto the kitchen deck. She hoped the crawling mess didn't eat its way out of the plastic bag and through the decking. Maybe the military needed to know about this possible new chemical weapon.

"What the hell did you do?" His face looked a little gray.

"Me? What did I do?" She poked a finger into his chest. The firm muscles didn't give. "When did you throw your last load of laundry into the washer?"

Black eyebrows shadowed his chocolate eyes. "I ..." His eyes flared wide open. "A while ago."

"I think there was some sort of meat in there." She shivered. "I've never seen anything so gross."

She took a deep breath through her nose. Her eyes watered. She went back to breathing through her mouth.

"I ... I ... I didn't look very hard for the source of the smell." He leaned out the door, his head hovering above hers. He inhaled and then hurried back into the kitchen.

Metal screeched as Adamski opened windows. She turned

as he pushed open the laundry room. He staggered as the stench washed over them.

"Do you have candles, spray, anything?" she begged.

"Living room. On the mantle."

She ran, any excuse to escape the cloying smell. In the living room she gathered matches and large candles. The candles looked like something a decorator had placed and admonished him not to light. Too bad. Sucked to be him.

Stripping off the gloves, she set the candles on the counter ad struck a match. Would the whole house blow?

Adamski returned from the basement with a fan. He plugged it in and aimed it at the open laundry door.

"You don't happen to have a gas mask?" she asked, only partly kidding.

"Don't I wish." He coughed a little.

She wanted to ask what he'd been thinking. She wanted to shake him. The man needed a keeper.

With the breeze from the fan, the candles and some spray he'd squirted into the laundry, Kate could finally breathe without her eyes watering.

"Mr. Adamski," she started.

"Alex. My name is Alex."

The strong, masculine name suited him. "What in God's name was in that washing machine?"

He ran fingers through his hair, making the thick curls stand up. His face turned red. "I think I might have dropped lunch meat in while I read the manual."

"Read the manual?" Didn't he know how to run a washing machine?

He rubbed a hand on his chin. His beard rasped against his palm. "Martha did my laundry. Up until she left me."

Kate threw her hands up. "She retired."

"Well, she's been working for me since …" Alex paused.

"Ever since I moved here. I never bothered with the laundry, or the dishwasher."

Kate had grown up in a privileged environment, but this man took the prize. How could he have survived without learning basic skills for metropolitan survival?

"I'll be updating your education. But first we have to fumigate the washing machine." And she meant *we*. He needed to be held accountable.

After mixing a batch of bleach, water and soap, she found a set of large gloves under the kitchen sink and handed them to Alex with a sponge and the bucket. "Wipe out the insides of the machine with this."

"Me?" Fear filled his dark brown eyes.

"You." She pointed at him. "I pulled everything out of the machine. Your turn."

He sighed. The gloves almost ripped as he tugged them onto his hands. With a sigh, he trudged into the laundry room. "God."

He wiped out the machine while she sipped another cup of coffee.

"Done," he called, stepping out with the bucket. Tears ran down his cheeks.

"Come on." She motioned him back to the small room.

"Do I have to?"

"Yes." She took a deep breath before entering. Once she showed him how to set the machine for a large load, she threw in the rags, added detergent and slammed the lid shut before running back into the kitchen.

"I couldn't figure out where the smell was from." He shifted on his size twenty shoes. "I thought it was the fridge."

She collapsed onto a barstool. Her hands could barely hold up her head. What waited for her in the fridge?

Her phone alarm rang. Four hours had passed already? She couldn't go to the office like this. She'd have to head home and shower. She'd planned to grab a bite to eat, but after that mess, she didn't want to touch food for a month.

Kate shut off the alarm. "I have to leave. Don't open the fridge. I can't take anymore today."

She hadn't made it through half a page of Martha's task list.

He fidgeted. Those big hands barely fit into the back pockets of his jeans. Jeans that stretched against a bulge she couldn't help but notice. Was it hands or feet or a nose that was an indicator of how well-endowed a man was?

"You'll be back tomorrow? You won't bail on me like the others?"

Her mouth dropped open. "How many people have bailed?"

"Four." His deep voice was a mere whisper.

Kate's mouth dropped open. Her mother had set her up.

ABOUT THE AUTHOR

Best-selling author of the BIG SKY DREAMERS and FITZGERALD HOUSE series, Nan Dixon spent her formative years as an actress, singer, dancer and competitive golfer, but the need to eat had her studying accounting in college. Unfortunately, being a successful financial executive didn't feed her passion to perform. When the pharmaceutical company she worked for was purchased, Nan got the chance of a lifetime—the opportunity to pursue a writing career. She's a five-time Golden Heart[R] finals and lives in the Midwest. She has five fabulous children, three wonderful son-in-laws, three granddaughters, two grandsons, and one neurotic cat.

Nan loves to hear from her readers so contact her through the following social media.

Printed in Great Britain
by Amazon